
★

Heavy darkness shrouded the trees, the pavement...

The bright lights and crowds on Duval Street lay only a couple of blocks away, and I pumped harder toward home. That's when a pair of bright headlights flashed on and moved toward me, slowly, relentlessly, threatening to block my path. I honked my horn and tried to pull aside, but the car kept coming.

In another moment I heard a scream. It took me an instant to realize the scream had come from my own throat and that the driver of the oncoming car had no intention of turning aside.

★

"...written with a light touch and plenty of offbeat appeal."

—*Booklist*

Previously published Worldwide Mystery titles by
DOROTHY FRANCIS

PIER PRESSURE
CONCH SHELL MURDER

DOROTHY FRANCIS

COLD-CASE KILLER

W⊕RLDWIDE®

TORONTO • NEW YORK • LONDON
AMSTERDAM • PARIS • SYDNEY • HAMBURG
STOCKHOLM • ATHENS • TOKYO • MILAN
MADRID • WARSAW • BUDAPEST • AUCKLAND

For my family.

COLD-CASE KILLER

A Worldwide Mystery/November 2008

First published by Five Star Publishing.

ISBN-13: 978-0-373-26653-1
ISBN-10:   0-373-26653-7

Acknowledgments

My thanks to the many people who helped make this book possible:

Maureen Moran, my agent; Ed Gorman, every writer's friend; John Helfers, my editor at Tekno; Mary P. Smith, Tiffany Schofield, my editors at Five Star; Dee Stuart, my first reader; Judith Pulse, my foot reflexologist; Jeremy Linsenmeyer, juvenile court officer of Tama County, Iowa; Richard Roth, Monroe County, Florida sheriff; Bill Crider, a gentleman from Texas.

Any errors that may have slipped into this book are my own and not theirs.

PROLOGUE

1982

THREATENING RAIN CLOUDS darkened Key West on this blustery afternoon. An eerie half-light honed the palm trees behind her apartment into dark skeletons that did a grotesque dance in the rising wind. Some Christmas Eve this was going to be! Heat from my excitement felt like a hot band binding my chest like a rope so I could hardly breathe. Why didn't that warmth reach my hands? Dyanne Darby. The cold metal of the gun and the silencer in my jacket pocket chilled my fingers. Dyanne Darby.

Today Dyanne Darby would regret giving me the brush-off.

Today Dyanne Darby would regret her Christmas Eve date with Randy Jackson.

Today Dyanne Darby would regret making me grovel for her affection.

Today Dyanne Darby would be beyond all regretting. The stench of boiled cabbage hung in the air as I climbed the outside steps to Dyanne's dingy apartment behind Sloppy Joe's. Boiled cabbage on Christmas Eve! Dyanne Darby wasn't the boiled cabbage type. I couldn't imagine her eating anything so common. Maybe lobster. Maybe caviar. The odor must be coming from someone else's kitchen. Maybe her friend, Nicole's. Maybe from Sloppy Joe's.

At the top of the steps, I tugged a rope that rang an old-fashioned ship's bell to announce guests. No response. I jerked the rope again.

"Who's there?" she called. "Randy? Is that you? You're way early."

I yanked the rope again. This time she opened the door a narrow crack. A crack. That's all I needed. Using an elbow, I pushed my way inside before she could slam the door in my face.

"Good afternoon, Dyanne." I let my voice grow soft. I undressed her with my eyes. "You're looking well today."

"How dare you barge in here like this!" She stepped closer to me, trying to strong-arm me out the door.

"Just stopped by to wish you a merry Christmas and make a date for tonight. How would you like dinner and an evening of dancing at the Rooftop Café?"

She laughed at me. "Don't try to play me for a fool. Surely you don't think you can show up at the last minute and find me waiting for you. Besides, you can't get reservations at the Rooftop at the last minute. I've had a Christmas Eve date with Randy for ages."

"A date you'll never keep, Dyanne. I don't like broads who play hard to get and laugh at me."

Fear flashed in her eyes and I felt the satin of her wine-colored negligee brush my hand as she tried to wedge her body around mine and escape down the stairs. I blocked that maneuver with my shoulders and hips, grabbed her arm, and flung her across the room onto the shabby couch.

"You're drunk!" she shouted. "Get out of here."

"You're not going anywhere, Dyanne. Not for a long time. We're going to have a cozy time together—a real holiday time." I sat down beside her on the couch. She jumped up, screaming.

"Help! Help! Nicole! Call the police!"

She kept on screaming and it was my turn to laugh. "Who do you think's going to hear you above all that wind and street noise?"

When she stopped screaming and I stopped talking, we could hear the rattle of the Conch Train making its rounds, the amplified voice of the driver pointing out the historic must-return-to-see spots on the island. And right below her window a Salvation Army guy rang a hand bell and bellowed requests for donations. She screamed again, but the sound blended in with the din below.

If she hadn't looked at her phone before she made a grab for it, I might have missed seeing it sitting on an end table behind a vase holding a single hibiscus blossom. I beat her to the phone and snapped the cord from the wall.

"Who you thinking of calling? Nicole? Police? Or maybe your loverboy, Randy. Where do you suppose he is now when you need him?"

She made another break for the door, but I tripped her and she fell flat. Gentleman that I am, I helped her to her feet. She stood, trying to regain her balance when I pulled the gun from my pocket.

"We're going to have some fun, then one sure shot's going to make you very sorry you ever heard of Randy Jackson."

"Stop!" she shouted. "Think what you're doing, you idiot! Nicole's just down the hall. She's going to stop by any minute now to show me her new Christmas dress."

I pointed the gun at her head and she broke into a run, zig-zagging around the room. I didn't try to catch her—just followed her with my eyes and my gun. Then she fooled me and dashed into her bedroom, slammed the door. I felt the vibration of the sturdy pine through the soles of my shoes and heard the click of the lock. Ha! Did she think a door could stop me! Even though I had a silencer on the gun, I waited until the Salvation Army guy was ringing at high speed before I shot and shattered the door lock, kicked the door open.

Empty room. I rushed to the open window. Must be fifteen feet to the ground. I expected to see her sprawled on the concrete below. But no. She hadn't jumped. I looked around the room for a moment. The closet. The only place she could be. I eased the closet door open inch by inch to heighten her suspense and fear.

A furry creature skittered across the room. Sensing her rising terror, I took my time poking my gun along the rod of hanging clothes—waitress uniforms, dresses, robes. No Dyanne. Kicking a row of shoes aside, I stepped into the closet for a better look. That's when I heard her. Whirling around, I saw her sliding from under the bed.

"Thought you could fool me? Give up, Dyanne. Nothing can save you now."

I prodded her to her feet with the gun barrel. Even then, she didn't give up. She ran back to the living room and headed for the door before I grabbed her arm and swung her around to face me.

"I never shoot people in the back, Dyanne. Choose the spot where you want to die."

"You mean you've shot other people?"

"So now you're going to try the old keep-him-talking ploy?" I laughed at her. "Be real, Dyanne. You've had your chance to please me. I can't count the number of times you've refused my calls. So now you're going to pay for making me play the fool. You're going to pay big. Do you think a few dates with Randy Jackson are worth your life? Think about it. Tell me you're sorry. I want to hear it from your own lips."

She said nothing. Fear leaked from her eyes. Or maybe it was anger. Or hatred. "I want to hear you talk, Dyanne. I want to hear you beg me for mercy."

She jerked her arm free from my grip and dropped onto the couch. "You coward!" She lifted her chin and said it again. "You rotten coward."

I squeezed the trigger. One bullet shattered her neck. The next two sent blood spewing down her chest. After that, I didn't need to check for a pulse. Her body slumped to the floor and I knew she lay dead. The cabbage odor disappeared into the stench of blood and death.

I knelt beside her and readied myself before I jerked her negligee aside. What she had denied me in life, I took in death.

After I finished, I was too smart to retreat down the outdoor steps where I had entered. Still breathing hard, I forced myself to calm down and ease across the room. I opened the door to the inner hallway. Walking along a carpeted runner and then down the inside stairs, I paused before I let myself out onto the street.

Smiling, I dropped a buck into the Salvation Army kettle.

ONE

MY NAME IS Keely Moreno and I'm proud of being the only professional foot reflexologist in Key West—maybe the only one in the Florida Keys. I'm not so proud of my reputation as an amateur detective. One important lesson my foot reflexology courses didn't teach me was how to deal with a corpse. Last year I'd learned that lesson on my own.

And it changed my life. Now I realize life is fragile and should be handled with care and respect. Last year I worked seven days a week. This year, I've eased up. I close my office on weekends and Wednesday afternoons. My new work schedule allows me to relax and spend more time with Punt Ashford, my long-time friend, the man who saved my life.

No more mystery solving for me! I'm aware of Randy Jackson's problem, and even though his mother, Maxine, is my cleaning lady, a woman I respect, I'm turning a deaf ear to her request that I try to help her son. Detective work can get a woman in big trouble.

This Wednesday morning I felt well and rested. Last night around midnight I'd managed to wake from a fitful sleep and throw off a recurring nightmare. I called it my Jude Cardell special. Even in death, my ex still managed to terrorize me in my dreams. But this morning I felt eager to meet the new day. I'd showered, given my hair its casual blow-and-go do, and dressed in my workaday khaki jumpsuit. I'd unlocked my office and stepped outside into the sunshine, when I saw a folded paper tucked under a corner of my business sign bolted to the door. Who'd left that? I'd heard no knock. Maybe Maxine, my first client of the day, decided to cancel her initial appointment and felt too embarrassed to give me the news face to face.

I opened the note printed in blood-red ink on a half sheet of notebook paper. After I read the words, my heart pounded. I stood frozen.

UNLESS YOU WANT TO DIE, DON'T STICK YOUR NOSE INTO THE RANDY JACKSON CASE. MOUSE-MILK.

I read the note twice, letting the words soak into my brain. Then the taste of fear, sharp and rusty, coated my tongue. I stepped forward to glance up and down the street, but I saw nobody near. My hands grew icy and the letters on my business sign wavered. I blinked, then blinked again until the words came into sharp focus.

ALTERNATIVE HEALING. KEELY MORENO.
FOOT REFLEXOLOGIST.

In spite of this warm March morning, I shivered.

Returning to my office-apartment, I closed the door before my grandmother in her shop next door saw me and hurried over to wish me a good morning. Gram had a weak heart and I tried to avoid stressing it with my problems. Who wanted me dead? And why? Could the note be some weirdo's sick idea of a joke? Sitting on the edge of my bed, I jammed the message under my pillow as if hiding it from sight might make it go away, might keep its words from threatening my life and my world. Unless you want to die. Unless you want to die. The words kept zinging through my mind.

Following my divorce four years ago, I'd stopped playing the doormat role of abused wife. With help from the Ashford family, I'd taken charge of my life and earned my professional certificate from St. Petersburg's International Institute of Reflexology. I've worked hard to set up my private practice on Duval Street. Many people are searching for new and promising concepts of disease prevention and healthful living. I have a thriving business in spite of the media and the police having hounded me about my involvement in the Margaux Ashford murder and the accidental death of my ex. But those things happened last year. Someone was after me now and I had no idea why.

My hands shook as I reread the warning then pushed it out of sight again. Someone knew I'd been thinking about the Randy Jackson case. Snippets of last week's conversation between me and Maxine Jackson replayed through my mind.

"Impossible, Maxine," I'd said. "It wouldn't help you or Randy for me to try to investigate a cold-case murder that happened two decades ago. I wouldn't know where to begin. I was only a child then."

I didn't tell Maxine that I found the idea of getting involved in the life of an ex-con repugnant. Criminals—the underbelly of society. No way did I want to be associated with people of that ilk. I considered Maxine a straight arrow, hardworking and honest as they come. I didn't fault her for Randy's problems, but neither did I want to get sucked into them.

"I need your help, Keely. You've solved one murder. You have detective experience. I think you can help me and my Randy now if you'll only give it a shot."

I like Maxine and I tried to ignore her pleading. "Believe me. I want no part of playing detective. Too dangerous. Too time-consuming. It would intrude into my professional work. Why don't you talk to Punt Ashford at the Fotopolus and Ashford Agency?"

"Your boyfriend?"

"Right. Punt and I are close friends, but more important to you, he and Nikko Fotopolus have opened a private detective agency here in Key West. They might be able to help you—and Randy."

"Keely, be real. No way can I afford to hire no private detective, and Randy, he don't have the purse for that high-falutin kind of thing either. So far, nobody on this island's been willing to give an ex-con a job. I can only afford your reflexology stuff because you'll let me pay you with my cleaning services."

The conversation that had been replaying in my mind stopped when Gram knocked and I glanced at my watch. I do three treatments on Wednesday mornings—eight, ten, and noon. Maxine was due for her first treatment and I needed to make sure my office looked its best. Right now I had trouble keeping my mind on such everyday matters as reflexology treatments ...

"Keely, you be up? Keely?"

"One minute, Gram. I'm coming."

I stuffed the note farther under my pillow. No. That would never do. I pulled it out again. I couldn't risk leaving it there. I folded the note and slipped it into the pocket of my jumpsuit, then finger-combed my dark hair before hurrying to open my office door and giving Gram a hug.

At seven in the morning, Key West throbbed with life. In the distance a cruise ship hooted a blast of sound into the day. I inhaled the scent of night-blooming jasmine that wafted on the tradewind. Looking down Duval, I saw some of the ship's passengers spreading across the island like a colony of fire ants following the scent of honey.

"I thought Wednesdays were 'no ship' days," I muttered in Gram's ear, enjoying the fragrance of freshly ground coffee beans that travels with her.

"The *Royal Sea,* Keely. She dock early this morning. Is a good thing. She carry many passengers—customers with deep pockets."

We locals consider cruise ship passengers a mixed blessing. They sometimes crowd us off our sidewalks and they jaywalk until the traffic snarls and stops, but they make our cash registers ring. For the most part, our smiles of greeting are genuine.

Closer by, I heard the clang of the Conch Train and the voice of the driver spouting island history and trivia to his passengers. The train rattled down Simonton Street one block from Duval, and I caught snatches of information about the old post office. I could imagine him pointing out the pink and purple bougainvillea blossoms trailing from vines twining in the palms or caught on the balconies of Old Town's Conch houses. Conch train drivers had a knack for keeping tourists looking up—away from the broken sidewalks that allow banyan roots to break through the concrete and make walking a hazard.

CELIA HERNANDEZ SUNDRIES. That's what the sign above Gram's doorway says. Since she arrived here from Cuba over forty years ago she's operated her hole-in-the-wall coffee bar where she offers specialty coffees, teas, and hard-to-find gourmet items to caffeine lovers, food hounds, and the local restaurants.

"What's up, Gram?" Her dour expression warned me of a problem.

"Is a sad morning that forces my begging."

"You know I'm always glad to help you, Gram. What's today's problem?"

"The usual. Cannot lift new bag of beans to countertop. Please to help me, then we sip a cappuccino."

"Sure thing. No problem." Although Gram pretends to be unaware of it, her appearance attracts as many people to her shop as do the sundries she sells. She wears her hair in a high topknot spiked with two tortoiseshell hairpins. Her golden hoop earrings and sandals along with her scarlet caftan and head bandeau give her the look of an aging female pirate. I never say the word "aging" within her hearing. At seventy-two Gram feels age challenged. She keeps her birthdays top secret along with the fact that she has to wear earplugs at night so she can sleep in spite of the Duval Street clamor. Gram's my favorite person and she knows I'd do anything for her.

"You have full schedule today, Keely?"

"Sure do. Three appointments this morning, and it's Wednesday, you know."

"Your afternoon for fishing, yes?"

"Right. Sometime I wish you'd close shop on Wednesday afternoon and boat into the back country with me. You love casting to the bonefish and 'cuda in the flats as much as I do." Although the early morning temperature hung in the seventies, I felt nervous sweat dampening my jumpsuit and I could hardly keep my mind on our chit-chat as the death threat in my pocket intruded into my thinking.

"No like to close shop for a whole afternoon. Folks even knock on my door during my siesta hour in spite of sign I hang in my window. People need my sundries."

We entered her shop and I breathed the fragrance of vanilla mingled with cinnamon. Behind the pine serving counter with its high stools, a steaming cappuccino machine dominated one corner of the room and an espresso machine the other. A hand-operated coffee grinder sat beside the gallon-size glass jars filled with coffee beans that lined the floor-to-ceiling shelves. I grew up in this shop, living with Gram in an upstairs apartment after my mother's death. In those days the scents of coffee lulled me to sleep at night like a silent lullaby.

Hoisting the jute bag to the countertop, I opened the drawstring and helped Gram transfer part of the beans into a gallon jar. Once we finished the task, I set the bag in a storage closet, but I declined her offer of a cappuccino.

"Got to get back to my shop, Gram. Maxine Jackson's my first client today. This'll be her first treatment and I need to be sure everything goes well. She's edgy about the whole reflexology scene and I want her to feel at ease."

"Maxine Jackson, your cleaning lady?"

"Right. Our cleaning lady." I smooched a kiss onto Gram's cheek and left her.

Sometimes Gram hates to admit she no longer has the time or the strength to give her quarters a thorough cleaning. That's where she and I differ. It doesn't bother me a bit to have someone else take care of the dust-and-mop scene. I've never numbered housekeeping among my talents.

Back inside my office, I placed the OPEN sign in my window. I was pulling the wicker screen that separates my living quarters from my business quarters into place when my telephone rang. I half expected to hear Maxine's voice begging to cancel her appointment.

"Foot Reflexology. Keely Moreno speaking."

For a moment I heard nothing on the other end of the line. That happened now and then. Maybe someone had dialed the wrong number. I started to hang up, then I heard heavy breathing. I thought I might be getting an obscene call when a muffled voice spoke. Man? Woman? The voice sounded so androgynous I couldn't be sure. But it didn't sound like Maxine.

"Did you find my note, Keely Moreno? Read it again and take heed. Poke into the Dyanne Darby murder and you're a dead woman."

TWO

I MANAGED TO REPLACE the receiver before it slipped from my fingers, and I felt my world closing in on me like a cast net closing on a school of pinfish. The feeling that an intruder lurked nearby rattled me. But how impossible! I'd yet to open my office for the business day. True, I'd unlocked the front door and stepped outdoors onto the sidewalk, but I'd been no more than twenty feet from my doorway even during the time I talked to Gram and helped her in her shop. The phone call could have come from next door, from across the island, from anywhere. I saw nobody nearby.

With belated presence of mind, I grabbed the phone again and punched "O" on the keypad.

"How may I help you?" the operator asked.

"Can you trace a call for me—the call I received at this number only a few seconds ago?"

"No, Ma'am. I'm not authorized to trace calls. That might be possible if you have a police order, if I have permission from an authority."

"Thank you." I slammed the receiver down. I wasn't about to instigate any action that involved the police. The next time I saw Punt I'd tell him about the call, show him the note—maybe. I've learned from experience that once a person tells another person secret information, she loses ownership of that information. Maybe for the time being I'd keep the threats to myself. Maybe. I felt too shaken to decide on that right now, but I was determined to calm myself and stop shaking. I couldn't expect Maxine to relax for her treatment if I came on like a basket case. I clamped my teeth together and they stopped chattering. But my hands still trembled.

I stood for several moments staring into the street. Nothing unusual there. Three teens drove past in a convertible, their boom box sending vibrations pulsing against my eardrums. A man and woman dressed in identical Hawaiian shirts and white slacks passed along the sidewalk and peered into my window, but the two men who were smiling at each other and holding hands as they walked along never looked my way. I knew people could see no farther inside my office than my desk and swivel chair. They couldn't see the patron's foam-padded bench, the small whirlpool footbath, or the adjustable chair that sat farther back in the patient-treatment area.

Turning from the window, I appraised my office, making sure everything was in order. Behind the treatment chair, bolted to one wall hung shelves that held towels and pillows along with the lotions I used during treatments—lemon, orange, jasmine. I inhaled deeply, still trying to calm myself. The only smells I found as soothing as those in my office were those common to the backcountry flats, the scent of the tradewind, the salt water, and the living-fish aroma of the sea.

Maxine showed for her first appointment early. No surprise there. People scheduled for first reflexology treatments seldom arrive on time. They either appear early in nervous anticipation, or they arrive late, reluctant to face a new experience.

"Good morning, Maxine." I put on a smile as I stepped forward to greet her, and once she stepped inside, I closed the door that opened onto the sidewalk.

"Morning, Keely."

Maxine's gold front tooth gleamed like a jewel when she smiled at me. Her body reminded me of a child's playground ball—firm, round, and fast moving. Today she wore blue polka dot bloomers—knee length—with a white tee shirt along with Nikes and red-and-white-striped athletic sox. I doubt that she realized how picturesque she must appear to others. She eyed my treatment chair with doubt.

"You sure this reflexology thing won't hurt me none?"

"That's a promise. If you experience any twinges of pain, you let me know and I'll stop the treatment."

"Then it might hurt? Right?"

"You may experience a slight discomfort at times. Maybe. But no pain. Why don't we get started? If you'll sit down and remove your shoes and stockings, we'll begin your treatment with a warm footbath."

Maxine backed from the padded bench and the footbath like a child trying to escape punishment. "Keely, 'splain me again about this here foot reflexology thing. Maybe better I should clean your place as always—for money instead of as a trade for treatments."

I sighed and smiled, and at last Maxine sat on the padded bench while I gave her my short information dump about the age-old practice of foot massage. She'd heard it in great detail before, but now she sat leaning forward and listening intently—her way of stalling, I guessed.

"Reflexology's an ancient form of pressure therapy, Maxine. The Egyptians knew about it and used it thousands of years ago. It involves applying focused pressure to certain known reflex points located in the foot. These points correspond to certain areas in the body." I pulled out a chart, again showing her the connections of foot parts to body parts, but she shook her head and handed the chart back to me as if it might burn her fingers.

"Don't want no truck with no charts."

I laid the chart aside. "The massage therapy promotes increased blood circulation to the affected body areas, relaxation in those areas, and a release of tensions. Reflexology has helped curtail pain for many sufferers. When doctors can't relieve a patient's pain many of those patients give foot reflexology a chance."

"And you're one of them people?"

"Yes. At one time I suffered from severe back pain. Pills helped, but the pain always returned. When doctors started talking to me about surgery, serious no-guarantees-promised surgery, I gave them the old cliché, 'Don't call me. I'll call you.' I backed off. Then I happened to read a magazine article about reflexology, and the information grabbed my attention. It didn't take much persuasion to get me to try this alternative to surgery. I signed up for a series of treatments in Miami."

"And they helped? How'd you happen to hurt your back?"

"Yes, the treatments helped." I ignored her second question. No need for Maxine to know my ex had inflicted my back injuries as well as many others that had healed. It embarrassed me to admit I'd put up with Jude's abuse for so long. I still had to find my way through admitting I'd been the wife of an abuser for years before I found the courage to face the danger of taking action on my own behalf.

"Reflexology offered no quick fix, though, Maxine. I stuck with the Miami practitioner for weeks, only seeing gradual improvement. Guess that was my way of avoiding the surgery. But after a while I knew the treatments were worth the time it took to drive to Miami as well as the expense. Today I'm pain free. Foot reflexology gave me my life back again, and the experience inspired me to use reflexology to help others."

I assisted Maxine in removing her shoes and stockings and then I snapped on the small whirlpool footbath.

"Hmmm." Maxine said no more, but she sat smiling as she breathed in the lemon-scented water and felt it swirl around her feet. When she's making up her mind about something, Maxine has a way of rolling her tongue up over her gold tooth and peering into the distance as if deep in thought. Finally she spoke. "So far, I like it, Keely. Like it a dadburned lot."

I didn't point out that we hadn't started the treatment yet, and I kept the mood light. "You'd be surprised at the sight of the feet that I've worked with, Maxine. Callused. Misshapen. And yes, just plain ugly and smelly. You have wonderful feet. They're firm and sturdy and I can tell you care for them well and wear shoes that give them the proper support."

"Got to take good care of my feet. You might say my feet are my bread and butter. Once those dogs begin barking, I'm through for the day."

After a few minutes in the footbath, I dried Maxine's feet on a soft towel, eased them into disposable slippers, and led her to the treatment chair that I lowered until her feet were in a position that allowed me to massage them.

"Want a pillow?" I asked. When she nodded, I placed a pillow under her head so she could look at me and we could talk during her treatment.

The moments I'd spent assisting Gram and preparing Maxine for her massage had helped take my mind off the threat in my pocket and the phone call. Now I wondered if Maxine had received such warnings, too, but I couldn't bring myself to ask her. Not now. Not yet. I lacked the courage to share my feelings. Maybe I needed to talk to Punt first—in private. Maybe.

Moistening my hands with mint-scented oil, I began massaging Maxine's left foot. She relaxed almost immediately, but when I concentrated pressure on her toes, she pulled her foot from my grasp and rolled her eyes.

"Hurt?" I asked.

"No," she lied. "No pain. Just a smidgen of pressure."

I eased the pressure and massaged her instep before I returned to working on her toes again.

"'Splain what you're doing, please." She raised her head from the pillow to look at her foot, and I wondered if she might get up and leave before I'd had a chance to do her any good.

"I'm breaking up tiny crystalline and calcium deposits in your toes, and that will help your blood circulate to the nerve endings in your sinuses and your pituitary gland. Those are the places where lots of headaches begin. You did tell me you suffered from headaches along with backaches, right?"

Maxine nodded and lowered her head onto the pillow again. I felt her relax and wiggle her toes. I knew additional crystals were beginning to break up. Now that she was more at ease, I massaged the sides of her feet in a way that could relieve sciatic pain. For a moment, Maxine closed her eyes and I hoped she might drift into a light sleep, but no. She began talking.

"Keely, we're friends, right? We're tighter than employer/employee, right?"

"Right. We sure are." I could guess what was coming next, but I saw no way to avoid it.

"Please help me help my Randy. That's all I'm asking. I've asked you before. Now I'm asking again. Just listen and give me some advice. I don't know how to fancy talk with the police and I don't want to say the wrong thing to them. Don't want to privy them that I know they did a rotten job."

"Rotten job of what?"

"A rotten job of finding Dyanne Darby's true killer. My Randy didn't murder that girl, but someone did, and me and Randy, we wants to know who."

THREE

"THE POLICE SHOULD better find that killer," Maxine continued. "Can you imagine my Randy's pure pain of having to rot in prison for years for a crime he didn't do?"

"It's beyond everyone's imagination." My stomach knotted whenever I thought of innocent people doing jail time. "People hate thinking about it, hate talking about it. That's because they have no answers."

"My Randy, he wears a mask to hide his feelings, to help him cope. That mask almost makes him look normal, but I know what it hides. Helplessness. Hopelessness. Deep, deep depression. And hate. Randy hates the authorities. That hate's a habit he's taught himself every day for twenty years. The habit of hate. It's a fearsome thing."

"Maybe he should try to blank out the past by stopping the hating, finding a job, and getting on with his life."

"Right now my Randy's a lost ball in high weeds. His whole being's been turned upside down. Find a job? You know the first thing bigwig bosses ask? They ask where he's been the past twenty years. He answers. They sneer. Then they prod him about his job skills. That's a laugh. In prison nobody helped the lifers to develop no job skills."

"Maybe he could return to school and train for some job that interests him." I applied more lotion and continued the massage, unable to change the subject without appearing rude.

"No money." Maxine sighed deeply. "Of twenty or so Florida inmates wrongfully jailed, maybe two or three got any pay to make up for their lost work years, their lost dreams. Everyone thinks money'd help, but you can't put no dollar value on human pain."

"I suppose not, but money would buy food for the table and new clothes. It'd pay medical and dental bills. It'd pay for gasoline and apartment rent."

"Some freed-convicts did get some loot. They had more problems than before."

"What kind of problems?"

"People crawled out of the woodwork demanding handouts. Friends. Family. Crooks. You'd be surprised how much attention a body can get by flashing a little cash. And there's another thing, Keely. The courts may say my Randy's innocent, but even so, many people think: maybe he didn't do it or maybe he did do it. In their minds, they still question the court decision."

I felt guilty as Maxine pointed out thoughts that had played through my own thinking when I'd heard about Randy's release. Since I said nothing, she continued.

"My Randy needs to track down the person who murdered Dyanne Darby all those years ago. That's the only thing that'll convince the public that he's really innocent, and that's what I want to help him do. Police hate admitting they made a mistake. I don't know where to start. Who's going to listen to a cleaning lady?"

"Maxine, you might start by remembering that many of the men and women on today's police force are new to their jobs. Only a few old-timers may know or recall a murder that happened over twenty years ago."

"Right," Maxine agreed. "That's why I need a private person, maybe you, to help me dig into the long-ago. I got no money to hire no detective, but you—you've shown everyone you know how to talk to the police and make them listen."

I massaged Maxine's feet, saying nothing. Last year during the uproar over Margaux Ashford's murder, I'd had no magic charms that had worked on Detective Curry or on any of the police force. After I'd found Margaux's body, I'd only done what I had to do to protect myself, my name, and my business. I'd listened to Detective Curry remind me over and over that the person finding a corpse was of special interest to the police. My learning the identity of Margaux's killer came as the result of a long series of eliminations on my part and a lot of life-saving efforts on Punt's part.

"Randy…is…bitter." Maxine's voice reminded me of a pair of shears snipping the words from a string. "I can't fault him for those feelings. Florida State Prison. My Randy, he spent years in a cement cell at Raiford while the real murderer walked Scot-free doing as he pleased. I went to visit Randy as often as I could afford the bus fare or gasoline for the car, but in the visitors' room, a glass partition separated us, making talk hard. And a guard always stood in the room listening."

I could think of no reasonable response. "Maybe that person walking Scot-free is a she. You don't know it's a man." I remembered the breathy voice on the phone.

"He or she, that person's still walking free. Maybe right in Key West. That thought scares the bejabbers out of me."

Maxine's voice took on a hollow, frightened quality that made me wonder if she had received a warning message, too. And perhaps a phone threat. I wanted to ask her, but I felt wary of hearing her answer. Nor did I want to tell her about my threats. If I learned that we'd both received threats, it'd be harder for me to refuse her request for help. Yet, I wondered what help I could offer. I didn't want to build up her hopes.

"I've read about Randy's case, his arrest, his imprisonment, but many of the details have slipped from my memory."

"They're still very fresh in mine, Keely. And in my Randy's. You willing to listen to them? You got time to hear me out?"

"You've traded me an hour's cleaning for an hour's massage. I can listen while I work. If you want to talk about your son, I'll listen, but I still can't promise you help."

Maxine squirmed into a more comfortable position. "Back in the 1980s Randy worked as a diver for treasure salvor Mel Fisher. You've heard of him, right?"

"Everyone in Key West hears a lot about Mel Fisher. Guess every boy who could swim and dive wanted to dive for him. Wanted to help find the sunken galleon *Atocha*. Punt's dad, Beau Ashford, was one of those boys. Punt, Jass, his twin sister, and I were high school friends and because of that, Beau and his first wife were my mentors for many years after the death of my mother. If it hadn't been for Mel Fisher's generosity to Beau and the Ashfords' generosity to me, I might never have been able to open this business."

It embarrassed me to realize that I'd been doing much more talking than Maxine. I hushed and listened for whatever might come next.

"My Randy was one of Mel Fisher's *Atocha* divers. In those days Mel had little money to pay the boys. He managed to feed them, and he housed some of them in an Old Town apartment so crowded they had to sleep in shifts. Dive. Sleep. Dive. Sleep. That formed their routine. My Randy had it a little better than most. He could sleep at home and that's what he did on most nights.

"In his time off, Randy dated Dyanne Darby, a waitress at Sloppy Joe's who lived in an upstairs apartment near the bar. When my Randy went to call for Dyanne one Christmas Eve, he found her lying dead with blood all around her."

I said nothing, but I empathized with anyone unlucky enough to find a corpse.

"My Randy, he rushed to her to see if he could help her, to see if she might still be alive. But no. She lay dead. Randy called the police for help. But instead of helping, they arrested him. Although he shouted that he was innocent, he faced a murder trial. People presented lies against him. They lied. And I think some jury members were prejudiced against him right from the git-go."

"Why would they be prejudiced?" I asked.

Maxine cleared her throat, then cleared it again. "My Randy had two or three arrests on his record. Minor things like shoplifting. Traffic problems. Nothing major."

"So he had a rap sheet." Criminals—the underbelly of society.

"That shouldn't have mattered in his murder trial. And to make matters even worse, each day's court happenings made national headlines. The bigwig judge turned into a grandstander. He enjoyed playing Mr. Important while he heard the jury verdict and then sent my Randy to prison."

"Randy's lawyer didn't appeal his case?" I asked.

"Oh yes, he appealed, but it did no good. I think he had a bad lawyer—a what-do-I-care lawyer. I couldn't afford to hire no lawyer for him, so the court appointed one. Not top-notch in his field. A low-notch lawyer. That's my opinion. Top-notch lawyers had so many clients they didn't have to depend on court appointments for a living."

I agreed with Maxine's assessment of court-appointed lawyers, but just then my office door burst open and Consuela flounced inside interrupting Maxine's story as well as her appointment. Her intrusion spared me from having to voice my opinion on court-appointed lawyers.

Today Consuela wore a bright purple sarong, five-inch heels, and a hibiscus tucked behind her ear peeked through the flow of her dark hair. Conseula's a wannabe writer, and her present state of excitement made me wonder if she'd finally found a publisher willing to publish her Spanish-First-Language book for children.

"Keely! Keely! I have good news for both of us."

Consuela's appearance seldom meant good news for anyone, but I smiled at her.

"What's up, Consuela?

FOUR

CONSUELA STOOD CLOSE to my front window, and I knew she hoped passers-by would look inside and admire her as they would an exotic picture. She misses few chances to seek the lime-light, and her actions made it clear that she thought nothing of interrupting me or my client in the middle of a treatment.

"I have the name of a new client for you—Ace Grovello." She did a turn in front of the window and waved at a friend passing by. "Perhaps you already know him?"

"No. I've never heard that name before. Tourist or local?"

"Local. And he's my new boyfriend."

"So what else is new? I mean you have a new boyfriend every few days." I stepped back to Maxine and continued her massage.

Consuela's gaze followed me and she scowled when she stepped closer. "Maxine! I didn't know you were Keely's client. I suppose you think I've been two-timing Randy."

"Randy don't blab to me about no girlfriends," Maxine said.

"Well, Randy and I have been dating—quite a few times, but that doesn't make him my significant other. We aren't in a serious relationship or anything like that. I have every right to date Ace or Gus or any man I choose to date whenever I choose to do so."

"Consuela, you have an appointment with me at ten." I glanced at my watch. "How about leaving Maxine and me alone now and telling me your big news when you return? This's Maxine's first appointment and I guaranteed her privacy."

"You're telling me, Consuela, that I'm intruding?" She took up her stance by the window once more, and I wondered if she intended to spend the morning posing there.

"Please don't get bent out of shape, Consuela, but we can talk about your big news later. I'm dying to hear more."

"Well, I don't want you to die, so I'll tell you right now as I intended to do all along. Is okay with you, Maxine?"

Without waiting for Maxine's response, Consuela continued. "Keely, we have a deal, you know?

"Refresh my mind, please."

"You know perfectly well what deal! You promised me a free treatment for every new customer I bring in who signs up for your introductory six-week series. Today I give you the name of Ace Grovello, my new friend. If Randy had told me his mama was interested in reflexology, I could have recommend her and earned a second freebie."

"Please, Consuela." I nodded toward the door. "If Ace Grovello comes in asking for treatments, I'll give you credit— as promised."

Consuela walked to my desk and helped herself to some brochures before she flounced from my office, slamming the door as she left.

"I apologize for the intrusion, Maxine. Guess I should have locked the door, but few people barge in unannounced."

Maxine chuckled and wiggled her toes. "No problem. No problem at all. In fact I'm interested in my Randy's friends. He doesn't talk much about his comings and goings. Like to know who he's hanging out with. What's Consuela's last name?"

"Nobody knows. She keeps it a deep secret—says really famous people don't need last names. Then she cites Cher and Madonna. And Boy George."

"Well, I hope my Randy don't go ga-ga over Consuela. He may fall like a ton of squid for the first woman who smiles at him. My Randy, he's had enough of being treated like pond scum. Wish I could warn him that Consuela has lots of fish in her sea."

"Don't see how you can do that without letting him know you've talked to her. Has Randy found a job yet?"

"He's looking. But no luck yet."

"Maybe you could give him some of your extra clients. Cleaning is an equal-opportunity job. Would he consider cleaning houses?"

"He might, I suppose. But who's going to want an ex-con roaming their home? Any little thing gets lost, he the first one they call a thief."

"What about the hotels? They're always advertising for cleaning people. I see Help Wanted signs in lots of windows."

"Same problem. What hotel wants an ex-con on the premises? Any little thing go wrong and my Randy, he'd be blamed. Anyway, I couldn't recommend hotel cleaning to him when I refuse hotel work myself."

"Maybe you could take on a hotel job and then after a few days, a week or so, pass it on to Randy. Think that might work? If he really needs a job, he can't be as picky as you are."

"No, that won't never work. I don't talk to hotel people. Don't want any of 'em thinking I'm even slightly interested in their offers. I'm not into cleaning up broken furniture and spring-breaker vomit in rooms that have held eight or ten kids besides the one or two who rented it. No way."

"I can't fault you for that." I sighed. "So you're Randy's sole support?"

"So far that's true. Last week he did win some money up on Ramrod Key. Boondocks, the tiki bar, has a mechanical-bull game on some nights. Last Wednesday they offered a prize to the guy who could stick on that bull the longest. Randy won. One hundred dollars. Not much, for sure. He gave most of it to me for groceries, but he held a little back for marijuana."

I wondered why Maxine was telling me this. "He's a user?"

"Afraid so"

"A dealer?"

Maxine hesitated. "Not a dealer. At least not yet. I hope he'll never deal drugs, but the temptation must be great. Read the papers. Headlines tell everyone there's big bucks in dealing."

"Big money, and sometimes death—if the deal goes wrong."

Maxine lay quiet and silent. Neither of us said more about drugs or drug dealing. I usually give a short first treatment, hoping the client won't be worn out and will want to return. Now I raised the chair to its upright position, and brought Maxine's shoes and stockings to her.

"Well, what do you think, Maxine? Are you willing to book another appointment for next week?"

I thought she might say no. I saw our work exchange deal flying out the window, but she surprised me. She paced across my office. She peered behind the privacy screen and into my apartment that she cleaned on a weekly basis. Then she stopped and faced me head on, meeting my eyes with her direct gaze.

"I received a warning note this morning, Keely."

For a few moments I could only hear the humming of the refrigerator.

"What sort of warning?"

I forced calmness and a casual tone. I needed to keep her talking. I wasn't sure I wanted to reveal my own note and phone call just yet. I really wanted Punt's advice before I talked about the warnings to anyone.

"The note, it almost scared me from leaving my house today." She pulled a scrap of paper from her bloomer pocket, unfolded it, and handed it to me. I read words almost identical in meaning to those in the note I'd received.

NOSE INTO THE RANDY JACKSON CASE AND YOU DIE.

I wanted to tell her about my note, but for some reason I held back.

"And this morning I also received a threatening phone call, Keely. Man? Woman? I couldn't tell. I'm guessing a woman. Don't know why. Guess it just sounded like a woman, maybe a woman with a head cold."

"What are you going to do about the warnings? Have you reported them to the police?"

"No police. Not yet. I don't know what best to do. Again— another reason I'm asking you for help."

"Who helped get Randy released from prison? He had to have had assistance from somewhere. Maybe those same people could help you now or at least offer you some advice."

"The preacher man, Reverend Soto, visits prisoners from Key

West. He's a real do-gooder. He's the one who suspected someone had framed my Randy. That preacher, he talked to important bigwigs at the courthouse, and he persuaded them to reopen my Randy's case. What could my Randy have done from a prison cell? Not much, that's for sure. His efforts would have amounted to nothin'."

"I read about the use of DNA evidence."

"Right." Maxine's gold tooth glinted as she smiled. "My Randy, he'd been locked away years before law men began using the DNA thing to catch crooks. Reverend Soto, he raised a DNA stink until authorities reopened Randy's case and used the DNA stuff."

I couldn't imagine the dignified Reverend Soto raising any kind of a stink, but I didn't argue the point. "And someone listened to him."

"Right. Someone listened. About that same time a college class in Illinois began raising a ruckus and proving that innocent victims in Illinois were doing prison time. Those college kids, law students the papers said, were helping get innocent guys set free. That's what Reverend Soto hoped would happen in my Randy's case."

"And it did."

"Yes. Finally. It took months. Reverend Soto prodded Attorney Shelley Hubble from the Hubble and Hubble Law Firm to bust her ass in Randy's behalf—pro bono. That means for free, Keely. Someone had raped Dyanne Darby. Shelley Hubble helped prove that the DNA samples taken from inside Dyanne's body did not match Randy's DNA. Randy got Dyanne's blood on hisself when he tried to help her, when he tried to tell if she might still be alive."

Maxine had been talking so fast I held up my hand like a traffic cop to slow her down. Her agitation hit a nerve in my brain. I knew I had to share my morning warnings with her, to let her know she wasn't alone. Or maybe I needed to let myself know I wasn't alone.

"Maxine, look at this." I pulled my warning from my pocket and began unfolding it. She snatched it from my hand, running her finger under each line, silently mouthing the words as she read.

"And minutes before you arrived here, I received a threatening phone call, too."

"Man or woman?"

"Like you, I couldn't tell."

"So what are we going to do about all this?" Maxine looked up at me as if we had suddenly become partners and as if I had the answer written on my forehead.

I drew the drapery across my office window and set up the CLOSED sign before I led Maxine behind the privacy screen and into my apartment. We sat on the edge of my bed since books and clothes and newspapers occupied both chairs.

"First, let's think of who might have known we'd been discussing helping Randy find Dyanne's killer. That's the thing that's scaring someone. Randy's been proved innocent of that crime, and someone out there feels threatened. That person doesn't want the case reopened. Somebody doesn't want the real murderer to be found."

"The real murderer, he likely the one who wrote these notes and made the phone calls." Maxine rolled her tongue over her gold tooth and stared across the room, deep in thought.

"Keely, who have you told about this?"

"Me? I've told nobody. I had no intention of getting involved in this murder case. No intention at all. I've spoken of it to no one—not even Punt. Maxine? Who have you told about it?"

When Maxine looked at the floor and hesitated before she replied, I knew she'd talked to somebody besides me.

"It's hard for me not to talk about my Randy. It broke my heart to see him in prison. Now it's breaking my heart to see him so hopeless and angry. Only a wee part of my brain admits that my own son, my Randy, in his anger and bitterness, could be a threat to society."

"Who've you talked to, Maxine?" I grabbed a ballpoint and some paper from the end table beside my bed. "Let's make a list. You've alerted someone you've talked to and now we both may be in danger."

Maxine squirmed and punched a bed pillow. "I talk to the people I work for. Talk comes easy for me. Especially talk about my Randy. There're the Smiths. The Currys. The Edmonds. The Gallaghers. The …"

I laid my ballpoint aside when I realized Maxine's list could go on and on. "You've talked to all those people, maybe asked them to help you help Randy, right?"

"Right." Maxine scowled. "I'd even hinted that you might be helping me."

I stood and glared at Maxine. "And I'm guessing those people you've talked to have talked to their friends, their families. When people talk about murder, everyone pricks up their ears. It's only natural. Everyone's interested. After all your talk, anyone on this island could know that you and I are interested in knowing who murdered Dyanne Darby." I picked up the ballpoint and threw it across the room. I shredded the notepaper and let it flutter to the floor.

"You're mad at me, aren't you?"

"You bet I am. You had no right to get me involved. I had no intention of investigating this cold-case murder. None at all."

"You had no intention of investigating." Maxine repeated my statement and then smiled. "Do you mean that's how you felt yesterday? That today you feel differently? Today you're willing to help me?"

"No. It doesn't mean that I'm willing to help you." I retrieved the ballpoint, ashamed of my temper tantrum. "But I can see that I'm already involved whether or not I'm willing. You have to help yourself, Maxine. I refuse to lift a finger in your behalf—unless you agree that both you and Randy will go with me to talk to Punt Ashford."

"I can't afford no private detective. No way. I told you that. My Randy can't afford one either. Why bother Punt Ashford to listen to us when we can't pay?"

"There's a chance that Punt might take your case—pro bono. For free."

"I know what pro bono means. I told you that. And I'm not going begging to Punt Ashford or anyone else."

"It might not be begging." I left my perch on the bed, hurried to my desk, and grabbed my phone. "If there's a search for the Darby killer, it'll be a high-profile case."

"You mean big headlines and all that."

"Right. Headlines and all that. If Punt was the one to bring Dyanne Darby's murderer to justice, the advertising would promote the Fotopolus and Ashford Agency. Such promotion might be more valuable to a new business than monetary payment."

"Won't beg. Jacksons no beg."

"With your permission I'll call Punt and ask for an appointment for the three of us—you, me, and Randy. How about it?" I wished I hadn't felt so trapped into this situation, but maybe Punt could ease me out of the action by agreeing that his firm would do the investigating for the publicity it might be worth.

"Do I really have a choice?" Maxine asked.

"Do I?" I countered. I started to punch in Punt's number.

FIVE

"WAIT," MAXINE JERKED my hand from the phone. "I'll have to ask my Randy before I agree to this. He may not want Punt Ashford's help."

I rolled my eyes. "As if Randy has a lot of choices! As if he can afford to be so high-handed." Then I pushed the phone toward her. "Go ahead. Call him. Get his promise that he'll go with us to talk to Punt if Punt's willing to listen."

Maxine shrugged and set the phone down. "No can do, Keely. My Randy, he's off island today."

"Off island where?"

"Yesterday afternoon he flew to New York City. The Big Apple." Maxine gave me an aggrieved look. "Never been there myself, but my Randy, he go and he fly first class. He's booked at Four Seasons hotel. First Class. You don't believe this, I can give you his telephone number at that posh hotel."

I looked into Maxine's eyes and her gaze met mine without wavering. "Please tell me why Randy has booked a flight to New York City. How does he happen to have money for a first class ticket, for a first class hotel? That makes no sense when you tell me he has no money to pay for an investigation that might clear his name in the eyes of a community that still may doubt his innocence. Someone might offer him a job if they felt him worthy of their trust."

"Important lawyers in New York pay Randy's tab. Reverend Soto's, too. Bigwigs. They're putting them on a TV program so they can tell the whole world what's happened to my Randy and to other freed ex-convicts. These lawyers and this TV station want the public to be aware." Maxine looked at her watch, tapped it with her forefinger. "If you snap on TV we can watch the program in a few minutes."

My gaze darted from Maxine to my TV and then back to Maxine again. "Do we have time to go to your place to watch?"

"Your TV broke?"

"No TV problem. But I want to see that program and there're too many chances for interruption here. Consuela's my next client and she may arrive early. I'll leave a note on my door telling her I'll be back soon and asking her to wait."

Maxine chuckled. "Can't imagine that one waiting for anyone, but come along with me then. We gotta hurry or we'll miss the start of the program."

I had no idea where Maxine and Randy lived. A few weeks ago, a friend had recommended Maxine's cleaning to me, and all my contacts with her had been by telephone. She'd parked her old Ford in the alley behind my office. The car looked as if rust might be the only thing holding it together. But I understood that. The salty tradewind in the Keys rusts everything but plastic. I took a half-breath. No point in dirtying my lungs with the alley's garbage and spilled beer smell.

"Maxine, you were lucky to find a parking place—even here in the alley."

"I know. But early morning is a good time to find parking— sometimes even on the street."

"Yeah, maybe. But I refuse to own a car. I let the tourists vie for the parking places. That's my green bicycle chained to the lightpost by my back door."

"I'm surprised someone doesn't cut the chain and steal it."

"Sometimes I wheel it inside at night if there's a parade or some other special after-dark activity."

"What if you need to go a long distance?" Maxine jingled her car keys as she opened her car door.

"Then I call Maxi-Taxi, but that doesn't happen often. On an island only two miles wide, almost everything's within biking distance. Of course bicycling to home appointments or to meet clients is unhandy and it takes time, but for the most part my clients come to my office."

Maxine eased her roly-poly bulk under the steering wheel. "Guess a body can park a bike almost anywhere there's a lamppost to chain it to."

"Right." Upon entering Maxine's car, I shoved a tin of Skoal lying on the seat aside and ducked to avoid a head-on collision with a pair of felt dice dangling from the sun visor. Maxine grunted as she tried to reach the dice, tuck them out of the way, but they kept falling down and she gave up that effort and concentrated on shoving the Skoal into the glove box.

"Randy's junk," Maxine explained as if I hadn't guessed. "He won the dice at a carnival before he went to prison and I had no heart for throwing them away. And now they stay put because Randy still likes them and because me and him, we share the car."

I needed a deep breath and I almost gagged on the smell of tobacco and stale cigarette smoke that clung to the car's interior. Randy Jackson made me shudder.

After we fastened our seat belts, Maxine revved the motor and we headed onto Duval and then turned toward the beach. Her radio was on and static crackling from her police scanner threatened to drown out any conversation until she snapped it off.

"Where do you live, Maxine?"

"Stock Island. Sometimes it's quicker to drive by the beach than to take Flagler with all its traffic."

Stock Island! I didn't know anyone who lived there, but I knew of its rough reputation as a service community for Key West. Marinas. Drydocks. Bars and taverns. Former home of the greyhound track. Gram said that in years past, men in dimly lit shacks on the island gambled on late-night cock fights. Don't know how she knew that. Gossip, maybe. Cock fighting's illegal now, but roosters still crow, and stray hens and chicks have become a nuisance in the lower Keys. Police kept busy on Stock Island.

On South Roosevelt, we passed elegant apartments and high-rise condos that overlooked the beach and the sea. This morning, orange-jacketed teenagers picked up empty cans and Styrofoam boxes and shoved them into canvas bags.

"Caught a few last night, didn't they?" Maxine chuckled.

"Right. Quite a few at that." The police always give the kids they cite for using false IDs or for being drunk and disorderly the chance to work off their fine in lieu of being arrested and having their misdemeanors reported to their parents. Today's workers projected a somber mood and moved with scant enthusiasm.

"Has Randy ever been to New York before?"

"Several times. My Randy, he's a pretty good talker once they get him to open up and tell his story. The program people ask him questions and he gives them the answers they're after. Why, he's been on the *Oprah* show and *Good Morning America*. Even spoke out on *Larry King Live*. Also he's done his talking on shows nobody's ever heard much about—like the one today on Public TV."

"What's it called?"

"*Wrongfully Convicted*. It's a special program sponsored by Florida Public Television."

"I've never read anything about Randy's TV appearances in the *Citizen*."

Maxine snorted. "Not likely you will, either. News people try to squelch the bad stuff whenever they can. Don't want no tourists thinking that ex-cons are roaming Key West streets right along with regular folks."

Traffic picked up near the airport then thinned again as we passed what used to be Houseboat Row. Only two small catamarans remained lashed to the seawall. After over thirty years of arguments and legal maneuvering between the police and the houseboat owners, authorities had finally forced the houseboat dwellers out. They'd left kicking and screaming for less picturesque and more expensive moorings at nearby Garrison Bight. I sorta missed them. They lent a certain ambience to the island, but then, I'd never had to deal with the water pollution near their boats. Nor the smell.

When we crossed the Boca Chica bridge, I looked down at fishing guides in their small crafts. Most of them were loaded with lunch coolers, bait, and fishing rods along with hopeful clients heading out for a day in the back-country flats. Fishing. Lots of sun. Calm winds. A great day. Fishing's what I'd be doing this afternoon.

Sunshine poured onto the golf course like liquid gold and also onto the ash-colored hill that rose close behind the fairways. Mount Trashmore. That's what the locals called the mound when the city used it as a landfill. Gas stations. Bait shops. Quick Chick Café. At MacDonald Avenue Maxine turned right and we passed a large marina before we entered a street lined with trailer homes. Some looked to be in good repair, but others looked as if a strong wind would blow them away.

"Wilma touched down here in several places," Maxine said as if reading my mind.

"But that hurricane happened almost two years ago."

"Takes some folk a while to get things going again." Maxine slowed down. "Lived here over forty years after my husband bailed out." She parked in a narrow slot next to an aluminum trailer with a blue canopy that formed a porch near the door.

I didn't ask about her husband or why he had "bailed out." Husband talk's off limits as far as I'm concerned.

Maxine has a green thumb. Pots of pink geraniums, white orchids, and lavender hibiscus marked the boundary of her outdoor living area. A bougainvillea vine twined across the top of the trailer, dropping scarlet blossoms on her doorstep. Her home stood out like a beauty spot on an ugly face.

"Randy grew up here. He's known only two homes. Stock Island and Florida State Prison. He was a good boy, Keely. Mel Fisher called my Randy one of his best divers and hardest workers. He spoke out for my Randy at his trial, but his words make no nevermind in that courtroom."

"Where did Randy go to school?"

"Key West High School. Got good grades, too. Never straight As, but good enough. Randy, he liked to read. Next to swimming and diving, he liked reading. And he liked the classics—those books most people pretend they've read. Well Randy read them. He told me that Shakespeare and Dickens and Tolstoy helped save his sanity during all those years in prison. Of course he liked Dick Francis and John D. McDonald, too. And who's the fella what wrote the westerns? Hillerman. Tony Hillerman. Randy like Hillerman's books, too."

After we got out of the car, Maxine unlocked the trailer, opened the door so I could enter, and then stood back. I'd just started to step inside her home when something darted across my path. I jumped, startled and frightened, but Maxine laughed.

"Meet Lavonna."

I turned to look at a small iguana—head and back green as an emerald contrasting with a long dark tail. Maxine opened the trailer door wide, and Lavonna entered first.

"A house pet?" A chill traveled up my backbone clear to my scalp. "She looks like a miniature dragon. Does she bite?"

"Only fruits and veggies." Maxine grinned and pulled a chunk of lettuce from her refrigerator and laid it beside a water dish on the floor protected by a piece of newspaper. The creature began eating. "Yes, she's my house pet but she runs free while I'm at work. I thought for a while she must be someone's pet, but nobody's ever come to claim her."

"And she doesn't run off?"

"She sticks around because I feed her. She's my work partner when we go to Mallory at sunset." Maxine snapped on the TV and began flipping through the channels. "Have a chair, Keely." She checked her watch. "Program will start soon."

"Your work partner?" I could barely cork all the questions that crowded my mind as Maxine channel skipped until she found the right station.

"Yes, my work partner. Lavonna and me, we do sunset with the buskers at Mallory two or three nights a week. It's a touristy thing. You ever go there?"

"Not at sunset. Too crowded. But what do you and Lavonna do? Is she tame?"

Maxine motioned to a camera on a shelf above the TV set. "I carry Lavonna to Mallory in a cage. She's tame enough in my home, but I don't want the crowds to scare her into running away. At the dock, I snap on her collar and leash. Then I gentle her with bananas and avocado treats while I offer to take her picture with the tourists. Some like to send a shot of themselves and an iguana back home to loved ones. I like to set Lavonna on a person's shoulder and sort of wrap her around the subject's neck."

"And Lavonna puts up with all that attention?"

"She loves it. I give her a treat after each shot I take. She rates lots of oohs and aahs and the crowd presses closer. Soon I have the snowbirds lined up and waiting for the privilege of posing with Lavonna. They're ready and willing to pay. One night I drew a bigger crowd than the French fellow with the trained cats."

I tried not to shudder, tried not to imagine the creature wrapped around my neck.

"Do you carry insurance, Maxine? What if there was an accident? What if Lavonna bit someone?"

Maxine just laughed. "Lavonna, she never bite. She's gentle. She likes to go to Mallory, likes everything about it—except that bagpiper. I keep my distance from that one and his noise."

The usual spate of commercials flashed on the TV screen and I hoped Maxine would mute them, but she didn't. She seemed to enjoy them—especially the one where the man demonstrating a vacuum cleaner pulled the spots from a Dalmatian. I looked around the trailer trying to imagine living in such confined quarters for decades.

The home would have made a good ad for promoting Maxine's housecleaning. Everything looked spotless. I even smelled the telltale aroma of chocolate-chip cookies. The bed built into the back of the trailer lay neatly made and the blue-and-white-polka dot bedspread matched the curtains at either end of the bed. I looked at Maxine's bloomers and wondered if Sears or Big K had promoted a fabric sale. Or maybe she'd mail-ordered it.

The middle of the trailer housed a built-in stove and refrigerator, both spotlessly clean, and we were sitting in the living room that consisted of two easy chairs and a couch.

"The couch folds out into a bed," Maxine said as if reading my mind. "That's where Randy sleeps—usually. On nice nights he sometimes sleeps in the hammock under the canopy outside the door."

Forty years. Forty years. The words replayed through my mind. Maxine had lived in a Stock Island trailer for forty years. A man's resonant voice brought my attention back to the TV screen. The Reverend Soto. He was well-known in Key West. Today he wore an ankle-length white robe with a mandarin collar. A green cord nipped the robe in at the waist and the green stole around his neck matched the cord. Soto sat in a captain's chair beside a small table that held books and papers. The man sitting facing him at the other end of the table wore jeans topped by a denim jacket over a crew-neck T-shirt. When he changed positions, squirming in his chair, I read the words Hog's Breath Saloon on his shirt. And he wore barefoot sandals.

"The guy closest to the camera's my Randy." Maxine whispered as if her words might be heard by the men on stage and interrupt the program.

"Oh." I'd sometimes heard people say, "Words failed me," and now I experienced that sensation. I'd never seen Randy Jackson before, but I'd built up a mental picture of him that in no way matched the reality on the screen. From Maxine's talk, I'd guessed Randy to be between 40 and 45, but he looked more like 60 or 65. His steel-gray hair hung straight to his shoulders, sometimes revealing the gold stud in his left earlobe. His piercing eyes were like blackened nail heads gleaming above a gray moustache and a scraggly beard that only partially hid a deep Z-shaped scar on his right cheek. I tried not to imagine him swigging beer from a long-necked bottle concealed in a brown paper bag.

Because of Maxine's roly-poly stature, I'd expected Randy to be short and stout, too. Wrong. He must have inherited his father's genes. Even sitting in his slouched position, his head rose above the minister's and he looked beanpole thin. The word emaciated sprang to mind.

Anger began to bubble deep inside me. Were the city slickers backing this program deliberately trying to make Randy Jackson look bad?

"Good morning, viewers. Welcome to this week's edition of *Wrongly Convicted.* I'm today's emcee, Reverend William Soto from Key West, Florida." Soto smiled into the camera. "I'll be introducing today's guest, Randy Jackson, our special visitor from my home town. Randy, say hello to our audience."

SIX

WITHOUT SMILING, RANDY gave a cursory nod toward the camera. The Reverend Soto said a few more words of introduction before the program broke for announcements. I reached into my jumpsuit pocket, fumbled past the mini–tape recorder I always carried to record patient comments, until I could pull out my cell phone. Keying in Punt's number, I waited. The more Punt knew about Randy and Maxine Jackson before he met them, the less I'd have to explain to him at the meeting I hoped to set up.

"Keely here, Punt," I said when he answered. "Please tune quickly to Public Network TV, and watch Randy Jackson." I broke our connection before he could respond, and focused again on the TV.

"Ladies and gentlemen," Soto said, "I'm sure you've all read about convicts who've been exonerated when their lawyers presented DNA evidence that proved them innocent. Our guest today, Randy Jackson, has experienced this situation. No. Correction, please. Randy Jackson is experiencing this—this ongoing nightmare.

"I and Attorney Shelley Hubble of Key West, Florida, brought Randy's situation to the attention of the sponsors of this program, and now we're bringing it to a larger audience, you viewers of this TV show.

"First and foremost, wrongly convicted prisoners want their freedom along with legal exoneration. But once they've achieved those things, society's backhand slaps leave them bitter and angry. Doesn't that describe, partially at least, the way you've felt since the court granted your freedom, Mr. Jackson?"

Randy straightened up and I guessed he wasn't used to being called "mister." Without smiling, he nodded in agreement.

"Let me give you some statistics." Soto rose and paced, looking almost regal in his clerical trappings. I prepared myself for an information dump. Okay. I needed to know more about ex-cons and how Randy Jackson fit into the picture. Soto smiled into the camera.

"In our rich nation, only a handful of our fifty states pay reparations to exonerated ex-convicts. New York and West Virginia have set no limits on what they pay, but California caps the total payment at $10,000. And our federal government? Pleas to federal officials might get a freed convict $5,000—if he has a good lawyer."

Soto stepped closer to the camera as he continued, and his stentorian voice demanded audience attention. "A statistician crunched some numbers revealing that one hundred ten exonerated inmates freed by DNA evidence had spent, collectively, over one thousand years in prison. But after doing years of jail time, they were freed to make a new life for themselves. Free? Yes. But for many of those men, their freedom brought neither a happy ending to their past imprisonment nor a happy beginning for their future freedom. But I'm going to let Randy Jackson share his feelings with you.

"Randy, where are you living in Key West?" Soto took his seat at the table.

Randy scowled. "I can't afford to live in Key West, so I'm living on Stock Island near Key West in a trailer home with my mother."

"Did she take you in willingly?"

"Yes, sir. She did. If she hadn't, I'd be a street person today."

"You'd like a place of your own?"

"I appreciate Mom's taking me in, but sure, I'd like my own place. I've got no money to buy a house or rent an apartment."

"Where do you work, Randy?"

Randy shrugged. "I'm unemployed. No job."

"Have you applied for work?"

"Many times. More times than I can count. I've scoured the help wanted ads in newspapers from Key West to Key Largo. I've appeared for interviews. When an employer learns I've once been convicted of rape and murder and that I've spent over twenty years in prison …" Randy shook his head and looked at the floor.

"Raiford. That's Florida State Prison, right?"

"Right." Randy's scowl deepened. "Florida employers hear the word Raiford and they show me the door. When I argue that I've been exonerated, they shake their heads. Seems to me they're convinced that 'exonerated' is a dirty ten-letter word."

"Do they give reasons for turning you down?"

"Sometimes they say they're afraid I've been influenced by the criminals I've associated with for twenty years. They're afraid their men employees will resent working with an ex-con and quit. They're afraid their women employees will be afraid of me and quit. It might not help me, but I wish accounts of my past arrests could be erased from my record. Wherever I go, that rap sheet follows me."

Now the audio control technician began blipping out Randy's profanity.

"I wish you could start over with a clean slate, too, and in time it may be so. But for now it's impossible. I take it that you find few jobs available in the Keys."

"Not so. Few jobs are available for ex-cons. Many windows on Duval and Front Street show 'help wanted' signs. Employers need waiters, dishwashers, bus boys. It's always been that way. The (blip, blip) employers don't pay wages that allow service workers to afford food and housing."

"You're willing to work in an entry-level service job?"

"Yes. I'll accept any (blip) job that gives me a paycheck."

"How old were you when the court sent you to jail?"

"Twenty-two. Almost twenty-three."

"You graduate high school?"

"Yes sir. My mom's still got my framed diploma hanging in her trailer house."

"You must have worked for several years between high school graduation and your imprisonment at Raiford."

"Right. I worked as a treasure diver for Mel Fisher. He was a big-time salvor searching the sea bottom for sunken Spanish galleons."

"You liked that work?"

"Loved it."

"Any dive jobs open now?"

"None open to ex-cons."

"Ever think of writing a book about your diving experiences?"

Randy shook his head. "No money there. At least not for authors. Oh, I read about a handful of writers making it big. But others work and starve trying to make a living. I'm willing to do honest labor for anyone who'll hire me."

"Thank you for your input, Randy."

The Reverend Soto looked into the camera. "What do you think, viewers? Do you agree with me that our justice system has failed society by imprisoning the innocent? Do you agree that although exonerated, these men remain silently condemned for life?"

Soto rose and stood behind Randy's chair for a moment before he spoke again. "Of course the court's mistakes are horrific, but, as the saying goes, help's on the way." The minister took his seat again. "During the past several years, concerned people have worked to establish innocence projects to free prisoners wrongly convicted. Today, concerned citizens are trying to help the exonerated ease back into society."

"Who are these people?" Randy asked.

"Organizers of the DNA Identification Technology and Human Rights Center are frontrunners in helping the exonerated. Their projects require funding, but we'll discuss that at another time. Right now, I want you viewers to hear more from Randy Jackson."

Soto turned once more to Randy who again had slumped in his chair. He straightened up. I held my breath wondering what he'd say next.

"Mr. Jackson, will you tell us of some of your experiences in prison? No sob story, please. Just your feelings about your false incarceration. I want our listeners to try to imagine their own lives, had they had the bad luck to have been in your shoes."

Randy leaned forward in his chair.

"To start at the beginning, I went one night to pick up my girl-friend, Dyanne Darby. She'd the night off from waitressing at Sloppy's and I'd promised her dinner at Pier House. We were celebrating the first month's anniversary of our first date. But that dinner never happened. I knocked at her door. No answer. I tried the knob and the door opened. When I stepped inside, Dyanne lay on the floor in a puddle of blood."

Randy looked at his feet. "Hate thinking about that time. It never entered my head to run. I approached Dyanne and checked for a pulse, finding none. I called the police. First thing I knew, I was being accused of a rape and murder I didn't do.

"I'll be first to admit I went to prison with a rap sheet that told of my head-ins with the law. But I'd never been in serious trouble. I had no street gang connections. I hung out with Mel Fisher's dive crew—my working buddies. But I did have an arrest for shoplifting. That was a big thing for kids to do during my senior year in high school. Police caught me lifting a dive mask at Boog Powell's marina. Later, I had a few arrests for underage drinking and traffic violations. But I'd faced no felony charges."

"Who was your attorney?" Soto asked.

"Attorney Ralph Mason—court-appointed since I had no money for a lawyer."

"Did you like this man? Did you feel he did his best for you?"

"No and no. I didn't like him or his superior nose-in-the-air attitude. He'd visit me reeking of beer. I think he even came in tipsy to the courtroom on one occasion. Anyway, the judge called a recess that day without saying why. But that's getting ahead of the story. Before my case went to trial, the police questioned me endlessly.

"I didn't change my story. I declared my innocence to lawyers and prosecuting attorneys and judges. Later, in the courtroom, people came forward and spoke against me—some of them I didn't know, people I'd never seen before. One woman I did know—Nicole Nichols, a friend of Dyanne's, testified that she saw me go into Dyanne's apartment and come out with blood on my hands. When I heard that, I shouted and caused a commotion, but nobody listened. The judge banged his gavel and ordered quiet in the courtroom, and the bailiff came to stand by my side.

"Nobody but my mom believed in me. Nobody. After the trial, the jury foreman said 'guilty,' and the judge sentenced me for a rape and a murder I didn't do."

Soto spoke again. "Tell our viewers about day by day prison life."

Randy leaned a bit farther forward. "I hated sharing space with lifers. Kidnappers. Child abusers. Rapists. Murderers. Those weren't my kind of people. I hated them. They hated me. The daily life-or-death need of having to get along with those (blip) turned me into a hard man at age twenty-three. I knew immediately that I must protect myself. The inmates were like wolves eyeing me, sniffing my scent."

Suddenly Randy stood and began pacing. At first I thought Soto would try to calm him or ask him to sit down again. But no. And Randy continued talking and pacing, stepping closer and closer to the camera. Even Maxine stood and approached the TV as if she wanted to reach out and touch her son's arm.

"I made a shiv from a spoon—a spoon they gave me with a meal. The guard never noticed anything missing when he picked up my tray. I hid the spoon in my mattress. At night I fashioned that spoon into a make-shift knife. The next day I stabbed a guy who propositioned and threatened me during recreation time. Didn't hurt him much. He never complained to the guards. But after that incident, I got more respect from those (blip) thugs I had to live with. A lot more respect."

"Did you feel that one of them might retaliate? If you had a knife of sorts, maybe one of them did, too."

"I watched my back," Randy said. "Every minute of every day and even at night I kept on guard. Back home I'd slept like ten dead elephants. No more. The least sound or unusual movement startled me awake. I hadn't been there long before someone would blame me for attacking them whenever I tried to defend myself. The guards tried to break my spirit. I spent lots of time in solitary. As I look back on it now, those days in solitary were some of my easiest days in prison. I could relax. I didn't have to worry about someone attacking or stabbing me while I slept. On the outside, I'd been an avid reader, and that past reading saved my life. Many hours I'd lie there in cold and damp and darkness recalling passages from Dickens and Shakespeare—even passages from Zane Grey and the Bible. The twenty-third psalm sustained me many times."

Now Soto rose again and stood beside Randy. "I'm afraid we have to draw this program to a close, Mr. Jackson. There are people and organizations trying to help you and others like you who have been exonerated of crimes. And I'm one of those people. We want a few necessary things for you—job training, for instance. We want affordable housing. We want you to have access to both physical and mental health checkups. But I have one more question for you, Mr. Jackson. Right now at this point in your life, what is the one thing you want most for yourself?"

Randy rose and stepped so close to the camera that his face filled our screen. The scar on his cheek flushed red as he scowled and screamed, "I…want…revenge."

The technician blipped some words, missed others he should have blipped, and Soto tried to ease Randy from front and center, but Randy held firm. "I intend to find the guy who murdered Dyanne Darby. I intend to find the (blip, blip, blip, blip, blip) and make him pay. Big time."

The cameraman cut Randy from the picture and focused on Soto, but it was too late. Everyone had seen the naked hatred on Randy's face and heard the rage in his voice. In that moment I agreed with Maxine. Randy Jackson could be a threat to society.

SEVEN

I WAITED FOR MAXINE to say something following Randy's outburst, but she stood silent as a stone. So did I. She felt protective toward "her Randy," and I wasn't ready to share my feelings with her yet. Randy Jackson wanted revenge. His anger put me on guard, but his sad story prompted me to identify with him. Me identifying with an ex-convict! How could that be! We both were well acquainted with the status of underdog. We'd both known extreme mistreatment and the ensuing hopelessness.

Randy and I had met, not in person, but through this TV show, and I have a strong belief that people never meet accidentally. Somewhere there's a master plan. People meet when there's a need for them to know each other. What was the need here? Randy was in an almost hopeless situation—a situation similar to my own when Jude Cardell controlled my life and I could see no way out. Now, Maxine was asking for my help. I locked my thoughts deep inside myself as we prepared to return to my office.

Snapping off the TV, Maxine picked up the leavings from Lavonna's snack and tossed them into a trash basket. She grunted a bit when she stooped to coax Lavonna to her and then grasped her collar. Her knuckles whitened from the effort of grabbing the countertop and hoisting herself upright. I wondered how she managed to clean houses when stooping and rising again were such a struggle. She needed to lose some weight? Easy for me to say. Not easy for Maxine to do. I wondered if she'd ever tried going on a diet. Weight loss might do her body more good than foot reflexology.

"Out you go, Lavonna." Maxine pulled the iguana toward the door and coaxed her outside with a tomato. Lavonna ate the tomato and then strolled to the palm tree that supported one end of a hammock. With little effort, she climbed the smooth trunk before disappearing into the greenery. I wondered if Randy ever slept in that hammock unaware that Lavonna might be watching from above. Lavonna the watch iguana.

"Aren't you afraid she'll run away? Is she safe outside?"

"Lavonna stick close by. She knows who feeds her."

Maxine didn't speak again until we were in the car and back on Highway One headed for Key West. Nor did I.

"Now you see why I need your help?" Maxine sighed and relaxed for the first time since turning off the TV.

"I can see Randy's having a hard time adjusting to his new world. His situation has changed a lot in twenty years."

"My Randy. He's like a firecracker with a sizzling fuse. This morning I think his ready-to-fight attitude scared Reverend Soto and likely the TV people, too—the very people who are trying to help him."

"You're right. His attitude could scare people." I almost blurted that I was one of those people, but I bit my tongue and swallowed the words. I had a lot of thinking to do.

"I'm worrying that one day all his bottled anger will explode unlessen he find Dyanne Darby's killer. Once the true killer's convicted and put behind bars, people will have to admit my Randy's innocent. Only then will they be sure."

Maybe. I said the word in my mind, remembering the long hair, the ear stud, the Hog's Breath Saloon T-shirt. "Finding the guilty one might help. I agree. I didn't realize people were giving Randy such a bad time. I understand his anger and depression."

"And hopelessness. That's the worst thing. He's lost hope for a better life."

The driver of an RV trailing both a pick-up truck and a twenty-foot cabin cruiser gave a blast on his horn when Maxine cut ahead of him and turned onto North Roosevelt. Maxine flipped him the bird and eased into the right lane. I looked the other way.

"When will Randy return from New York?"

"On a seven-fifteen flight tonight. I'll meet him at the airport."

I smiled at the thought of Randy passing through airport

security. People traveling in and out of the Keys usually face extra scrutiny including a thorough baggage mauling and a body-wanding that can reach the point of embarrassment. Then I scowled; guards might be just as likely to pass Randy through quickly, thinking nobody carrying drugs or weapons would appear dressed so obviously like a crown prince of the under-world. Instead, they'd scrutinize some white-haired grandmother type and give her the treatment with their wands and X-ray machines. But since 9/11 I never complained about extra security. The guards can't guess which granny might carry a bomb tucked under her garter.

I gazed across the bay where sunlight made the water surface look like crumpled aluminum foil. A slim jogger pounded along on the sidewalk between the street and the bay, leading his Great Dane on a leash while a woman wearing headphones power-walked, nodding to a rhythm only she could hear. Gulls screamed and wheeled overhead. Pelicans perched like icons on dark coral rocks that studded the shallows. In the distance three sailboats caught the salt-scented breeze and skimmed across the water, their white sails taut. I seldom tired of the sea scene and I kept my eyes averted from the string of fast food cafés, auto repair shops, and hotels on my left, pretending they didn't exist.

When we reached Garrison Bight, only one fishing boat remained in its slip. I could hardly wait to get my own boat in the water.

"Hopeless." Maxine said the word with a sigh. "That's how my Randy feels."

"Maybe Punt can help. I know you've had no time to get Randy's permission to talk to Punt, but surely you can persuade him to agree. You heard me call Punt before Randy's TV appearance. Punt's a wealthy guy from a wealthy family, but he knows firsthand what it's like to be down and out on booze and hard drugs. He knows how it feels to have society against him. Punt can identify with the underdog, and after hearing Randy's story, I think he'll be willing to try to help him. And if Randy's smart, he'll accept all the help he can get." I still couldn't admit my own feelings of identification with Randy. Maybe it was enough just to put him in touch with Punt.

Maxine inched the Ford down Duval, honking and narrowly missing three girls wobbling on rented mopeds. Tourists seldom read news about tourists' moped accidents. They never make the front page. Stopping in front of my office, Maxine double-parked long enough to let me out. Motorists behind us honked and shouted.

"I'll call you this evening, Maxine. I'll try to make us an appointment with Punt. You try to get Randy to talk with him. Okay?"

"I'll try, but I'm making no promise." Maxine drove away as if oblivious to the traffic snarl she had caused.

Consuela sat waiting, perched on a bar stool in Gram's shop and sipping a latte.

"Finish your drink," I called to her before I entered my office. "I need to make one short phone call."

Hurrying inside, I checked my phone for messages. None. Punt seldom ignored my calls. I punched in his number again. No answer. Drat. Had he seen Randy on TV? I willed myself to be calm. I couldn't give Consuela a reflexology treatment if my hands were shaking. I didn't know what scared me the most—the person who wrote the warning note, the one who made the telephone threat, or Randy Jackson himself. Identifying with Randy didn't make my fear of him disappear.

Consuela, now wearing a lime-green sarong with a matching shoulder purse, made her usual whirlwind entry into my office. Sitting down uninvited, she kicked off her spike heels and plunged her feet into the footbath before I'd had time to add the frangipani scent to the fresh water. Consuela always insisted on frangipani, maybe because I'd told her it was one of the most expensive fragrances I offered.

"I suppose you watched the program, Keely."

"What program?" I pretended ignorance. It graveled me that Consuela knew so much about my business, my activities.

"You know good and well what program." She deliberately splashed water onto the floor. "The TV program Randy Jackson just starred on in New York. I watched it, too. People treat Randy rotten."

Starred? I had to admit Randy had upstaged Reverend Soto. "Yes, the public's been very unkind to him. I didn't realize …"

"I have a late date with Randy tonight. He's going to tell me all about his trip, his first-class plane cabin, the big-time hotel—the whole thing. When my writing makes me famous I'll know about those important things from personal experience. I'll have opportunities to experience them for myself."

"I'm sure you will, Consuela. Where are you and Randy going for your date tonight?" I wondered how a guy like Randy could afford any place Consuela would consider appropriate for a famous writer-in-waiting.

"Randy's got no money. I know that. But his charm makes up for that. We'll relax at my place. I've made conch chowder and a Key lime pie—his favorite foods."

Consuela left the footbath and walked to the treatment chair without bothering to slip into the slippers I'd provided. I sighed and said nothing about the puddles she left on the floor. When she lay back in the chair, I raised the footrest and I didn't offer her a pillow. Didn't want to talk to her if I could avoid it.

"Need a pillow, Keely. Got plenty to say to you this morning. You rude to me earlier. Didn't like that at all. We are long-time friends, yet you keep me waiting for my appointment. Don't like that none, either."

"I apologize, Consuela, I'm sorry. I know I'm a few minutes late, and I'll work with you a few minutes longer. This morning you interrupted Maxine's treatment. That's why I had to ask you to leave. It was Maxine's first treatment, and she felt wary of being tipped back in the chair."

"Consuela accepts your apology." She brushed her flowing hair aside and adjusted the pillow beneath her head. "I would like to help you find Dyanne Darby's killer, Keely. We would be doing the world a service."

I didn't doubt that Consuela would like to be in on any murder investigation. Her kind thrived on excitement—and male attention. Had it been possible she would have worn her boyfriends like charms on a bracelet.

"Why do you think I'm trying to find Dyanne Darby's killer? I've no plans to get involved in a mystery that happened when I was a child. No way."

I worked on Consuela's big toe and felt the crystalline deposits break up. I knew she must have felt twinges of pressure, but she never flinched. She often complained of headaches and she believed my reflexology treatments kept them at bay.

"I think you've decided to help Randy and his mother because you're a kind person, Keely. You have a good heart and you like to help people—underdog people like the Jacksons. You deny this?"

I didn't reply.

"Okay, so I tell you the honest truth. I know you be the one who tries to help Randy because he hint that to me. He say a friend of his mother found one killer on this island and that she may help him. Now who could that be except you, Keely. Who?"

EIGHT

I DIDN'T GIVE CONSUELA a yes or a no. Instead I released her left foot and began manipulations on her right foot.

"Let me help you with your investigation, Keely. I know the people you need to talk to. Know some of them well."

Again, I made no response.

"Well you can go on saying nothing, but I'm eager to admit that I've been trying my best to help Randy find the rotten person who let him sit in jail all those years."

"And just what have you been doing?" I hated breaking my clam act, but I've found it's a good plan to know what esoteric activities Consuela has in mind.

"I've been talking to people on the QT. Very quietly. Very subtly."

I squelched a smile at her oxymoron. Her attitude worried me.

"Who've you been talking to?"

"The divers. The old-time divers who worked for Mel Fisher back in the eighties. Some of those guys still live here. Some of them I know well. Very well, indeed."

"What do you think they can tell you that will help Randy Jackson? So Randy says they all worked together. They hung out together. But that doesn't mean that one of them murdered Dyanne Darby. And if one of them did, he'll certainly never tell you."

"See?" Consuela crowed. "I knew you were interested in that murder. Let me help you, Keely. You, me, Punt Ashford—we'll be detective partners."

"Which divers have you been talking to? And what have you been saying to them?"

"Some of the divers you may know. They're older now. Not many of them dive for hire these days."

"That figures. Punt's dad, Beau, used to work for Mel Fisher, but he hasn't done any serious diving for years."

"You met Gus Helmer a while back. You remember him, right?"

"How could I forget?" Rough, tough Gus Helmer. Of course I remembered him. Didn't she know Gus was one of my current clients?

"Gus used to be special to me, but he married now. Some Miami woman." Consuela grinned. "Now I only see him when wifey goes to visit her mother. But I talk to Gus about Dyanne Darby and Randy. He remembered them—and the murder."

I sighed and kept my thoughts to myself. Gus Helmer's a shrimper who owns and operates the *Pink Gold*. He's a bulldog of a man, not a big guy, but tough acting. At the time Punt and I first met him, he lived aboard a dry-docked boat near the shrimp docks. He doubled his fist a lot when he talked to Punt and Punt respected that. He shrugged a lot when he talked to me, explaining his romantic activities. His attitude won him little respect from me, but live and let live. Who was I to judge him?

"So you've talked to Gus. Who else?"

"Slone Pierce. Slone and I go back a long ways. Today he operates his own salvage business. He travels anywhere in the Keys where there's work. He also married now and his wife, Nicole, say I can only talk to him if she's present. That cramps my style a whole lot, but I did talk with the both of them about Randy. Don't think Slone knows anything about the Dyanne Darby murder."

I hoped Consuela was right. I massaged her left arch and then her left heel. Slone Pierce reminded me of a trained seal, sleek, heavy set, handsome. Don't blame Slone's wife for not wanting him to talk to Consuela.

"But I want to talk to you about Ace Grovello."

"Your new boyfriend, right? And a diver, right?"

"I tried to tell you about him this morning—you know, the guy who may sign up for your treatments and earn me a freebie. Well, Ace used to dive for Fisher. Made some good finds, too—a gold doubloon, for instance. Mel let him keep it. Ace had it mounted and now he wears it on a chain for everyone to see. If

I'm good to him, he lets me wear it for a day or two, but it's important to him and I always have to give it back."

"Consuela! You're a common slut!" The words slipped out before I remembered that wise businesswomen don't use crude names when speaking to a customer. I blame my life with Jude Cardell for my in-depth knowledge of a vocabulary I seldom use.

"How dare you talk to me like that!" Consuela started to leave the treatment chair, but I forced a smile and gently pushed her back down.

"I'm sorry, Consuela. Tell me more about Ace. What does he do now?"

Consuela stayed in the chair and pouted for a few moments before she replied.

"I'm no slut, Keely Moreno. A slut sleeps with any guy she meets on the street. I only sleep with the ones I love. And because I'm no slut, I can accept your apology. Ace runs a bed-and-breakfast on Whitehead Street. The Sand Dollar. Sometimes he invites me to stay all night there in the off season. Very neat place. Always full in season."

"Who else, Consuela? Who else have you talked to?"

"Reverend Soto. He worked for Fisher, but he helped spring Randy from prison. I doubt that he the one who murdered Dyanne Darby. Unless he did it and now tries to throw suspicion from him by doing good works. People do stuff like that sometimes.

"And then there's Punt's dad. Beau worked for Fisher, too. But he's such a Mr. Big nowadays in Key West I can't suspect him. I housecleaned for years for Beau and his first wife. I don't think Beau would murder anyone."

I finished Consuela's treatment, massaged her feet with scented oil—frangipani, of course, and then helped her from the chair. She padded barefoot to her shoes and slipped into them.

"Keely, since I've done all this early-on investigation and told you all about it, how about letting me help you find Dyanne's killer? It might give me something to write about. Writers need ideas. And helping you would win me brownie points with Randy. Right now he's my favorite boyfriend."

"I am not going to get involved in this murder case. Don't you see what you may have done by questioning those divers? You may have alerted the murderer to the fact that Maxine wants help in looking into the Darby murder and that all the divers are under suspicion."

"Do you really think so?" For once Consuela looked crestfallen.

"Yes, I really think so. Your antics make me furious and they make no sense. Why do you feel that one of the divers's guilty? It could have been anyone. The culprit may live far from Key West. Over twenty years have passed."

Consuela stared into the distance as if that idea had never crossed her mind. Then she snapped her fingers and glared at me.

"Keely Moreno, you have no imagination. A good detective needs imagination. It is easy for me to believe that one of Randy's dive buddies was jealous of Randy. Hated him for dating Dyanne Darby. That jealous person may have gone into a rage. He could have killed Dyanne in order to keep Randy from having her. Sometimes jealous lovers behave that way. Don't you agree that this could have happened?"

"No. I don't agree."

Consuela flounced from my office without paying. But I knew she'd be back and pay up the next time she had a migraine.

One more client and I'd be free for the afternoon, but the morning's warnings made me wary. With both Maxine and Consuela talking up the possibility that I might be looking into the Darby murder, they'd put someone on guard. I wondered who.

Maybe I shouldn't go fishing alone. Before I decided to stay home, a marriage counselor's voice replayed in my mind. Fear is a response. Courage is a decision.

Living in fear was no longer an option. I had started to lay out some clothes for my afternoon on the water when my phone rang. I didn't answer and my mouth went dry. If the call was a client, he would try again later. Wouldn't he? I waited.

The phone rang again. I hated that it took so much courage for me to answer my telephone. Rats! I picked up the receiver.

NINE

"KEELY!" PUNT'S VOICE flowed across the line. "Sorry I didn't catch your call a few minutes ago. What's up? Gonna ask me to go fishing with you this afternoon?"

"Oh, Punt. I need to talk to you. Did you tune in to Randy Jackson's TV appearance this morning?"

"Caught part of it. First half, maybe. Then a client arrived and I missed the rest of the show. I remember reading about Randy Jackson quite a while back. Exonerated on a murder-one rap, right? But how come you're suddenly so interested in him?"

"It's a long story." I stopped talking, trying to organize my thoughts so Punt wouldn't guess I'd been scared to answer my phone. "Keely? You still there? Keely?"

"I'm still here. But …"

"The long story. Let's hear it, please. I can tell when something's giving you the nervous fantods. How's this Jackson person important to you? From what I saw of him on-screen, he didn't look like your type."

"My type of what?" I tried for a light touch. "Seriously, Punt, I need advice. I like to stick up for the underdog, but Randy Jackson looks and sounds like such a lowlife I feel confused." I couldn't bring myself to tell him about the warnings. Not yet.

"And Jackson's your current underdog? You're asking your favorite PI for help?"

"Perhaps. At least I'm trying to talk Randy Jackson and his mother into making an appointment with you. They need a private investigator's help, but they can't pay. I thought maybe you could at least listen to Randy's story—pro bono."

"Pro bono work's never my favorite kind of employment. But you can tell me about it while we're out on the water. Deal?"

"I'd planned to go fishing, but some unsettling things have come up since early this morning." I caught my breath. "But… I'm still going fishing. I decided that for sure before you called and I was hunting my jeans and boat shoes when my phone rang."

"Courage is a decision, right? That motto that can get you in big trouble if you take it too seriously. I can't guess what's bugging you today, but why don't I pick you up around one o'clock and we'll head for the back country together—in my boat. Let's enjoy the afternoon before we start worrying about Randy Jackson and his problems."

"What about your office, your clients? With your partner busy in Tallahassee, you could miss an important client if you close your office."

"This afternoon you'll be my important client and I won't tell Nikko. Pro bono. No retainer required or expected. See you at one."

Punt cut our connection before I could protest. But I wouldn't have protested. We'd shared an on-again off-again romance since high school days—on, when he'd been a good student and the football hero; off, when he'd been a school dropout and a druggie. And off during my four-year marriage to Jude Cardell. Following my courage-is-a-decision divorce, Punt and I became close again. He was drug free by then, but still a beach bum. We fell in love and he proposed marriage, but my emotional scars along with my terrifying nightmares made me wary of all men. For weeks, those scars wouldn't let me share his bed for even one night, let alone for a lifetime of nights.

I stretched out in my apartment to rest for a few minutes before my next appointment—Gus Helmer. Reflexology treatments wear me down both physically and mentally. I almost dozed until I heard Gus knock on my back door. Jumping up, I hurried to admit him, wishing Consuela hadn't talked to him about the Darby murder. I couldn't help wondering if Gus had been the person spouting threats and warnings.

Gus always entered through my back door, parking his rattle-trap car in the alley where it might be towed away at any moment. But somehow that never happened. Guess Gus thought it ruined his tough-guy image to be seen at my front door reporting for re-flexology treatments. As usual, the faint aroma of shrimp wafted around him. I willed my hands and my voice into steadiness.

"Morning, Keely. Great day outside."

"Right, Gus." He followed me to the footbath and I closed the drapery across my office window, reassuring him that nobody would see him inside. Nor could anyone see me. Today I wanted to be visible, visible to anyone who might come to my aid if I needed help. But I left the curtain closed.

Gus wore his sandy hair hanging straight in chin-length wisps that matched his freckles. His tank top revealed a multitude of tattoos. Snakes. Hearts. Spacecraft. You name it and Gus could point it out somewhere on his arms and chest. I didn't name it. Sometimes I wondered if his tattoos covered his whole torso, but I wasn't about to ask.

"Shoulder's been a-paining me this week. Need a fix there." He kicked off a pair of black flip-flops and waited while I ran fresh water into the foot-sized tub. After I started the whirlpool, he plunged his feet into it and I let him enjoy the motion of the water for a few moments before I directed him to the treatment chair.

"What kind of lotion do you prefer, Gus?"

"Lime. That sounds good for today."

Gus's weight made my chair creak and groan, and although he had huge feet, they were easy to manipulate. I picked up his right foot first.

"You been doing extra exercise of some kind that started the shoulder pain?"

"Just the usual. Lowering nets. Managing the dragging. Winching the catch up."

"When did the pain start?"

"February the second. I marked it down in my log book. Like to keep track of things of importance. Shoulder pain's important to a shrimper."

To my surprise, Gus fell asleep only a few minutes into his treatment and I felt more at ease. A sleeping patient was unlikely to rise up and murder me on the spot. I had to awaken Gus when I finished his treatment and he apologized for dropping off.

"Been working for ten nights in a row. Brought the *Pink Gold* in early this morning. Now I got to get back to the dock and help the crew unload. Good catch. I'm not complaining. Good catch. I marked it down in the log."

As soon as Gus paid me and left, I relaxed and locked my office, skinned from my khaki jumpsuit, and pulled on jeans, T-shirt, and boat shoes. I jammed my cell phone into my pocket, but when I started to hurry to Gram's shop to tell her my after-noon schedule, my phone rang again. My throat tightened, but I had to answer. I half expected another threat, but instead a deep resonant voice said my name.

"Miss Moreno?"

"Yes?" My voice came out high-pitched but firm.

"Ace Grovello here."

"Yes. How may I help you?"

"We haven't met in person, but our friend Consuela is insist-ing that I try your services as a foot reflexologist. She guaran-tees you can cure my upper back problems. Do you have any openings?" He hesitated for a moment, then added, "Perhaps an opening as soon as tomorrow?"

"Thank you for calling, Mr. Grovello." I managed to lower my voice to its usual pitch. "Consuelo always plays the role of eternal optimist. I never guarantee my treatments as sure cures for anything. She knows that. But I'm willing to meet you and to talk with you about how reflexology treatments might be able to help you."

"Fine, Miss Moreno. Would you have any free time tomorrow?"

"Tomorrow morning my first time slot's open. If you'd stop around nine o'clock, I'll talk to you about your specific problems."

"Nine o'clock it is. I'll be there."

"Thank you. I'll look forward to meeting you—to helping you."

Ace Grovello. I tried to forget that he was one of the former divers Consuela had talked to about Randy. His name had a pleasant ring to it and I rolled it around in my mind as I hurried to Gram's shop. Gram had taught me long ago that it's never safe to go boating without telling someone where you're going and when you expect to return. She obliged by being my safety net, but I usually returned about the time I said I would.

"Have fun, Keely," Gram said once I'd told her my plans. "I know you be safe when you be with Punt. You be smart to marry that man. Handsome. Rich. Employed."

Three customers sitting at her coffee bar grinned and I felt heat rise from my neck to my forehead. "Come on, Gram. No match-making today. We're going out to catch bonefish—maybe a permit. Be back before dark."

Punt arrived, double parking his vintage Karmann Ghia in front of Gram's shop while I grabbed a sweatshirt, stuck the CLOSED sign in my window and pulled the drapery more securely across the glass. Gram's customers pretended they weren't scrutinizing Punt, but I knew they were eyeing his rangy build, his thick auburn hair caught in a ponytail at his nape, his mirrored sunglasses.

His yellow convertible barely had room for 2 passengers, but we both loved its low-slung frame and its black leather bucket seats, loved to see people gawk at this rebuilt relic of the 70s as we drove through Old Town. Had anyone asked, Punt would have been flattered to stop and tell them all about his rebuilding the VW right in his carport at Ashford Mansion. Today nobody asked.

"Yo, mama," a teenager called and whistled. "Travelin' our route?"

"Way to go, man," his buddy shouted, giving us thumbs up.

I looked at Punt and we both pretended not to notice our audience.

Punt didn't press me for answers to the questions I knew must be flying through his mind. Good. Maybe I needed to calm down and think things through. We drove slowly to Seaview Marina, parked in a visitor's slot, then entered the marina office.

The building reminded me of an above-ground cavern. Voices and motor noises echoed as they bounced off the ceiling high overhead where boats of all kinds and sizes peeked from storage slots. My mouth watered and I could almost taste the aroma of the hotdogs sizzling in a countertop broiler. They masked the ever-present and less enticing odor of diesel fuel and sweeping compound.

"Yahoo!" I threw my head back, shouted into the cavern, and

waited for the echo. The guy at the sales counter jumped, startled. Two guys working on their motors dropped their wrenches. A third man looked at me and gave a low whistle. I guessed that all of them had always wanted to shout a yahoo inside this place but had never had the spunk.

"Keely." Punt grinned. "You okay?"

"Sure. Just want to be sure that people notice our presence here this afternoon."

Punt led the way quickly to our lockers where we selected our tackle for the day. "Something's really bugging you, right? Not like you to be a noisemaker."

I didn't answer. Punt shrugged.

"Spinning rods or fly rods?" he asked. "Your choice."

"Spinning, okay?" I liked to use a fly rod when I was alone in my own boat, but with two people aboard, spinning rods were easier to manage—fewer back lashes, tangled lines, and taut tempers.

I refilled a thermos with fresh water from a spigot and bought us two boiled conch sandwiches and a couple of sodas from the vending machine while Punt purchased a package of frozen squid and half a dozen live shrimp from the bait boy.

"Great day for fishing," I said when we left the building. My boat shoes thunked against the planked dock, then I felt the gentle sway of the floating catwalk runway leading to the slip where Punt tethered the *Sea Deuced*.

He stepped over the gunwale and into his skiff before he turned to offer me a hand. The fiberglass boat floated like a sleek mermaid. Punt took pride in his role as captain. He polished the brass fittings and teakwood trim and kept the twin outboards in top-notch order. Before viewing the *Sea Deuced,* I'd never ever seen a fishing skiff with a carpeted floor. Punt also had recently added a silent electric motor to the boat's bow and installed an elevated poling platform above the motors aft.

"Where shall we go?" Punt secured our rods in the caddy beside the console before he dipped a bucket of sea water into the bait well and added the shrimp. I unwrapped the package of squid and set it on the bow to thaw. "The Tortugas?" he asked. "I know some keys out that way, secret places, safe spots with sandy coves."

"Sounds good to me." I liked the word safe. Sandy beaches are hard to find in the Keys because the coral reef offshore slows the waves before they smash into the shore-line rocks and grind them into sand. I sat on the passenger seat while Punt eased the boat from its slip and held to a no-wake speed until we reached open sea. Once he revved the motor and put the boat on plane, sunshine glinted on the V-shaped wedge of water ahead of the bow. Sea water frothed on my arms, and I tasted salt on my lips. For the moment I forgot my fears. I always felt safe with Punt. I smiled. I could think of no place on earth I'd rather be and no one I'd rather be with.

The motor roar made talking impossible until we reached Punt's chosen cove.

I'd fished this spot before, but since he thought it a secret place, I didn't tell him. He switched off the big motor and raised it from the water before he eased to the bow and plugged in the battery-operated electric motor. I walked aft and cast the anchor, watching the orange mushroom-shaped weight sink into the gray turtle grass three or four feet below us. The electric motor made hardly any noise. Later, it would allow us to ease into another cove without alerting any fish that might be nearby.

We began rigging our rods. Punt baited with a shrimp, but I pried a piece of squid from the frozen block and threaded it onto my hook. I made a couple of practice casts, standing at the side of the console.

"Why not stand on the bow, Keely? You can see 'em coming better from up there. I'll stand back here on the poling platform."

We stood in our respective spots and at the ready, but no fish finned through the crystal clear water. After a half hour of watching and waiting, I sighed.

"Want to hear about Randy Jackson now or later?" I could tell I was more eager to talk than Punt was to listen and that surprised me. Maybe he knew more about Randy Jackson than he'd let on.

"Let's give the fish a few more chances. I know you're all keyed up about something, but time on the water has a way of relaxing a person—of making molehills out of mountains."

I sighed, knowing my mountain would remain a mountain.

"We can always talk, Keely, but fishing's a sometimey thing. I'll ease us to another spot—a lucky spot." He pulled the anchor.

I stepped from the bow while Punt used the foot pedal on the electric motor to point us in a different direction and into a different cove. And again we cast anchor then waited under the cloudless sky. Punt spotted the permit first.

"To your left, Keely. Ten o'clock. Put that squid in front of his nose."

I saw the fish swimming toward me over a bed of turtle grass. Drawing my arm back, I made the cast, but the permit darted like a torpedo to our far right out of range.

"Drat!"

"Hey. Watch this." Punt dropped his shrimp right in front of a small 'cuda that had been stalking the permit. His rod tip bent toward the water and the sea frothed as the 'cuda took the bait and jumped. Silvery gray. It splashed back into the sea and Punt fought to keep the rod tip up. The 'cuda jumped again then headed toward the horizon. Punt played the fish, raising the rod tip, reeling in line. During all that activity, my attention had wandered from my rod, and I got a strike that almost jerked my tackle from my hand. The sudden action surprised me so I struggled to keep from falling overboard. Punt looked over his shoulder to see what was going on, and in that instant his 'cuda broke free and disappeared.

"Didn't want that one anyway. Next one'll be bigger—and hungrier."

"Sour grapes, Punt. You can't fool me. You goofed." I'd regained my balance and I began fighting the fish on my line.

"It's a bone, Keely. And a big one. Go easy. It's a brag-about catch if I ever saw one. Let's see you bring it to the boat."

TEN

FOR AN INSTANT I SAW the silvery body flashing through the water and I let it run for a few yards before I raised the rod tip and reeled in line. The fish and I played that strenuous game for the next half hour. My arms ached and my breath snagged in frenzied gasps by the time I brought the fish to the boat—both of us exhausted.

"Good one, Keely. Bet it'll go eight or nine pounds. Maybe more." Punt jumped from the poling platform and came to the boat side, grabbing a landing net on his way.

"I want to release it." I admired the silvery body, the black eye staring at me. Then the fish gave one more surprise lunge in an unsuccessful effort to escape. "I don't intend to keep it, Punt. Bones are no good for eating."

Punt leaned over the side and scooped the fish into the landing net. "Okay. You don't need to keep it, but before you release it, I want to snap a picture. Proof, you know. Proof to show any doubters who might give us an argument when we get back to the marina. Hold the net a minute, okay?"

I took the net he thrust into my hands, feeling the full weight of the fish. Punt scrambled to open the storage bin under the passenger seat and pulled out a camera and a steel tape.

"I'll hold the net, Keely, while you step onto the bow again. The tape's weighted. It'll stand upright while you hold the fish near it. Let the tail touch the bow and be sure the nose is on the level with a number on the tape. When you're ready I'll snap the pic and we'll have our proof."

Inserting my fingers into a gill slit, I managed to lift the fish into position next to the tape and Punt clicked the shutter. He clicked it twice to be sure he had a good shot.

"Done! Now let's lower it into the water." We eased the bone back into the net and then submerged it in the sea. "It's just lip-hooked, so it'll be an easy release. Let me get my pliers."

I lifted the net to boatside again while Punt removed the hook with one deft movement. Moving quickly, I submerged the net and lowered it from under my catch, but the fish didn't move. For several moments it lay motionless as a bathtub toy.

"I hope it's still alive." I prodded the fish's tail with the net, eager to see some movement. Then I leaned over the side, grabbed its tail, and pulled the fish back and forth to get water flowing through its gills.

"It's alive." Punt leaned over the side, too, and we both pulled the fish through the water. "It's finding its bearings, getting ready for a long run."

Punt knew the drill. Suddenly, water splashed in our faces as the bonefish took refuge under the boat for a few seconds before streaking toward the open sea. Big fish with their beauty and speed always left me awestruck and I watched this one out of sight while Punt pulled the anchor.

"Snack time. Agreed?"

"Agreed!"

Punt pointed the boat toward the beach where mangroves grew into the water, their brown roots arching like stiff ropes along the shoreline. Island builders. That's what conservationists called the mangroves. The trees showered their seeds into the sea, and in due time new plants sprouted from the brine.

Punt eased the boat a few feet from a cove before he cast anchor again. I grabbed our lunch and Punt pulled a blanket from a storage bin. Pausing, we both rolled up our jeans before we splashed into the water, stopping a few feet from shore to rinse fish slime from our hands. Once ashore, we smoothed the sand, spread the blanket, and plopped down to rest.

"Some fish, Keely. I'm going to enter it under your name in the marina's bonefish contest. That specimen could be the winner."

"Forgot all about that contest. What's the prize?"

"Lots of honor and glory around the marina and in the *Citizen,* of course, but also a slip for your skiff—rent-free for a year."

"Not bad."

I handed Punt a soda and a sandwich then unwrapped one for myself. Aah! Minced conch and dill pickle mixed with relish and mayo. Paradise. I gulped the first bite then slowed down and enjoyed the rest of the sandwich. And the sunshine. And the tradewind.

"Life doesn't get much better than this."

Punt allowed me the cliché. "Few wintertime fishing days turn out to be so nice. It's more usual to face high wind and rough seas."

"Conch sandwiches always taste better on the beach," I said. "Wonder why."

"Everything's a lot better on the beach." Punt reached to pull me toward him and I didn't resist. We lay in a loose embrace and I enjoyed the touch of his warm lips against mine. For a moment it was easy to shove thoughts of Randy Jackson, the warning note, the phone call from my mind. We kissed and we kissed again as we snuggled into an even closer and warmer embrace. I wanted it to last forever, and I knew Punt wanted it to evolve into something more intimate. But neither of those things happened. A raucous shout snapped us to attention. In a skiff about fifty yards offshore, a couple of men were training binoculars on us.

"Damn!" Punt stood and shook his fist at them. I ducked behind a mangrove. "They're just teenagers," Punt called.

I peeked. The intruders retreated a few yards, but not because Punt scared them. They were bent on teasing us and making pests of themselves. They took turns using the binoculars.

"Forget them, Punt. It's too nice a day to let kids spoil it."

Punt sat again. "But they scared you. I suppose you'd rather be thinking about Randy Jackson."

"Not rather. But I do need to talk to you about him and some other stuff. Wish you'd seen all of that TV show. The program was an effort to make people aware of the plight of exonerated ex-convicts."

"I got that much from the lead-in. Randy did a lot of jail time before the courts found him innocent, right?"

I told Punt a few more of the program's highlights. "But the show ending evolved into a climax that almost blew viewers away like kites in a gale. Randy, in madman mode, approached the camera until his face filled the screen. His expression could have scared anyone who saw it into thinking he might still belong behind bars. Reverend Soto, the program emcee, jerked Randy off camera, but too late. He'd already announced the one thing he wanted most—revenge."

"I'm guessing that's how a lot of people might feel—a need for revenge—were they in Randy's position. No job. No money. No anything."

"That's what I need to talk to you about. Besides revenge on society in general, Randy wants to see Dyanne Darby's killer arrested, convicted, jailed. If that happens, he thinks employers would be willing to believe he's innocent and offer some jobs."

"A good goal, I'd say." Punt took another swallow of soda.

"Maybe a worthy goal if he could accomplish it without being a danger to society—to the person or persons he thinks may be guilty. Randy scares me. I think he's the type of guy who may hit on his chosen target first and ask questions later—perhaps from another prison cell."

"Well …" Punt stared at a cormorant floating on an updraft far above us. "I realize Randy's mother's your cleaning lady, but why are you making Randy Jackson's problem your problem?"

"Because I empathize with him. Because I empathize with his mother. I know what it's like to be down and out."

"So do I. We both know that."

"Maxine wants me to help them find the culprit in this cold-case murder. I told them I didn't want to be involved, that I didn't think I could help unless it might be to point them toward a good professional detective. You."

"I'm flattered you think I can help."

"Investigating's your business—yours and Nikko's. Will you talk to Randy and Maxine? Give them some advice? Pro bono?"

"I suppose I could do that. Do you know who Randy suspects of killing Dyanne Darby? What's his thinking? He's had twenty years to mull it over."

"I haven't talked to Randy in person. But Consuela's clued me in to her eclectic thinking."

Punt groaned and gulped the rest of his soda. "What's Consuela got to do with it? How'd she undulate into the picture?"

"She's presently dating Randy Jackson—among others, of course."

"Of course. I'm afraid to ask you who Consuela thinks may have murdered Dyanne Darby over twenty years ago—when Consuela couldn't have been much older than ten or eleven."

"Yeah, right. I know how you feel, Punt. Anything Consuela says should be taken with a grain of sand. Her opinions are usually worth about that much. But she sometimes does use a bit of logic. She thinks one of the divers who worked with Randy at the time of his girlfriend's death might be responsible. That's fairly straight thinking—for Consuela. She's calling the motive jealousy, you know, if-I-can't-have-her-nobody-can. She could be right, you know."

"How does she know who those divers were? Seems to me it might make more sense for the killer to have offed Randy. Then he'd still have Dyanne alive and well and all to himself."

"Strong point. Why not Randy instead of Dyanne? So there are two ways of looking at that murder. Randy gave Consuela the names of some of those divers he considers potential suspects—Beau being one of them."

"Dad! Cool your jets, Keely." Punt stared at me, and I hoped he'd begun taking my words seriously. The case was hitting too close to home for his comfort. "I know Dad'll be able to give us an airtight alibi once he and Jass get back from England."

"Give us an alibi? Us? I want nothing to do with this case. Nada. I'm doing my part by suggesting the Jacksons talk to professionals—you and Nikko."

"Consider the 'us' a slip of the tongue. What other divers did Consuela mention besides Dad?"

"One of the first was Gus Helmer. Remember him?"

"The shrimper who works the *Pink Gold?*"

"Right. He's one of my current clients. And she mentioned Slone Pierce, and Ace Grovello, and Reverend Soto. They all worked for Mel Fisher in the early eighties, and they're all still living and working in Key West, but no longer as divers."

"Reverend Soto? Ridiculous! Consuela's a few innards short of a chum bag. According to what I remember reading about the case, Soto's the person who fought to get Randy released. Soto and Shelley Hubble. Consuela's crazy and I don't want anything to do with her and/or Randy Jackson."

"I'd hoped …"

"There are lots of things I'd do for you, Keely, but investigating people Consuela suspects of murder isn't one of them. Please don't ask me to get involved with Consuela. She's a wannabe writer out to use you—or me—to make a name for herself."

"Punt?" I'd buried my guilt at not stepping forward to help Randy and my fears for as long as I could. "Punt, there's something I haven't told you."

Punt sighed. "Give. But if it involves Consuela, I'm unlikely to change my mind about the Randy Jackson case anytime soon."

"This morning I found a threatening note on my office door." I imagined alarm bells going off in Punt's mind as he stared deep into my eyes. "Maxine received a similar note. And later we both received death-threat phone calls."

"What'd the note say? What'd the caller say?"

Repeating the note contents to Punt was like reading an etching engraved in my brain.

"Why didn't you tell me sooner?" Punt sat up and looked toward his boat.

"Guess I thought I could deal with my problems on my own. Then I changed my mind when you refused to help Randy. My working alone on the case wouldn't be fair to the Jacksons. They need the best help they can get—you and Nikko, once Nikko gets back from Tallahassee."

"Show me the note. I might be able to get some fingerprints off it at the office."

"It's at my apartment. In my jumpsuit pocket."

Punt stood and we began folding the blanket. "Come on, Keely. Let's go."

"Does this mean you'll help the Jacksons investigate the Darby murder?"

"Yes, now that you're involved. You don't think I'd turn you down, do you? When can the four of us get together for a meeting?"

"I can't speak for the others for sure, but how about tomorrow after my last patient? If that suits you, Maxine, and Randy, it's a plan." I carried our sandwich wrappers and soda cans as we splashed into the water and boarded the boat. Punt ground the motor three times before it started then I clutched the edges of the passenger seat for support as he gunned the boat on plane and we skimmed across the water toward Key West.

At the marina Punt tipped a dockhand to care for his boat, a chore he usually preferred to do himself. I knew then for sure that my news about the note and phone call had caught his full attention. He broke the speed limit getting to my office, but no cop stopped us. Nor did one appear when he parked in a no parking zone.

"Where's your door key?" He held out his hand and I dropped the key into it. "Wait here while I enter first."

I waited, hovering close behind him.

"What be going here?" Gram hurried from her shop. "Car in bad place. Police have it towed. At owner's expense." Then she stood in front of the Karmann Ghia as if she might try to protect it with her life.

"It's okay, Celia," Punt said, stepping outside. "I'm going to find a better parking place right now." He drove away and Gram and I waited in my outer office for a few minutes. I'd just finished telling Gram about my big bonefish when Punt returned. Gram was eager to see my romance with Punt flourish, so she told us goodnight and disappeared into her shop.

"No sign of a forced entry," Punt said, checking both my doors. "Now show me the note."

I grabbed my jumpsuit from the bedroom chair and pulled the note from the pocket, spreading it on the bedside table so he could read it.

"Very amateurish."

"Think maybe some kid's trying to scare me?"

"I might think that if Maxine hadn't received a similar note. Do you have a Ziploc bag? I'll take the note to my office and check it for prints."

I found a baggie and Punt had slipped the note into it and was tucking it into his shirt pocket when we heard a sharp thud along with the sound of shattering glass.

ELEVEN

DASHING INTO MY OFFICE, I saw a gaping hole in my front window and a chunk of coral rock lying on the floor beside my desk. Duct tape held a note on the rock. Broken glass crunched underfoot and rough edges of the rock cut into my hand as I grabbed it and opened the note. Punt and I studied the scrawled message.

TAKE CARE, KEELY—UNLESS YOU REALLY WANT TO DIE.

"Same kind of writing." Holding the paper by the edges, Punt turned the note over, but there was nothing on the other side. "Same kind of ink." He laid the rock and the note back where we'd found them and reached for his cell phone.

"Wait. What're you going to do?"

"Call the police. I know we shouldn't have touched the crime scene, but the idea of someone threatening you, putting you in danger…Too late for regrets now."

"Crime scene?" I looked from the coral rock to the hole in my window while Punt keyed in 911. I hated to admit that my office, my home, was a crime scene.

"You can't let someone get by with threatening you— damaging your property. We have to report this to the police."

I wanted no interaction with the police, but I trusted Punt's decision and I went along with it with no argument. By that time Gram and a few tourists had come running to my office doorway, gawking, spouting questions. With her earrings bobbing and her long skirt swishing, Gram pushed ahead of the others and rushed to stand beside me while she glared at the shattered glass, the rock, the note.

"What vandal do this, Keely?" She turned toward my apartment. "I call policia."

I pulled her to my side and patted her arm. "Punt's calling the police. It's all right, Gram. Nothing's been hurt but the window."

"No be all right. You be in danger. Someone try to hurt you."

We managed to shush Gram. In a few minutes two cops that I'd met many times elbowed their way through the onlookers and began questioning us. At the sight of the uniforms, the tourists began to back off. No surprise there. Nobody wants to be involved, but everyone wants to know the skinny.

"Don't anyone leave," Officer Bremmer ordered. The onlookers froze in place—at least for the moment. They reminded me of Key deer caught in a car's headlights. Both cops looked as if they might have been linebackers for Florida State. Jeff Bremmer, the tall, red-haired one did the talking. Officer Hillie Hilsabeck, balding and burly, guarded the door, making sure nobody entered or exited. After Jeff studied the situation for a few moments, he pulled a small notebook from his pocket and clicked a ballpoint ready for action.

"Whose property is this?" he asked.

I stepped forward. "Mine, Jeff. It's my business office and living quarters."

"Your name, please." He spoke as if we were strangers and I went along with it.

He fired the usual questions at me, pausing only when I gave my occupation as a professional foot reflexologist. I guessed he'd forgotten about my occupation—or maybe he had aches and pains he thought I might be able to help. I've learned to view people as potential customers. Even cops.

"Any idea who might have done this?"

"No."

He turned to the crowd. "Any of you see anyone heave the rock, run off?"

Nobody spoke. He eyed the onlookers, making each one squirm and look away.

"Those of you with no business here may leave. Do so now, please."

Once the crowd left, Officer Hilsabeck picked up the rock and the note. Hillie Hilsabeck. We'd been on a first-name basis, but for now he was Officer Hilsabeck.

"I'll take the evidence to headquarters and have it dusted for prints. Nothing further we can do now. Call us if you have more problems."

"That's all you can do?" Punt stepped forward blocking Hillie's exit.

"We'll have a bike cop patrol this address frequently through the night," Jeff said.

Both officers left, and Gram began scurrying around picking up glass shards and dropping them into my wastebasket.

"Let me do that, Celia," Punt said. "You'll cut yourself. Why don't you make us lattes and we'll join you in a few minutes."

Gram scowled. "What you do about window? One touch and it fall."

"I've some leftover building scraps at my office," Punt said. "We'll nail a piece of drywall over the window and call a repairman in the morning."

"How you get drywall from your place to this place?" Gram asked. "Tiny yellow convertible won't hold nuttin'." Then she flashed a smile as if suddenly realizing that a successful matchmaker shouldn't criticize a prospective groom—or his car. "But don't worry none. I got friend with truck."

Gram disappeared for a few minutes, and by the time she returned, we had cleaned up the glass shards and a jeans-clad man wearing a baseball cap pulled low on his forehead sat waiting outside in a pickup.

"Go with Jose, Punt. Show him to your office and the drywall."

When Gram spouts orders, people tend to obey—even Punt who's never been a fast study when it comes to taking orders.

"I stand outside and guard the window hole until you return," Gram said. "Go now. Vaminos. Be off." She pulled a long tortoise-shell hairpin from her topknot bun, brandishing it like a dagger.

I saw Punt cork a grin at the idea of Gram's fending off a vandal with a hairpin. True night blanketed the island now and

I felt the sea air cool my face and dampen my hair. Gram and I both stood on the sidewalk outside my office. I kept my cell phone in hand, but nothing threatening happened. Nobody accosted us. Punt soon returned with hammer, nails, and drywall and after he and Jose covered the hole in my window, Punt slipped him a twenty.

"Want me to stand guard tonight?" Jose smiled and pocketed the twenty. "I park in front. Keep one eye open. Nobody bother place while Jose on guard."

Punt gave him another twenty. "Do it, okay?"

We went to Gram's shop and enjoyed lattes. She'd added my favorite cinnamon flavoring to mine. When we rose from the bar stools to leave, Punt took my hand.

"Keely's staying at my place tonight, Celia."

"But…" Gram started to protest, but her matchmaking skills kicked in and she nodded agreement. "I no approve of such… shacking up. But want safety for Keely."

I gave her a goodnight kiss, locked my office door, and slid into the Karmann Ghia beside Punt, trying to forget that someone on this island wanted me dead.

"We could make this a regular thing, Keely." Punt grinned at me. "All you have to do is to say yes. It would make Celia and me happy to see us living in wedded bliss."

"I wish it were that simple. It wouldn't be fair to you. You deserve better than a part-time companion, but that's all I can offer until I get my head on straight."

Punt gave me a sideways glance. "Looks straight enough to me."

"I'm still seeing a therapist, but sometimes I don't think she's helping. She seems to be suggesting I deal with the past, get over it, and move on."

"Sounds like a plan to me—as long as you move on to my place on a permanent basis. Keely?"

I loved Punt and I wished I could agree to move in with him. But as long as my Jude-oriented nightmares kept terrorizing my sleep, I knew I had to keep my own apartment. No fair making Punt share the fallout from my past. My divorce had ended Jude's abuse. His death had ended my fear of him. I wondered what it would take to end the horror-filled dreams that threatened to make every night a challenge.

"Keely?"

Snapping to attention, I looked into Punt's eyes as we paused at a stop light. "Yes?"

"Have you considered forgiving Jude? Don't toss me a quick answer. Think about it. Give it some deep thought."

I glared at Punt. "You think I should forgive him after all the pain he put me through? All the humiliation? All the …"

"I'm asking you to consider it. After Dad and I forgave each other for our various transgressions, our reconciliation forged a stronger bond between us."

"But Jude's dead. And if he were alive, I'd want no part of a reconciliation. I want to forget him."

"Nothing would please me more than to have you forget Jude Cardell. But first forgive him. Think about it, okay?"

I gave way. I couldn't be so hardheaded as to refuse to think about a request from a man dear to me. I placed my hand on his arm. "All right, Punt. I'll think about forgiving Jude. I'll talk it over with my shrink. Maybe she can help. It could be a part of her get-over-it-and-move-on advice."

"I won't mention this again. The bait's on your hook. Right now we've got to think about these threats."

"We've?" I felt a surge of hope. "Then you've decided to investigate the Darby murder?"

"Decided to investigate for your sake, that's for sure. I won't decide about helping Randy Jackson until I meet him."

I didn't see how Punt could help me without helping Randy, but I said no more. Punt pulled into the carport at the Ashford mansion, parking beside Jass's lavender VW, and I peered around us as if someone might be hiding on the premises waiting for me to appear. Waiting. Waiting to pounce. But nothing seemed amiss. Yet.

I glanced up at the widow's walk. Because the widow's walk with its perimeter lights was one of Key West's favorite tourist attractions, Jass had left the bulbs burning while she and Beau toured England. The huge three-story mansion with its gingerbread trim and wrap-around galleries on each floor reminded me of a white wedding cake with the widow's walk making a platform for a bride and groom.

Beau, a long-time widower, had leased the mansion to Punt and Jass when he married Margaux. I led the way up the stairs then stood aside while Punt unlocked the door. When we stepped inside the one large white-walled room, I looked around warily.

"Relax, Keely. You're in no danger here."

"I know that. But I feel as if I'm being watched...followed."

I tried to cork my fear and enjoy the apartment. Punt had used white wicker furniture to divide the space into living-dining room, bedroom, and kitchen. Dive flags, boat flags, and flags from foreign countries decorated the walls. They gave the apartment a nautical look without the usual clichés of rope-framed seascapes, life buoys, and fishing nets dotted with dried starfish.

I crossed the white tile floor of the entryway and walked into the living room where a jewel-toned couch and chairs formed a conversation area around a coffee table.

"Want to change from our fishing clothes and go out to dinner?" Punt began pulling off his sweatshirt. "Or if you're not too particular I could nuke some leftovers and we could eat here."

"Let's eat here, okay? I really don't want to go outside again. Had enough excitement for one day."

"Meaning that you don't find my cooking exciting?"

"I find almost everyone's cooking exciting—except my own. Let's stay here where I feel safe."

"It's a plan. How about a shower and some fresh clothes?"

"A second plan." Punt's round bed and the mirrored ceiling above it sometimes bother me if I stop to wonder who he might have shared the area with before I dropped back into his life. But tonight I put such thoughts from my mind. I opened the closet where Punt had reserved a section of the clothes rod for my things and pulled out a robe and slippers. I headed for the shower with Punt close behind me.

We skinned from our clothes, then with the warm water flowing over our bodies, Punt pulled me to him, kissing me, holding me tight, then lathering us both with jasmine-scented soap. The temptation to stay in the shower forever lasted until the water began to cool. At last Punt turned off the stream and we stepped onto a fluffy bath mat. Punt dried me and I dried him, touching each other in very private places before we slipped into our robes.

"No reason this couldn't be a permanent arrangement, Keely."

No reason, I thought, except for Jude Cardell who continued to haunt me from the grave, who continued to remind me of my weaknesses and shortcomings, who even in death forced the memory of his demanding body into my dreams.

"Maybe, Punt. Maybe soon."

"Have you told your therapist of my invitations?"

"Yes. She's on your side. All the way."

"Better do as the good doctor says."

"At least for tonight. That's for sure."

"I don't want you in fear. I want you in love." Punt punctuated the words with another kiss.

"Would you settle for a combination of the two?" I asked.

"I'm not ready to settle."

"I can understand that." I followed Punt to the kitchen where he brought cooked rice from the freezer along with a closed carton.

"What's that?"

He grinned. "I cannot tell a lie. It's leftovers from last week. I enjoy cooking and creating specialties, but Su Ying at the Chinese Garden does a much better job with chicken and cashews than I do. It's my favorite."

"And mine." Punt's been on the wagon ever since drying out at a Miami rehab center, and tonight he mixed non-alcoholic Yellow Birds with just a touch of banana flavoring. We enjoyed the drinks and the meal, lingering over coffee. At last I helped load the dishwasher before we sat together on the couch, listening to an album of Andy Williams and Frank Sinatra golden oldies. In spite of the romantic music, my mind kept replaying visions of someone tossing a coral rock, writing a death threat.

We avoided talking about those things, and after we went to bed and turned out the lights, Punt had his own way of taking my mind off everything unpleasant. I snuggled against him until the warmth of our eager bodies escalated into a fiery heat that threatened to consume us.

Afterward, we lay in a loose embrace. He fell asleep first, and when I heard his even breathing, I tried to sleep, too. But replays of the past two days' happenings kept zinging through my mind. Warning notes. Threatening phone calls. A chunk of coral through my window. And on top of all those images, I could still see Randy Jackson's face on the TV screen demanding revenge.

In the night stillness, I reflected on the truth that Randy and I shared a lot in common. We were survivors. I refused to let the death threats get me down. I'd survived my mother's murder, Jude's abuse, months of near poverty before I was able to open my business. But those things weren't as mind-numbing as Randy's twenty years in prison. I hated admitting that Randy and I had a lot in common. Maybe everyone's a survivor of some soul-deadening happening they hide deep within themselves. As Gram says—we're all in this together.

Throughout the night, Punt seldom moved, only now and then reaching to touch my arm, my thigh, as if to make sure I still lay close. Although calmed by his nearness, I slept fitfully, worrying about the threats, about my office window that would have to be repaired. At midnight bells pealed from a distant church. At two o'clock I heard cats yeowling somewhere on the Ashford property. At four o'clock garbage trucks began their banging and clanging in spite of city ordinances forbidding such noise at that hour. Key West, the city that never sleeps. Tonight I believed it.

In the morning shortly after seven, I slipped from Punt's bed, and into one of the jumpsuits I kept at his apartment. I let myself outside and tip-toed down the steps.

Sunshine began to warm life into the island. People were hurrying toward Garrison Bight and the daily party boats. Closer at hand a cruise ship towered over the scene at Mallory Dock—a scene that included many homeless men and women sleepily awakening to greet their day whatever it might be. The police were supposed to keep the Mallory area clear of vagrants, but many times the cops were lenient, closing one eye to the offenders who usually wanted nothing more than a safe place to sleep under the stars.

It was over two miles to Duval Street, and along the way the salt-sweet tradewind barely overcame the stench of spilled beer and other debris I hate to think about. I knew the walk to my office would do me good and perhaps clear my head of the fears that threatened to set up permanent camp in my mind. I tried to avoid thinking of Punt waking up without me at his side. But he'd know where I'd gone and he'd understand—in a way—I hoped.

I'd passed Sloppy Joe's, which hadn't opened for the day, and I'd almost reached Fast Buck Freddie's where a few tourists already stood peering at the eclectic clothing and souvenirs in the window. Across the street, two guys loitered near the wall outside St. Paul's Episcopal taking turns drinking gin straight from the bottle.

I walked faster, suddenly feeling vulnerable and alone. I'd almost reached my office when a man stepped from my doorway and sauntered toward me, looking me up and down as he approached. One hand hung at his side, his other hand formed a mound in his jacket pocket. I wanted to run.

TWELVE

WHEN WE MET HEAD-ON, the man smiled and I swallowed the scream that clogged my throat.

"You Keely Moreno, right?"

I nodded, wary at meeting anyone who hadn't telephoned ahead for an appointment.

"Jose Mendez here. We meet again." He held out his hand and I shook it, embarrassed that I hadn't recognized him as Gram's friend, the truck driver.

"Good morning, Mr. Mendez. I recognize you now, but my office doesn't open until nine o'clock."

"Maybe you'll make an exception in my case." He grinned and pulled a paper from his pocket and thrust it toward me like a flag of truce. It crinkled in my hand, reminding me of yesterday's early-morning threat. For a moment I couldn't bear to look at it.

"I'm here from my day job at Strunk Lumber. Last night I was moonlighting with my own truck, picking up a few extra bucks on the side. I kept guard over your shop, and Punt Ashford asked me to repair your front window this morning."

"Oh." I relaxed. "Oh, wonderful! I really need your help, and I apologize for failing to recognize you immediately."

"I'm ready to work now if it suits you. Got my tools here in my truck. Probably could finish the job before you open for the day."

"That'd be great, Mr. Mendez."

"Jose, please."

"That'd be wonderful, Jose." I'd been so busy eyeing him that I hadn't noticed the Strunk Lumber truck parked at the curbing a short distance from my doorway.

"Then I'll get right to work. Hope a little pounding won't bother you none."

"I'm sure it won't. I'm pleased to get the window repaired so soon."

A quick repair is almost unheard of in Key West and I knew Punt must have pulled a lot of strings with both Jose and Strunk Lumber to make this one happen. I watched for a few minutes while Jose brought two sawhorses and a crowbar from his truck and began prying off the drywall he and Punt had nailed in place the night before.

"How'd you happen to break a window like this one, Miss Moreno? Plate glass—takes quite a blow to knock a hole in it."

"An accident. Take care not to cut yourself." I unlocked my door and stepped inside before he could ask more questions that would remind me of last night's threat. Gram swooped outside her shop to serve as sidewalk supervisor and to offer Jose a cup of coffee when he finished the job.

The repair took almost two hours and Jose had to call Strunk's for help, unable to handle the large sheet of glass alone. After he'd cleaned up the mess and stored his tools inside the truck, Gram invited us both to her shop for coffee. I declined her offer when I saw a middle-aged man heading toward my office, leading with his stomach as so many men of his age do. After thanking Jose for the repair and Gram for her invitation, I stepped inside my workplace.

"Mr. Grovello?" I asked, smiling, as he entered. "I've been expecting you. Consuela's references are always valuable to me."

"Ace. Just call me Ace."

Ace had the Mack truck look of most of Consuela's boyfriends—big, burly, semi-handsome. He differed from the others in that his body had gone to flab, and he wore Italian loafers, chinos, and a golf shirt instead of barefoot sandals, jeans, and tank top. I noticed the glint of a gold doubloon hanging from a chain around his neck. The keepsake of a successful *Atocha* diver, I thought, remembering Consuela's words as well as the pendant doubloon Punt's dad always wore.

"Looks as if you've had a problem here." Ace glanced at Jose's truck with its Strunk Lumber logo.

"Nothing important," I white-lied and forced a smile. "A problem window. Do sit down and let me tell you about foot reflexology and how it may help you."

"No need to give me the hard sell." He laughed. "Our friend Consuela's already done that. I'm ready to see some action." He remained standing, peering at the bookcase near my desk, then at my shelves of lotions and towels, my treatment chair.

"In that case we'll go right ahead and get started." I led him to the client's bench and filled the footbath, adding lemon-scented fragrance and snapping on the whirlpool. A half smile curved his lips when he inhaled the aroma and he nodded his approval.

"Please remove your loafers and socks and let this water swirl around your feet for a few moments. It'll help relax you."

"No tension here, Miss Moreno. I'm loose as a goose."

"Please call me Keely. Great that you feel at ease. Some first-timers arrive tense as fiddle strings and it takes a few moments for them to relax." Ace Grovello's actions belied his corny loose-goose imagery.

His fingers fumbled at his loafers and it took him three tries to remove each shoe. After pulling off a sock, he folded it in thirds and placed it inside a loafer before removing the other sock and dealing with it in a like manner. Then he carefully lined up both shoes until they lay parallel to the footbath. He stared at the swirling water a moment, before he eased one foot into it and then the other without saying a word.

"Do you live in Key West, Ace?"

"Lived here all my life. Used to dive for Mel Fisher. Right now, I run a B&B near the far end of Whitehead Street. The Sand Dollar. One of the best inns on the island. At least that's what my customers tell me. I get lots of repeaters."

Ace stared at his feet as if he thought they might disappear. I kept the conversation going. "That's a beautiful pendant you're wearing."

Ace brightened and grinned. "It's an artifact from the *Atocha*. Mel Fisher presented it to me after I made a spectacular dive and found an emerald ring once worn by the queen of Spain. Mel had a lot of divers working for him, but he always named me as his favorite. Yes, that's what he said many times—Ace, you're the best diver in the whole bunch."

I didn't tell him that Beau Ashford wore a doubloon half again as big as his. Never a good plan to antagonize a customer. Ace and his bragging began to grate on my nerves, but I listened and smiled while he spouted details about his many impressive finds.

"Why, I'm the one who helped Mel find the mother lode, Keely. Oh, the gold we brought up that day! Mel had worked for years searching for that mother lode, and I'm the one who helped him find it. Me. Ace Grovello."

Could I stand a whole hour of this? I took a deep breath and handed him paper slippers.

"Let's move to the treatment chair, Ace. Sit and relax in it, then place your feet on the footrest while I lower your head. Relax. Relax. I'll get you a pillow to make you more comfortable."

Ace clutched the sides of the chair like a child visiting the dentist for the first time, but he relaxed some when I placed a pillow beneath his head and began massaging his feet with rose-scented oil.

"Are you having pain in some special area of your body, Ace?"

"Oh, a few twinges here and there."

Men! How they hated to admit weakness. "Can you be more specific? Each part of your foot corresponds to a part of your body. When a body weakness appears, it may be because blood and nerve functions have slowed. This may allow acids and calcium to form in your joints. If you can pinpoint your pain, I can be of more help to you."

"Left shoulder. Get a few slight morning twinges in that left shoulder. Not every day, but now and then."

I smiled, translating that to mean his left shoulder was killing him and he could hardly haul himself out of bed in the mornings. I began with a general massage of his left foot before I zeroed in on the area below his small toe. He jerked his foot away with such force it slipped from my hands.

"Easy, woman. Easy on those toes. You digging in with all ten fingernails?"

"No. I never do that. You're feeling inner crystalline deposits breaking away." I picked up his foot again, eased up my pressure, and continued to work the area as gently as I could. At the same time, I tried to take his mind off any discomfort he might be feeling. "Tell me more about your diving experiences. You must know information that no other people know."

"Right. I sure do." He thought a few seconds before he continued. "Bet you never heard that the divers, well most of them, had a fear of gold. It was a love/hate relationship. They loved gold, yet sometimes it scared the bejabbers out of them."

"Fear of gold? I never heard of that."

"Well, that's the pure truth. Those guys were afraid of the gold. Once a diver surfaced carrying a valuable chain or some coins, we crewmen whooped and cheered for a while, but we could hardly wait to get back to land and offload those finds. And for good reason, too. Lots of bad things happened when we had gold aboard a dive boat—enough frightening incidents to make us all superstitious."

Ace began to relax and I encouraged that with another question. "Can you tell me about such an incident?"

"Well, one night after we'd made several big finds, I lay asleep aboard our dive boat *Northwind*. The craft was nothing but a diving platform. Unseaworthy. Dangerous. But that didn't make me no nevermind back in those days. At age twenty I knew for sure I'd live forever. That night, suddenly I heard a voice shouting, 'Take care! Take care!' I jumped up. Took me a few minutes to shake myself awake. I ran toward the bow where the voice had seemed to be coming from. The boat rocked in high waves and I saw a canvas bag near the edge of the deck. A narrow, flat bag, and it was about to slide overboard.

"I flung myself onto it—almost slid overboard myself. But I saved the bag. Turned out it held gold salvaged from several days' dives. Me, Ace Grovello. I'd saved it. The guys made me out a hero, but I'd only done what I had to do. We headed for shore early the next day and offloaded that gold onto Mel's dock."

"You really believe something had put a curse on that gold?"

"I've thought about that night a great deal. Don't know what to believe. Maybe someone, maybe Mel himself, had been careless with that sea bag. Or maybe spirits long ago lost in the sea were trying to reclaim their own. But I know what I heard. A warning voice woke me up that night."

Ace's story made me shudder. It saddened me to think of all the people—people with families and hopes and dreams—that had perished when their galleons floundered on the coral reefs. But by the end of that story and a few others in which Ace always played the hero, I'd dubbed Ace my windbag du jour. I finished his treatment, brought him his loafers and socks, and offered him a glass of lemonade.

"Thank you for being a good patient, Ace. I hope the treatment will help relieve your shoulder problems."

"That's to be seen, isn't it?"

Ace drank the lemonade, setting the empty glass on the bookcase beside my desk as he pulled his wallet from his pocket, withdrew bills, and paid in full for my advertised special of six treatments. I opened my appointment book, ready to schedule a new date and time for him, but my telephone rang and while I was talking to another client, Ace left without rescheduling. I really didn't care if he returned, and I'd give him a refund if he asked. If Consuela spent much time with that guy, she'd more than earned her freebie.

I called Punt to thank him for having the window repaired but got no answer, and I left no message. I wanted to see his agency become a success and I hoped he was out with a client. Next, I phoned Maxine although I knew she might be working somewhere, but she answered on the second ring. I had hardly wished her good morning when she blurted her news.

"My Randy, he agree to meet with Punt Ashford. He didn't give me no argument. None at all. Oh, Keely, I'm so grateful to you for giving us this opportunity. You think Punt Ashford will agree to see us?"

"Yes. I've already talked to him and we're to meet him this afternoon after my last appointment. You're to bring along your threat note so he can examine and compare it to mine. That doesn't mean he'll take the case. It just means that for starters he'll listen to us. Why don't you stop by here and we'll go over together?"

"Will there be a parking place at Punt's office?"

"Yes. He has a parking slot for clients."

"Good. We'll see you this afternoon."

After I replaced the receiver I sighed. I knew that sooner or later I'd have to meet Randy Jackson, but I didn't want to meet him alone. It comforted me to know both Maxine and Punt would be present once we reached Punt's office.

My eleven o'clock appointment cancelled, but Consuela swished through my doorway to check on Ace. Her purple spandex shorts held my attention for a long moment, then I sighed. Maybe I was a tad envious of Consuela's looks, her glamorous outfits. I wondered what it would be like to be beautiful and to dress like a runway model. I quashed my thoughts and smoothed the collar of my jumpsuit when she spoke.

"Did he show up?"

"Of course. I gave him a treatment. He paid—and left."

"Not make a second appointment?"

"Not then. But don't worry. He paid in full. You'll get your freebie even if he stops treatments and demands a refund." That appeased Consuela and she left.

Punt stopped by in person to check the window job and to mention waking up to an empty bed. I thanked him for the window repair and made the usual excuses for the empty bed. He accepted them with grace and an invitation to lunch. We walked the short distance to Kelly's on Whitehead Street. Punt requested garden seating and the waiter led us to a table surrounded by hibiscus bushes, sea grapes, and palm trees. We ordered grouper sandwiches—my favorite midday meal. My mouth watered in anticipation as I opened my sourdough bun, picked up a lime wedge and squeezed juice onto the fish.

After we finished eating, Punt pushed his mirrored sunglasses to the top of his head, picked a pink hibiscus from a bush, and tucked it behind my ear.

"Everything set for this afternoon?" he asked.

"Right. Randy, Maxine, and I'll be at your office around four. You have my note and Maxine'll bring hers. We're both grateful to you for agreeing to hear our pleas."

"Your plea, Keely. I'm hearing theirs, merely because you're so involved. No more threats today?"

"None. Were you able to get any fingerprints from my note?"

"No. Too many smudges on the paper."

"Maybe Maxine's note isn't as smudged as mine. Punt, do you know Ace Grovello? One of Consuela's many friends? I gave him a treatment this morning."

"I've heard of him. Runs a local B&B, I think. How'd you like him?"

I shrugged. "He's okay, I suppose, if you like braggers. To hear him tell it, he found the *Atocha* gold all by himself."

Punt laughed. "Don't fault him for that. Sometimes Dad gets carried away with his own Mel Fisher stories. But they're fascinating."

"Right. I enjoy the ones Beau writes about in his column for the *Citizen*."

I hated to see our lunch end. I always felt safer with Punt near. He walked me back to my office where I treated my next two patients and then waited for Maxine and Randy to arrive. I couldn't help shuddering at the thought of meeting and associating with an ex-convict.

THIRTEEN

A LITTLE AFTER FOUR, a client called to reschedule an appointment and I was talking when I saw the Jackson car double-parked in front of my office. Randy ignored the honking and catcalls when traffic piled up. He unfolded his tall frame from behind the steering wheel, turned, and spat a stream of tobacco juice on the tire of the car behind his before he walked to my door. Cutting my phone call short, I rose to meet him. I felt impressed with his coming to the door instead of honking for me. But I felt irritated with his spitting, his arrogant disregard for the drivers behind him.

Randy towered over me, and the tradewind whipped strands of coarse gray hair off his face, revealing the Z-shaped scar on his cheek, a scar so nasty-looking it made me want to glance away. The breeze also revealed gold studs in both earlobes. I wondered if they were *Atocha* gold souvenirs from his diving days. I forced a smile and looked up into eyes that smoldered like burning coals. He wore a shark's tooth necklace and a Half Shell Raw Bar tee. A tin of Skoal inside his shirt pocket left a round impression on the thin fabric. He didn't return my smile.

"Move it along, buddy," a man shouted from an RV camper that seemed wider than Duval Street.

"Where are the cops when I need them?" a blonde-haired girl called as she flipped him the finger. If Randy heard or saw the complaints he ignored them.

"Miss Moreno, I'm Randy Jackson." He spoke as if I didn't know, hadn't guessed. He extended his hand and I shook it. It felt like holding a bagful of nails.

"Just call me Keely, please." I followed him as he sauntered to the Ford, waited while I settled onto the front passenger seat, and then continued his saunter to the driver's side. I turned, expecting to see Maxine in the back seat. But no. Hairs rose along the back of my neck. I sat alone, trapped in a car with an ex-con.

Once behind the wheel, Randy burned rubber as he floorboarded the accelerator, leading the vehicles behind us like a surly Pied Piper.

I corked a desire to jump from the moving car until I heard what Randy had to say. "Where's Maxine? She promised to attend this meeting with Mr. Ashford."

Randy stared ahead. "Ma's late getting off work. She'll meet us at his office."

I almost believed him, wanted to believe him, until I heard a telltale rustling behind us. I turned, seeing nobody. Someone lay hidden on the floor! My mouth filled with more saliva than I could swallow. I wiped the drool onto the sleeve of my jumpsuit as I grabbed the door handle, ready to leap into traffic.

"Hey, woman, relax." Randy shot his arm in front of me, slammed me against the seatback and jerked my grip from the door handle.

"Where are you taking me? Who's hiding in the back seat?"

He kept me pinned to the seat. "Chill out. You're hearing Lavonna back there. No sweat. She's caged and on the floor."

For an instant I couldn't speak. I didn't relax, but I gave up leaping from the car. When Randy put his hand back on the steering wheel, I felt ashamed. Randy Jackson probably hated being alone with a frightened woman as much as I hated being alone with him.

"Lavonna?" I asked once I found my voice again. "Maxine's taking Lavonna with her, with us, to see Punt?"

"Since the day's cooling down, Lavonna'll wait in the car while we talk." Randy remained stony-faced. "When we're through with the talking, Ma'll go directly to Mallory." He peered at the sky. "Good picture-taking time. Sun's out. No clouds."

Only when we reached the Fotopolus and Ashford office, left the car, and started inside did I see Maxine approaching on foot and in full regalia. Gone were the polka dot bloomers and white

T-shirt. This afternoon, Maxine and her work partner would look like a matched set. Maxine wore green Capri pants and matching sandals with a gray golf shirt. A black do-rag knotted around her head completed her costume. I suppose I should have warned Punt, yet no words could fully prepare a person to meet Maxine.

Punt met us at the door and our footsteps grated on the terrazzo floor. Randy eyed the austere office. Desk. Chairs. File cabinets. Telephones. The shallow Waterford bowl on Punt's desk that I had given him was the only art object in the room.

I said nothing about my fright. After I introduced Maxine and Randy, Punt offered us straight-backed chairs, pulling a third one from Nikko's side of the office. Once seated at his desk, he studied Maxine and Randy for a moment before he spoke.

"Keely tells me that each of you has a problem. Correct me if I'm wrong. Keely and Maxine have received threats. And Randy, you want to investigate Dyanne Darby's murder—a very cold case. Right?"

We all nodded.

"Let's talk about the threats first." Punt removed my note from the baggie in his desk drawer. "Maxine, have you brought your note?"

"Yes." Maxine pulled the threat from her purse.

"Let's spread them on my desk and study them. I want to be sure, as sure as is possible, that the handwriting on the notes is identical."

Punt stood while the three of us approached his desk. Maxine laid her note beside mine on Punt's blotter. The four of us studied the notes as if they might have been signed and we stupidheads had missed seeing the signature.

"What's mousemilk mean?" I pointed to the word with my fingernail. "I've never heard it before."

"Maybe it's the guy's signature," Maxine said. "A nickname. That's the only way it makes any sense to me."

"Could be, I suppose," I said. "Mousemilk. A very strange nickname."

Punt smiled. "Mousemilk's a coined word—fairly new, a buzzword you might hear from would-be hotshots in the business world. I think it refers to an activity or business plan that, if implemented, would prove to be more trouble than it's worth."

"Maybe it's a warning that I'll be wasting both my time and my life if I begin investigating anything for Randy," I said.

Randy shrugged. "Looks to me like the same guy wrote both the notes." His voice boomed into the room. "Paper and ink the same. Look at the words, the slant of the letters. Same downhill slant on both pages."

"No mention of mousemilk in my note," Maxine said.

"That could be significant, Maxine," Punt said. "And you're very observant, Randy. But we can't be sure a man wrote the notes. It could have been a woman. We can't rule out that possibility."

"What woman would want to prevent an investigation?" I asked. "What woman would have motive?"

"The woman who may have lied at Randy's trial," Punt said. "Nicole Nichols."

Randy and Maxine glanced at each other in surprise. I looked at Punt, knowing for the first time that this case had grabbed his attention. He had to have done some research, looked into some facts, maybe read a transcript of the trial, to have known the name of the female witness who had lied.

"Did you know Nicole Nichols, Randy?" Punt asked.

"Yes. She was a close friend of Dyanne's. Lived in the same apartment house."

"Did you like her?" Punt asked.

Randy shrugged. He began to remind me of Gus Helmer with all his shrugging. Maybe a guy had to be an expert shrugger to get Consuela's attention. Maybe that mannerism was the part of Randy's charm that turned her on.

"I suppose the note writer could have been a broad." Randy paused, looking thoughtful. "But more likely the man who murdered Dyanne wrote the note. A killer would have more motive for protecting himself than a…liar. And maybe Nicole Nichols lied to protect some man, a friend, a lover."

"Good point, Randy," Punt said. "But we still don't know if we're looking for a man or a woman. The notes give us few clues. Let's consider those telephone threats. What can either of you tell me about the call you received? Wording? Tone of voice? Either caller use the word mousemilk?"

I let Maxine speak first.

"Surprise left my mind blank. Can't remember the exact words the caller used. Heard no mention of mousemilk. I'd remember a word like that."

"Could you tell if the caller was a man or a woman?" Punt asked.

"Can't be sure. I get lots of calls from ladies wanting my cleaning services. Sometimes calls from men, but mostly from women. But this person, he talk slick as spit—smooth, quick, but the voice had a phony sound to it—like maybe someone trying to speak in disguise."

"He talk?" Punt asked. "There we go again, assuming a male made the calls. Maybe a woman was trying to disguise her voice."

Maxine shrugged. "His voice. Her voice. Don't know which. Couldn't tell if it be man or woman." She looked into space, curling her tongue over her gold tooth.

"What about you, Keely?" Punt asked. "Man or woman on the line?"

"I don't know. Now, when I look back on it, I think the caller was trying to disguise his/her voice. And doing a good job of it, too."

"Very good job of it," Maxine added.

I picked up my note. "Punt, I want you to investigate, to see what you can learn."

"I've already learned that there are no clear fingerprints on your note and probably none on Maxine's note either. I'll check later to be sure."

"Then what do investigators do next?" I asked.

Punt sat down and motioned us back to our chairs. A good sign, I thought. He could have motioned us out the door.

"Randy, who do you think had motive to murder Dyanne Darby? You must have some strong feelings about this case, about the killer."

Randy nodded. "Very strong. I want to know more about Nicole Nichols. She lied under oath, but I don't think she murdered Dyanne. I think a man did it—a jealous man with strong motive."

"What man?" Punt asked.

"Could be one of several," Randy said. "Maybe one of Fisher's divers. We all hung out together. Several of them had the hots for Dyanne, but she chose to date me. I don't think she went out with anyone else."

"Hold it one minute," Punt said. "Why wouldn't such a killer have murdered you rather than Dyanne if he wanted to date Dyanne?"

"Don't rightly know," Randy said. "Some people like a thing and if they can't have it, they don't want anyone else to have it either. Only way to be sure that doesn't happen is to get rid of the thing. Follow me?"

Punt nodded and I guessed he remembered that I'd told him Consuela had suggested almost the same reasoning. "That's one way of looking at it, I guess. So who are some of the men, the divers, you suspect?"

Randy scowled and his whole face darkened while he began ticking names off on his fingers, the same names Consuela had mentioned. "Gus Helmer. Slone Pierce. Arnold Soto. Ace Grovello."

"The Reverend Soto?" Punt asked. "The man who helped get you released from prison? Don't you think he's an unlikely suspect?"

"You never know what goes through another person's mind. Maybe he killed her, regretted it later, and tried to make amends by helping me."

"That's right, Randy." Punt smiled and nodded. "One never knows. But I know the other divers you mentioned. They're all businesspeople. No white-shirt-and-tie types, but they all make honest livings. Gus does dry-dock boat repairing and he's captain of his own shrimp boat. Granted, he's a tough character. Wouldn't want to anger him in a dark alley. Slone Pierce owns and operates a salvage boat. Ace Grovello runs a B&B. I'm not saying any one of these men is innocent. I'm just saying the odds are against any one of them being a murderer."

"You asked my opinion." Randy rose and began pacing. "Those are my top picks, but there are others. Your father, Beau, for instance. I've had a long time to think about these people and they all still live in Key West."

"My dad, Beau, isn't a killer. Known him all my life. He's a straight arrow. As for the other divers, yes, they do still live in the Keys, but I'd think a killer might move away and never return. If the Darby girl's murderer has left the area, we could be faced with a wild chase that could lead almost anywhere—or nowhere."

"I can't pay." Randy lowered his voice to a growl as he continued to pace. "Got no money. Got no job. Got no friends—except Ma. She's the only one stuck by me all these years." He paced faster, arms hanging like steel gaffs at his sides, hands clenched into fists. As his anger grew, his facial scar brightened.

"I'll work pro bono," Punt said.

"Jacksons won't accept no more pro bono charity." Maxine rose, went to Randy, and pulled him back toward his chair, but he jerked away from her and picked up the chair as if he might throw it.

"Easy, Randy." Punt approached him and when he reached for the chair, Randy glared at him, then spit a stream of tobacco juice into the shallow bowl on Punt's desk.

For a moment nobody spoke, then I jumped up and faced Randy. "How dare you spit that disgusting stuff in here! How dare you!" Randy lowered the chair. Punt stepped forward, trying to pull me back, but I jerked away, picked up the Waterford and thrust it at Randy. I was on a roll and I forced my voice to a deadly calm. "Apologize to Punt, then clean the bowl." I pointed to the lavatory down the hall. "You wash this bowl. Return it to the desk where you found it. Now!"

What had I done! My face flushed. I stepped back surprised at my outburst and expecting Randy to aim his next quid at me. Instead, he took the bowl. In moments we heard running water, and then he returned to the office and set the clean bowl on Punt's desk.

"Thank you." My stomach felt like a knotted rope.

"You're welcome." Randy scowled and sat down.

Maxine spoke to Punt in the ensuing silence as if nothing unusual had happened. "If we accept your pro bono investigating, then I expect you to trade it for my pro bono cleaning. Your home. Your office. Either one you prefer, or maybe both. I come once a week. I clean Keely's place on Saturday mornings. Maybe

I could do your office on Saturday afternoons. My Randy will help if'n there's heavy-duty stuff needs doin'."

Randy began pacing again, more rapidly this time. I knew Punt would want an ex-convict around his apartment or office about as much as I would. The air was thick with too many ultimatums.

"Maxine, I appreciate your offer, but I have a cleaning service. I can't dismiss those workers without reason. They've done excellent work for me both here at the office as well as at my home."

Maxine looked crestfallen, then she jutted her chin toward the ceiling. "Then if you won't let us pay in some way, we'll do our own investigating. We won't accept charity. Randy has several ideas. We'll follow them on our own."

I could tell from Punt's expression that he wanted no part of being responsible for Randy's proceeding with the investigation on his own.

"Maxine, I want to level with you and your son. I'm taking on this case because I want to protect Keely. Keely's safety means a lot to me. After hearing your story, Keely's story, and after doing some nosing around at the courthouse, you'll have a hard time calling me off this case anytime soon. All bills will go to Keely Moreno."

"Thank you, Punt," I said. "Of course I'll be responsible for the cost of your investigation."

FOURTEEN

RANDY STOPPED PACING and the redness gradually drained from his scar when he and Maxine started to leave Punt's office. I followed them to the door.

"You have a way home?" Randy turned and looked at me. "Be glad to drive you once I get Ma and Lavonna settled at Mallory."

My stomach got the knotted-rope feeling again when I thought of being alone in a car with Randy—especially after the tobacco juice scene.

"Thank you, Randy," Punt said, "but it'll be my pleasure to see that Keely gets home. I thank you both for bringing this case to me. I look forward to meeting with you again in the near future as my investigation in Keely's behalf continues."

"Thank you, Mr. Ashford," Maxine said, heading for her car.

Neither of us spoke until we heard the Jacksons leave.

"Punt! What have I snared you into? Exonerated or not, Randy Jackson makes me want to run in the other direction."

"He doesn't scare me. And you know how to make him back down. I can empathize with him and his plight. Don't think you snared me into anything. Let's say I'm taking the case because someone I love has been threatened. Let's say I'm taking the case for the experience it'll give me as a fledgling PI. Let's say I'm taking the case because our justice system forced a rotten deal on Randy and he needs all the help he can get."

"There's no way I can ever thank you enough, Punt."

"We both know that isn't so." Punt drew me to him in a warm embrace, and we pulled apart reluctantly.

"I wish Randy didn't send out such negative vibes, Punt. I try to believe he's innocent of the Darby murder because the law now says he is, but his anger scares me. Newspapers are always carrying news about some guy who thinks he's been shafted by society and who retaliates by shooting everyone in sight. That could happen to Randy—to us. When his scar turns scarlet as a stop light, it's time to take care."

"You're saying we have to protect ourselves from Randy and his temper as well as from Dyanne Darby's killer?"

"That's my take on the situation. And I think Maxine feels that way, too. I'm guessing she's afraid of her own son and what he might do in a fit of rage."

I peered outside into the waning afternoon. At the end of the block people hurried toward Mallory. Punt set the "closed" sign in his window, pulled the shade.

"Punt, how about going to the dock long enough to see Maxine and Lavonna in action? Lavonna's her pet iguana."

"She had it with her?"

"Yes. Caged in her car. She and Lavonna do a candid camera thing."

Punt rolled his eyes. "Not fond of iguanas, but we'll go toss her a buck or two."

I didn't tell him what Maxine expected of her customers, and when I started to open the door, his serious tone stopped me.

"I did a little research on DNA testing this afternoon, the sort of testing that helped free Randy. Found an interesting fact or two."

"For instance?" I paused, joining him at his desk where he pulled a file.

"One fact struck me as interesting." Punt held a sheet of figures before me and I tried to scan it as he continued talking. "I knew DNA evidence was inadmissible in court before about 1984, and it wasn't until much more recently that Florida authorities began consistently taking DNA samples from convicted burglars."

"Are you saying Randy has a rap sheet of burglaries?"

Punt shook his head. "Not saying that at all. Research has shown that many criminals convicted of homicide have previously been convicted of burglary."

"You've lost me somewhere, Punt. Are you saying that one crime leads to another? Like burglary to homicide?"

"Sometimes, but not always, of course. My idea's a long shot and it may lead nowhere. That happens to PIs a lot, but I think it's worth considering. Randy gave us the names of guys he thinks might have killed Dyanne Darby. We might get a lead by …"

"We?"

"Yes. As in you and me. We. I've appointed you my chief assistant. Okay?"

"What can I say?"

"Yes. That's what you can say—all you can say."

"Okay. Yes. Reluctantly. I accept, but with many doubts about my investigating ability."

"As I started to say, we might get a lead by running the names of Randy's suspects through the police database. If any of them has a burglary on his rap sheet, that's a person we should give some in-depth attention."

"But you said all burglars don't commit murder."

"Right, but an interesting percentage of them do—or may. I suggest that it's a place to start investigating."

"So how do you—we get into the police database? You think the cops are going to give a PI the time of day?"

"I know one who might. Jeff Bremmer. We both know him. I gave him some street-talk info in my beach bum days. It may have saved his life, but for sure, it won him a promotion. He owes me one."

"Can you call him now? Think he'll be on duty tonight?"

"He was last night." Punt picked up the phone and keyed the police station. To our surprise Jeff answered the call and Punt switched the phone to conference call so I could hear the conversation.

"Punt Ashford here, Jeff. And my friend and associate, Keely Moreno, will be listening in."

"Glad to hear from you, Punt. How can I help you and Keely?"

I listened while Punt made his request and gave him four names to check out. "How long will it take you to get some info?"

"A day or so, with luck. Without luck, a little longer. That soon enough?"

"Fine. Give me a call, okay?"

Punt replaced the receiver, turned out an overhead bulb, and snapped on the nightlight and the security alarm. "Guess that's all we can do for today. But it's a start. You wanted to go see Maxine's act?"

"Why not?" When we stepped into the humidity of the late afternoon, a cruise ship hooted its farewell hoot. Punt took my hand while we walked to Green Street, cut through an alley to Front Street, and then through another alley and onto the parking lot that paved the way to the dock. The smell of popcorn hung in the air and the drone of a bagpipe grated on our eardrums. Remembering Maxine's words about Lavonna and the bagpiper, I urged Punt in the opposite direction.

A mime with gold-painted skin and clothing stood lighthouse still on a pedestal, only allowing herself the motion of winking when an onlooker tucked a bill into her waistband. Farther on, a tarot reader snapped cards onto a black table decorated with a crystal ball, fanned out a deck of ESP cards, and laid down witch's wand.

"Want your fortune told?" Punt asked.

"Not right now, thanks."

"Some of the old timers aren't around tonight," Punt said. "I haven't been here for ages. Maybe they've retired. Remember Will, the guy who walked the high wire? And the Key Lime tart lady? She sold the best brownies on the island."

"And Key Lime tarts?"

"Yeah. Those too."

"And where's Uncle Sam with his twenty-two dollar bills? Remember how he used to fold the bills into rings? I used to have one for each finger."

We bought hotdogs and lemonades and sat on the edge of the dock, dangling our feet over Key West harbor while we ate. A stray dog snatched my hotdog, but Punt bought me another. After we ate, we stopped to watch a man whose esoteric commands urged trained cats to sit on pedestals and then jump through a burning hoop. Poor cats, I thought. Did they enjoy that act? Where was PETA?

After we'd seen more than enough of the cats, we crossed from the main dock to the bricked patio at the Hilton Hotel where a few other buskers plied their trade—a magician, a contortionist.

"There she is, Punt." I nodded at a potted palm a few steps from an open-air café. There Maxine's camera flashed and people oohed and aahed while a plump lady laughed and let Maxine untwine Lavonna from around her neck.

"Want your picture taken, folks?" Maxine looked at Punt and me and grinned. "Good souvenir to send up north to the family."

I backed away. "Another time, thanks."

Punt stepped forward. "Okay. Let's see you do your thing." Punt and Lavonna eyed each other, then Lavonna allowed Maxine to drape her on Punt's forearm. The camera flashed again, recording Punt and Lavonna for posterity.

Punt bowed and flashed Maxine a ten-dollar bill. I guessed he hoped his overt generosity would set a precedent for other customers who sometimes tended to be notoriously stingy. Easing our way through the crowd, we found a spot where we could watch the sun drop behind the horizon. We clapped at the end of that ritual bit of drama right along with the tourists as if Mallory dock presented the only place in the world where the sun would set this evening.

"How about tonight, Keely? Want to stay at my place again? I'd like to have you where I know you're safe."

I wanted to say yes. There's nothing I would have liked better than to spend the night with Punt. But I knew I'd be giving up a bit of my hard-won independence if I gave in to my fear—and maybe to Punt. Jude had taught me that many men seem to have an inborn need to curb a woman's feeling of freedom and independence. But maybe not all men. Surely Punt was an exception. I tried to instill that thought in my mind.

"I appreciate your offer, Punt, but I'll stay at my apartment tonight. Thanks to you, the window's fixed. I'm not afraid. Got strong door locks plus a grandmother who sleeps with one eye open."

"I'll drive you home, then." Punt bought us ice cream cones to eat on the walk back to his office and I tried to drown my inner fears in the sweet taste of coconut-pineapple sherbet packed into a waffle cone. Once in the convertible, we took a long route to my apartment. We drove out of our way to pass the beach, knowing there'd be no swimmers at night—only the full moon shining on the silver-tipped waves.

At the White Street Pier, a couple stood, bending to read the names on the Aids Memorial plaques embedded in the concrete. A man approached, carrying a long-stemmed rose. After studying the memorial names carefully, he found the one he'd been seeking. He kissed the rose and laid it down, positioning it carefully three times before he bowed his head as if in prayer. Moments later he turned and walked away.

We, like many of our associates, had lost friends to the HIV virus. We didn't speak again until we reached my door and Punt parked in the only space available—a tow-away zone. He leaned toward me and we kissed before we parted. I'd closed my apartment door and had headed for the shower when Gram knocked and called to me.

"Keely? Keely, sorry to bother at this time."

I hurried to open the door. "What is it, Gram? Come on inside."

"Can't sleep, Keely." She put her hand on her chest. "The heart it be aching and I have accident. Drop pills down sink drain. All gone." She held up an empty pill bottle.

Gram takes nitroglycerine for her angina pains, and she's had these problems often enough that we don't panic. She's usually careful to avoid running out of her medicine.

"Let's take a look, Gram. A pill might be caught right at the mouth of the drain. Maybe I can retrieve it if it's hanging in the stopper mechanism." I pumped calmness into my voice. The pills might be caught in the gooseneck pipe under the sink, too, but my plumbing skills were limited. Would the pharmacy be able to replace her prescription this late in the evening?

We hurried to Gram's shop and I followed her up the narrow steps to her apartment—a sitting room, 2 tiny bedrooms, a kitchen with a small table and chairs. When I had lived with her, I slept in one of the bedrooms. The apartment looked scant and crowded to me now, but during the time I lived there I never remember feeling cramped for space.

Gram snapped on the light in the bathroom and we peered into the sink. No way. No pill there. Maybe she'd placed an extra pill bottle in the cupboard. I opened the rough cupboard that my grandpa had made from the rowboat he and Gram had used to escape from Castro's Cuba in the early sixties. They'd sent my mother ahead of them to Miami by Pan Am on the Pedro Pan Airlift for children. She'd lived in a Catholic Charities orphanage until they claimed her over a year later. But forget all that now! I needed to hurry, and my heart began to pound. I seldom came up to Gram's apartment, and family tales, family memories all but overwhelmed me.

"No pills," Gram said. "I look good."

"No big problem." I tried to keep calm to help keep her calm. "Why don't you let me make you a latte and then I'll go to the pharmacy for more medicine?"

And that's what we did. Gram lay down on her sitting room couch and I ran downstairs and mixed the espresso and steamed milk.

"Amaretto," Gram called from upstairs. "A touch of amaretto, please."

I added the amaretto flavor and took the latte to her. "Enjoy, Gram. I'll be right back." I called the pharmacy first, making sure they had her prescription and asking that they have it ready when I arrived.

I seldom ride at night and my bike has only a dim headlamp. My hands trembled in my nervousness, in my hurry as I unlocked my bicycle. I planned to take a shortcut, to turn and ride a few blocks off Duval, down a seldom used side street that would let me avoid the string of tourist traffic leaving the Mallory sunset activities. I pedaled only a few minutes before I braked to a stop. In my distress over Gram's chest pain and her urgent need for the nitro, I'd forgotten my own danger. How stupid could I get!

I hadn't ridden far and I made a fast U-turn and headed toward home. I'd take a Maxi-Taxi to the pharmacy, ask the cabbie to wait while I bought Gram's pills, and then drive me home. Or, maybe I should have called an ambulance for Gram and headed for the ER. I should have thought of that! Hindsight. Well, I could still call the ambulance once I reached home if Gram would allow that. She hated ambulances and sirens and hospitals. "Too much ado over nothing," she'd say.

Turning toward home at the next corner, I began pedaling faster. I thought I heard someone shout my name, and for a moment I relaxed. Maybe Punt had tried to phone me and then had called Gram when I didn't answer. Maybe he'd come looking for me. No need for a taxi or ambulance. Punt would take me to get Gram's pills. I craned my neck, looking around for the Karmann Ghia, but I saw nobody nearby. Heavy darkness shrouded the trees, the pavement.

The bright lights and crowds on Duval Street lay only a couple of blocks away, and I pumped harder toward home. That's when a pair of bright headlights flashed on and moved toward me, slowly, relentlessly, threatening to block my path. I honked my horn and tried to pull aside, but the car kept coming.

In another moment I heard a scream. It took an instant to realize the scream had come from my own throat and that the driver of the oncoming car had no intention of turning aside.

FIFTEEN

THE SOUND OF TIRES against concrete grated against my eardrums and I choked on exhaust fumes. When the oncoming car began moving more quickly, toward me, I made a last-ditch effort to save myself. Yanking my handlebars to the left, and using all my strength, I thrust my weight onto the pedals. The car didn't crash into me head-on, but I felt it thud against my back fender, heard the crunch of metal against metal.

My bike tilted to one side, and losing my balance, I fell with the weight of it dropping on top of me, pinning me to the ground. Dirt and grit coated my tongue when my head hit the street, but after the initial shock, I managed to wriggle from the twisted wreckage. Fight or flee? Although I wanted to run, my feet and legs refused all mental commands. Nor could I get a good look at the car that had run me down. Its headlights had blinded me. I had been unable to discern either make or color.

I couldn't tell if a man or a woman drove the car, but an atavistic voice from within warned me to run. Before my divorce I'd attended a police-sponsored lecture on self-defense for women. I'd never been brave enough or strong enough to defend myself against Jude and his abuse by using any of the life-saving techniques the lecturer suggested. Now I had no choice. I had to act in my own behalf.

Don't get into a car with a stranger. The words began playing back to me like a recording set on fast forward. Once your attacker gets you in his car, you're a goner. He's almost sure to rape and murder you. Fight for your life. That's all you have going for you—your will to live. Give him a knee to the groin. Bite him. Kick his shins. Stiffen your fingers and go for his eyes.

Or his ears. Don't be afraid to hurt him. That's your chief goal. Remember it's your life or his.

If there's any distance between the two of you at all, even a few inches, your best chance of survival is to scream and run. Attackers hate screamers. Their success depends on your fear, your silence. So scream like hell's chief devil all the time you're running away from the crime scene.

What if he has a gun, you ask. My answer remains etched in marble. Run. Scream. Your best chance of survival lies in your ability to run. Run toward anyone you see on the street. No people? Then head for a lighted building. No lighted building? Then head for a hiding place. Any hiding place. What if he shoots? Half of attackers won't shoot. You have a fifty-fifty chance of making a running escape. If he does shoot, you have a fifty-fifty chance that he'll miss. If he makes a hit, you have a fifty-fifty chance that your wound won't be fatal. Run and scream, but don't get in that car. Never.

Even with all those words skimming through my mind, somehow I managed to wriggle from under my bicycle and crawl away from it. Run? Impossible. Perhaps the driver couldn't see me. The car drove on, catching my bicycle seat on its fender and dragging my bike with it. My left shoulder felt numb. My right knee throbbed. Something warm and wet oozed down my right cheek and the rusty taste of blood coated my tongue. Somewhere I found the strength to stand and run. Slow motion. Although I managed to move into the shadows of thatch palm near the roadside, my throat closed like a vacuum, locking a silent scream inside me as the car slowed down.

"I'm warning you and Ashford," a muffled voice called from the car. "Drop the Darby case. Give it up! You can reason with Punt. Call him off!"

Someone had been waiting for me, watching for me to leave my apartment. Hoping and praying my assailant wouldn't do a U-ie and turn to run me down again, I peeked from my hiding place and caught my breath—waited for the pain in my side to ease. When the revving of a motor followed by the squealing of tires told me I was safe, at least for the moment, I plopped onto the ground to rest, unsure of where I was. I'd felt rough ground underfoot and now the rising moon illumined scrub palm growing at the side of the road. A salt scent told me I sat close to water—maybe the sea, but more likely low-lying wetlands or perhaps an abandoned canal.

I shuddered. Sometimes alligators wandered onto the golf course on Stock Island, but they dislike salt water. They wouldn't travel this far. My fear of fire ants loomed greater than my fear of gators. Using both hands against the ground, I pushed myself to my feet. I remembered past episodes of fire ant bites. I forced myself to keep moving and I tried to wipe my face on the sleeve of my jumpsuit. The ripped sleeve hung dangling in the slight breeze like a flag at half mast, making face wiping difficult. I thought blood had stopped oozing from my head wound, but I couldn't be sure. My knee throbbed, and when I rubbed it, I felt bare skin. The leg of my jumpsuit hung in shreds.

My bike. I had to find it, to pull it from the street before a car hit it and totaled it. I reached into my pocket. No cell phone. I needed a telephone. And who would I call? Not the police. They'd ask too many questions I couldn't answer—didn't want to answer. Driver a man? A woman? Make of car? No police—not yet anyway. And I wouldn't call Gram. She had problems of her own right now. I hoped she'd fallen asleep in spite of her chest pains. Sometimes they eased up when she kept in a prone position.

I sighed and kept trudging toward Duval. I could decide whom to call later. Or maybe I could walk all the way home. It seemed that I had walked a long distance before I stumbled over the remains of my bicycle. When I managed to lift it, I couldn't straighten the handlebars, but the pedals were okay. The spokes in the front wheel were bent and some of those in the back wheel had been forced from the metal rim. They pointed in all directions like broken fingers on a maimed hand.

I pulled the crippled bike from the street and up onto a small terrace where I laid it under a tree. I hated to abandon it, but I couldn't push it forward. But neither could anyone else. That thought consoled me. The bike should stay where I left it.

No sidewalk lined this little-used street, and the houses, all without lights showing, were few and far between. I finally recognized it as an area where the city planned to build low-rent apartments for service workers. I guessed that some old houses already had been razed in preparation for the new construction. I limped along facing any traffic that might approach. People had parked trucks and boat trailers here and there along the road's edge, and when I saw a vehicle approaching, I ducked out of sight.

I looked to my left, and far in the distance I saw the lights on the widow's walk at Ashford Mansion. Relief flooded through me, then I groaned to myself when I realized I'd become lost on my way to a pharmacy right here in Key West where I'd lived my whole life. Maybe hitting my head on the concrete had left me disoriented.

After walking a short distance farther, I saw a single headlight. It approached more quickly than I could duck from sight, drawing close beside me and stopping. A motorcycle cop—not a person I wanted to see right now.

"Hello, Miss. Officer Brady here. Can I be of help?"

My voice sounded ragged when I forced a response. "No thank you, Officer. I'm heading home and doing okay."

He trained his flashlight beam on me. "You don't look so okay, to me. Care to tell me what happened?"

"I'm fine, officer. I'm just going to…to visit a friend."

"Can you give me an address?"

"No. I'm not sure of the address."

"Look, lady. Show some ID, please."

In my hurry to get to a drug store, I'd jammed a couple of bills into my pocket and rushed out the door. "No ID with me. Sorry."

Officer Brady said no more. Instead he radioed for backup help, and in a few minutes a squad car arrived. No sirens wailed, but blue lights flashed, sending eerie shadows into the street and the sky. Officers Bremmer and Hilsabeck identified themselves, and I sighed. Friends—of sorts. From their expressions, I knew I must look a mess. The little strength I'd mustered faded away. I made no fuss when they helped me into the back seat of the squad car.

"Where are you taking me, Jeff? Please don't take me to the police station. There's no time for that. I've done nothing wrong.

I was going to CVS. I need to pick up pills for Gram. She's having chest pains. I need to get nitro to her quickly. Can you help? She dropped her pills down the drain and …" I sensed myself babbling.

"Try to relax, Keely." Hillie's cello-like tone helped calm me.

"Please get her pills to her. Don't worry about me. I'm okay."

Hillie radioed Officer Brady and ordered him to pick up and deliver Gram's medicine and help her take it.

"No problem," Officer Brady replied. "Know her place well. Best espresso on the island."

"We're taking you to the hospital, Keely," Jeff said. "Emergency room. Care to tell us what happened? Someone mug you?"

"Am I under arrest?"

"No, of course not. You don't have to answer any questions right now. We'll let the medics check you over and ask the questions. Then we'll work from there." Jeff activated the siren and we turned several corners before we sped along Truman Avenue, running three stop lights before we crossed the Boca Chica bridge and headed down the street toward the hospital.

Once inside the ER, I ignored the medicinal smell, the sound of rushing feet as an orderly hurried toward me. I glanced into a wall mirror near the admission desk, catching a glimpse of someone I hardly recognized. Me. My hair lay matted to my scalp. My forehead still oozed blood. And my clothes hung in tatters.

"No ID," Jeff told the admission clerk. "But I know her. Keely Moreno."

"Miss," the clerk said. "Isn't there someone we can call in your behalf?"

With great reluctance I gave Punt's phone number. Almost immediately, a nurse and an orderly eased me into a wheelchair and pushed me into a hospital room where the nurse helped me into a hospital gown. I felt too exhausted to complain about the gown's air vents down the rear. Once I lay on my back on their hard bed, they didn't matter.

The nurse had covered me with a warmed blanket, and I lay dozing when a doctor arrived. He asked only a few questions before he began ordering X rays, treating my abrasions, and administering shots. I don't know how long I slept, but when I awakened, Punt sat on a chair beside my bed and pink and gray shafts of light lit the sky.

Punt rose to give me a kiss, and in spite of myself I burst into tears. He waited until I calmed down before he spoke.

"What happened? Who did this to you? Do you feel like telling me about it? Maybe you need to sleep some more."

"I've had enough sleep and I want out of here—want to go home." I ached all over but I sat up, forced my legs over the edge of the bed. "A car hit me while I was riding my bike to get some pills for Gram. Don't know who it was. No idea."

"It didn't stop?"

"It slowed down a little but it didn't stop."

"What kind of a car was it?"

"Big. That's all I can tell you."

"Man driving? Or a woman?"

"No idea at all."

"The person say anything?"

I lowered my voice to a whisper. "Just a warning to back off the Darby case. And Punt, whoever it was knows you're involved too. The person said your name. Someone must have been watching when we met at your office this afternoon."

"Yesterday afternoon, Keely. Today's Friday. You've been here all night."

Punt rang for a nurse while I was getting up, testing my legs to see if I could stand. He'd brought me fresh clothes and although I moved slowly, I stood almost dressed before the nurse arrived. She didn't bother to hide her surprise at seeing me up and about, and after she made me sit down so she could check my vital signs, she insisted that the doctor must see me, too. So we waited for almost an hour before the doctor strolled in, checked me over again, and gave his permission for me to leave the ER with the understanding that I'd see my family doctor for a follow-up visit at the first opportunity. Nobody said anything more about the police, and I certainly didn't intend to bring up that subject.

I filled out forms at the admission desk, then Punt offered his arm for support as we left the hospital and walked toward the Karmann Ghia. The sun, slipping from behind some morning clouds, began to warm the day.

"What about the police, Punt? They asked questions. I didn't have my ID with me. Am I supposed to report to them?"

"I've taken care of their questions. Forget them for now unless you want to press charges against someone."

"No charges. Don't know whom I'd press them against. Oh, Punt! Thanks for your help. What would I do without you?"

"Yes, what! Think carefully about that. You need me. I need you. We need each other." He helped me into the car, sealing my lips with his kiss, and then propping my head against a pillow he'd brought along.

"Gram will be having a fit. She needed medicine. She'll know I didn't come home last night."

"Relax, Keely. I called Celia the minute the doc said you had no broken bones and weren't seriously injured—anyway, no injuries that wouldn't heal in a few days—or weeks. The police delivered the nitro to her. I'm guessing she had a restful night."

When Punt crossed the Boca Chica bridge, I spoke up.

"I need my bicycle. It's a mess, but I need to get it to a repair shop. I abandoned it somewhere a few streets behind Duval. Maybe in Bahama Village."

"It'll probably be right where you left it."

Punt was right. We passed Emma Street and two unmarked streets—a common thing in Key West. Then I saw it. The bike lay there looking like a twisted cry for help. The Karmann Ghia offers little storage space, but we managed to cram the crumpled bike in behind the bucket seats and Punt drove to the Moped Hospital where a mechanic guaranteed to return it to my doorstep the next day. Maybe. Good fishing weather put the maybe in lots of be-done-tomorrow promises.

"I want you to follow the doctor's orders, Keely," Punt said as we left the repair shop then reached my office. "Cancel today's appointments. Sleep until you wake up. I've arranged another meeting with Maxine and Randy, but it can wait until you're out and about and feeling fit again. Give me a call."

Gram met me at my door, aghast at my cuts and bruises.

"All this happen on my account. Keely. Keely. Now it be my turn to take care of you. To bed with you. Now."

I was so glad to see Gram up and around that I let her boss me, let her turn back my covers and plump my pillow and bring me a cinnamon latte. I hated to take a day off to sleep, but I agreed to do that. Punt cancelled Friday's appointments for me. After hearing my promise to "sleep it off," he gave me a farewell kiss and left.

It was hard to fall asleep when the full impact of my injuries reached me. I could be the next murder victim.

SIXTEEN

WORRY DIDN'T KEEP ME awake for long. Nor did Gram's fussing over me. Nor did Punt's insistence on paying an off-duty policeman to do surveillance on this end of Duval Street. I slept like a tarpon in frigid water. When I finally woke up, it took me a few moments to get my bearings. My watch said midafternoon on Friday. I closed my eyes again. My whole body felt like a rusty scupper, but I managed to limp to the shower. Hot water sluicing over my body made me believe that I'd live to see another day.

After I checked in with Gram, repeating the whole story of last night's attack, we agreed to call the incident an accident and say no more to the police—at least not right then. I called Punt and we made tentative plans for the rest of the day, including a meeting with the Jacksons. In a few minutes he called me back.

"The meeting's on. I'll come get you and we'll meet Maxine and Randy at my office in half an hour."

"Maybe your office is bugged."

"I checked. No wires. Someone lurked outside watching us yesterday. No matter. Nothing we can do about it. Our lurker already knows we're investigating the Darby murder. Our meeting today will tell him for sure that we haven't backed off."

When Punt arrived the top was up on the Karmann Ghia. Maybe for safety. Maybe for privacy. I didn't ask. I inhaled a slight smell of canvas all the way to his office. Maxine's Ford occupied the visitor's slot and we all entered the office together. She was wearing her blue-and-white-polka dot bloomers again. Maybe she had several pair. Maybe they were her uniform like my khaki jumpsuits were my favorite work outfits. Punt and

Randy both wore jeans as usual, but today Randy's T-shirt advertised the Parrot Heads and Jimmy Buffett's Margaritaville.

Shoes and chair legs grated against terrazzo as we settled ourselves in a semicircle in front of Punt's desk. I saw to it that Maxine sat between me and Randy. I hoped Punt wouldn't mention the attack I'd suffered last night. And he didn't. I'd worn a long-sleeved shirt that hid most of my abrasions.

Randy spoke first. "We need to get DNA samples from the dive guys I mentioned yesterday. Helmer. Grovello. Soto. Slone. Those four for starters. And maybe Beau Ashford. DNA saved my ass—got me out of Raiford. Maybe it can help me again."

"How do you collect DNA samples?" Maxine asked. "We don't know how that's done and we don't want to go at it in a way that might make the suspects suspicious."

Punt grinned. "Everyone carries DNA with them, Maxine. It's found in hair, in skin, or…"

"Or in shit and semen, right?" Randy gave me an insolent glance as if to see if I found his language shocking.

"Yes," Punt agreed, without pause. "Or in other body fluids—blood, sweat, and saliva. Sometimes it's easy enough to get DNA specimens—if you go after them in a nonoffensive way."

"Next time Gus or Ace come for treatments, I'll request a lock of hair for my scrapbook." I laughed and Punt broke in before Randy could suggest more personal ways of DNA collection.

"In the long run, DNA specimens may point out Dyanne Darby's killer, but before we go after any specimens, we need to lay careful groundwork. Let's think this DNA business through carefully. Randy, what would you do with DNA specimens if you're lucky enough to get a few?"

"Take 'em to the cops." Randy scowled. "You got other ideas?"

Punt shook his head and smiled. "Before we go to the police, we have to be sure the police are interested in this case. Otherwise, they'll be irritated because we're wasting their time."

I sensed that Punt used the word "we" to discourage Randy from taking the investigation into his own hands and acting on his own. I tried to avoid imagining how he might go about collecting DNA samples.

Randy glared at Punt. "You thinkin' those dumb bastard cops aren't interested in finding Dyanne's murderer?"

I knew from the way Randy's scar began to glow that his anger might be reaching the boiling-over stage.

"That's right, Randy. They may not be interested. Sometimes the authorities say that a person's being exonerated doesn't prove his innocence, that it merely proves that prosecutors couldn't prove his guilt beyond a reasonable doubt. Sorry if that news shocks you, but that's the way it is."

"But…but…" Randy spluttered.

"Faced with unresolved murder cases, police rarely pursue additional avenues of investigation—especially if years have passed since the first investigation."

"That's unfair," Maxine said. "I think it's their way of covering up."

"Sometimes it seems that way," Punt agreed. "But prosecutors have legitimate reasons to abandon cases. Many murders become almost unsolvable with age, because witnesses have died and memories have faded. The evidence is old. The trail's cold."

Randy began pacing. "I'm going to make the police listen, to reopen this case."

"The police will be interested only if we can prove that the DNA donors or would-be donors are actually suspects—people who had both motive and opportunity for murdering the Darby woman." Punt looked directly at Randy. "No point in presenting DNA from what the authorities might consider a random sampling of people who might not have any bearing on this murder that happened two decades ago."

"Prove opportunity?" Maxine asked. "After all them years it would be purty hard to do that. Who could prove what any of them divers did on the night of the murder?"

"Right," Punt agreed. "It'll take lots of in-depth investigating to learn those necessary details. But it may not be such an impossible task as it seems at first glance. Once we have the needed facts, then Randy's absolutely right. A DNA sample, used by the right people and in the right way, could pinpoint the guilty person."

"The police have the DNA sample of the semen found inside

Dyanne's body on file someplace," Randy said. "All we need to do is to match it up with identical DNA."

"All we need to do?" I sighed. "That could be a very large job."

Punt nodded. "Big job, but not impossible. It'll take time and effort, but …"

"But there's a lid for every pot." Maxine grinned. "That's what my grandma always said—a lid for every pot. We work at the DNA thing, and we'll find a match."

"So how do we start?" I asked. "First things first. Maybe we can lay the groundwork for an investigation and make the police be responsible for collecting the DNA. How do we learn what Gus Helmer was doing on a certain night decades ago?"

"The exact night was December 24, 1982," Randy said. "That's the date of the murder. Christmas Eve. Hard to forget that date. I'd bought Dyanne a pair of earrings as a Christmas gift— black coral earrings a diver brought me from a deep dive off the coast of Belize. Never did get to give them to her."

"The murder date may be a help," Punt said. "Lots of people remember what they did on Christmas Eve, but maybe not on a Christmas Eve twenty years ago unless something very special happened that year. Test yourselves. Can any of you remember what you did on that Christmas Eve in 1982? Memories fade with time."

"So here's an angle," I suggested. "If we have opportunity to question those suspects about that 1982 Christmas Eve, we should pay special attention to anyone who comes up with a glib answer. If someone asked me that question, I'd have to think a long time, recall many other Christmas Eves before I could remember exactly what I'd been doing in 1982."

"Right," Maxine agreed. "I only remember 1982 because of the murder."

"That could be true of the divers, too," Punt said. "Let's use that fact to our advantage. I think those dive boys would remember that date with no trouble at all."

"They'd remember the day in full detail," Randy said. "And the guilty one would have an alibi rehearsed and memorized."

"Let me suggest another starting point for our investigation,"

Punt said. "Let's think about Nicole Nichols, the woman who gave false testimony at your trial."

"The bitch that lied about me," Randy said, "who pretended to be Dyanne's friend."

"You said you knew her?" Punt asked.

"Yes. I knew her. Slightly. She and Dyanne lived in the same apartment house. We double dated a couple of times."

"Who was her date?" Punt asked.

"One of the divers. Slone Pierce."

"I've been checking on her," Punt said. "I learned that her name's now Nicole Pierce. She's been married to your diver friend Slone for over seventeen years."

"Holy shit!" Randy exclaimed.

"Nicole Nichols Pierce," Punt said. "Let's think more about this woman. At Thursday's meeting, someone suggested that Nicole might have lied to protect the guilty person. Maybe we can call on her, question her and get her to admit her lie."

"Not likely if she was protecting her boyfriend," Maxine said. "Maybe her husband-to-be."

"Maybe not," Punt agreed, "but she still lives in Key West—right on Flagler. Talking with her, asking her a few questions, would be a starting point no matter what she has to say to us."

"Why would she admit lying now after so many years?" Maxine asked. "Surely she's not that dumb. Maybe someone bribed her to lie. Money talks."

"I have something here that may help us." Punt reached into his desk drawer and removed some papers. "This is a copy of the transcript of Randy's trial."

"Where'd you get it?" Randy jumped up and grabbed the papers, checked them briefly, then tossed them back onto Punt's desk.

"I got them on loan from Attorney Hubble—Shelley Hubble. Court reporters take notes at a trial, but unless there's a controversy over the trial, the notes may never be printed in hard copy. The Reverend Soto and Shelley Hubble had many questions about Randy's trial. At their request and payment of a fee, the court ordered a hard copy transcript of the court reporter's notes.

When I told Shelley we planned to investigate this cold case, she was interested enough to make me a copy of the transcript."

"What do it say?" Maxine asked. "How we going to use it to find the murderer?"

"First I want us to talk to Nicole, to ask her a few questions."

"Think you can get an appointment with her?" I asked.

"Private investigators don't make appointments in a case like this," Punt said. "Ruins the surprise element—gives the person time to fabricate a tale."

"We'll barge in on her unannounced?" Maxine asked.

"Yes. There are no laws against visitors knocking on someone's door. But we don't want to scare her. It might be best if Keely and I talked to her alone."

"No way." Randy jumped up, his scar blossoming. "I want to be along on this visit. I insist. That bitch's words helped lock me in prison. I want to meet her eyeball-to-eyeball and ask her the why of her damn lies. If you go see her, I go." Randy paced from his chair to Punt's desk and back several times before Punt answered him.

"All right, Randy. Maybe we all should go. But we have to remember that she may have been covering for a killer. And if she walked that way once, she'll likely walk the same path again. If that's the case, she'll almost certainly warn the killer that we've been snooping around asking questions."

"We'd all be putting ourselves in danger." I said the words, hating to admit the truth yet knowing we already were in danger.

"That's not why I wanted Keely and me to talk to Nicole alone," Punt said. "Confronting two people isn't as frightening as confronting four. We get this woman scared and she may clam up—not say a word that might help us."

"I'd be more than happy to scare the shit right out of her," Randy said, but he sat down and his scar faded. "What are you going to ask her, Mr. Ashford?"

"Hold on one minute, Randy. Before I have a chance to say anything to her she may slam the door in our faces. If that happens, there's no way we can enter her home without a court order. As a PI, there's probably no way I could get a court order.

The trial's over and done. Nicole won't want to see your case reopened now or ever."

"But she lied," Randy said. "She lied."

"Yes, she did," Punt said. "But your defense lawyer never tried to prove that. Because of that omission, and because of the surprise of our visit, we may be able to confront her with her lies and use them as a wedge in the door to get her to talk to us. It's a long shot. You had a rotten defense lawyer, Randy. When I checked into his record this morning, I learned he died five years ago."

"No help there," Maxine said.

"Maybe there is help there, Maxine. He later lost his license in the state of Florida because he appeared in a courtroom drunk. I might be able to arouse doubt about his sobriety during Randy's trial. Of course it's too late to backtrack, to do anything about that now. But judges know that court-appointed lawyers are sometimes bad news for their clients. I might be able to convince today's judge that Nicole lied and that Randy's lawyer's weak defense allowed her to get away with perjury."

"What good would that do now?" I asked.

"If Nicole lied, she's probably carried guilt about her lie with her all these years. The threat of Randy accusing her of perjury might make her reveal who persuaded her to perjure herself." Punt sighed. "But all of this is merely speculation. I think the first and the most logical thing for us to do is to pay a surprise visit on Nicole Nichols Pierce."

"When?" Randy asked, jumping up. "Right now?"

SEVENTEEN

WITH RANDY AT THE READY, Punt did a slow-motion performance of rising from his captain's chair and placing his copy of the trial transcript in his briefcase before he turned and locked his file cabinet. I sensed from his deliberate movements that he wanted to make sure Randy knew who headed this investigation—Punt, not Randy.

"Yes, Randy." Punt spoke calmly, and Randy backed off a few steps. "Now would be an excellent time for us to call on Nicole Pierce. I telephoned a friend at the marina and learned that her husband's on a salvage job near Marathon. Some guy's sailboat sank in high winds and Slone's trying to winch it up. Even if all goes well with the job, Slone won't be in until late tonight."

"Let's go." Randy headed for the door.

"Maxine," Punt said. "Is it okay if we all go in your car? One car arriving at the Pierce home will be less conspicuous than two."

"Especially if the one is gray—not yellow," Randy said. "Don't know why a rich guy like you drives that old klunker."

"Inverse snobbery," Punt said, grinning.

"We'll take our car." Maxine led the way outside and we all piled into the Ford for the short ride to the Pierce home. Flagler carries a plethora of traffic, but this end of the avenue offers few tourist attractions to catch a visitor's eye. We had no trouble finding curbside parking directly in front of a row of one-story stucco homes. I remembered the neighborhood well. I tried to forget the frosty reception and the curt invitation to leave that Punt and I had received when we visited here a year or so ago, seeking information from Slone Pierce.

Punt led the way through the gate in the coral rock privacy

fence, stepped onto a pine-planked porch littered with old air tanks and damaged face masks, and rapped on the door. At first I thought nobody would answer, then a curtain parted at a front window, dropped back into place. Punt knocked again, and in a moment the door opened a crack and the pungent scent of nail polish remover mingled with cigarette smoke reached us.

Nicole Pierce brushed a strand of bottle-blonde hair behind her left ear while she sized us up—and gave us ample time to size her up. Short. Middle-aged. Heavy-set. Her double chin formed a collar of flabby flesh that supported her coarse features. Her bloodshot eyes and no-smile lips gave her the dragged-out look of a barmaid who'd worked an eight-hour shift and needed a hot shower and a long rest. Clutching the thin panels of a thigh-length swimsuit cover-up together at the waist, she greeted us.

"Yes?"

"Mrs. Pierce, I'm Punt Ashford. My dad and Slone used to dive for Mel Fisher."

"Yes?"

"These people with me are my friends, Keely Moreno, Maxine and Randy Jackson. We'd like to come in and talk to you for a few minutes."

Nicole backed up a step and turned her head as a racking cough shook her body. Behind her on an entryway table, a cigarette smoldered in an ashtray. I thought she might close the door in our faces. But no.

"What's your business with me? What have you come here to talk about? I just got off work and I'm really not in a talking mood." Her voice carried the deep huskiness common to pack-a-day smokers and heavy drinkers.

Punt flashed his identification and although she peered at it, I doubted she could read it from behind the mesh of the screen door. So far she hadn't let on that she recognized Randy's face or his name, but I knew she had because when she spoke next, she directed her words at Randy instead of at Punt.

"Please state your business. I'm not sure …"

"May we come inside?" Punt asked again.

To my surprise, she opened the door and stood back so we

could enter. She scooped the top of a wetsuit off a chintz-covered couch and brushed two broken snorkels from a chair in front of a console TV.

"Please have a seat."

Punt chose a chair beside a window and Maxine, Randy, and I sat in a row on the couch like cormorants on a phone wire. I could identify with Nicole's lack of interest in housekeeping. The room looked clean enough, just "lived-in" messy.

Once we were seated, Punt drove to the point. "We want to talk to you about the Randy Jackson trial in the early eighties—about your testimony at that trial."

Nicole Pierce stood up immediately. "I have nothing more to say about that trial. I don't care to discuss it with you now or ever. Nor do I want to discuss it with anyone else. I want you to leave…now."

Punt didn't budge from his chair. "We'll only take a few minutes of your time, Mrs. Pierce." Punt kept his voice warm and friendly and he turned on a heartbreaker smile that I knew well. "Your testimony at Randy's trial carried a great deal of weight with the judge and jury. Are you aware that Mr. Jackson spent twenty years in prison?"

"I'm aware."

"Randy feels that you misrepresented him. He feels that you …"

"You lied." Randy's scar began to flame as he interrupted Punt and scowled.

"Easy, Randy." Punt stood to pat Randy's shoulder.

"Easy, hell!" Randy rose and turned his wrath on Nicole. "You bitch! How can you sit there and face me calm as low tide after the rotten thing you did to me?"

Nicole jumped up. "Get out of here, you murderer! All of you get out of my house before I call the police." She reached for the telephone sitting on an end table near the couch and jammed the receiver against her ear, listening for a dial tone. I could hear it from where I sat, but I didn't know how to stop her.

"Calling the police is your privilege, Mrs. Pierce," Punt assured her, keeping his voice low and smooth and his smile in place. "But we hope you won't do that. We haven't come here to make trouble for you concerning a trial that ended two decades ago. We had hoped you'd help us."

"Help you in what way?" She paused with her finger still poised over the telephone number pad.

"The authorities have exonerated Randy in the Dyanne Darby case. Surely you've read about that."

"Yes. I read all about that. I still think he's guilty as sin no matter what the court says or does. I didn't recognize him when you first arrived here or I'd never have let him inside. Again, I'm ordering all of you to leave."

"Mrs. Pierce, DNA evidence proved without a doubt that someone else murdered Dyanne Darby. You, like many others, may still have totally unfounded doubts about Randy's innocence."

"You bet I do!"

"We now feel there's only one way to totally clear Randy's name and help him ease into today's society. That way's to find Dyanne Darby's true killer and to get that person behind bars. That's what we hoped you'd be able and willing to help us do."

"How can I possibly do that? In what way do you think I can help you?" She set the phone back onto the end table, but she still remained standing, kept her gaze on it as if she might pick it up again at any instant.

"Please sit down and hear us out," Punt said. "You could help us by admitting you lied under oath. That's what we'll tell the police right now—if you force us to by calling them. We'll tell them we can prove that you lied. Perjury's a serious crime."

Nicole remained standing, folding her arms at her waist until she realized that position allowed her cover-up to gap. She clutched the cover-up to her body again, this time managing to tie strings at the neckline and the waist.

"You're thinking that if you tell the police I lied, and if they can prove I lied, then I'd be in big trouble?"

"That might be true," Punt said. "Or maybe not. It's hard to guess what lawyers, judges, juries, and the police might do. But it's something for you to consider."

Nicole sat again and jutted her ample chin toward the ceiling. "You're suggesting I could be brought to court on a perjury charge?"

"I'm saying that's a possibility," Punt said.

"Well, I say no way. I didn't lie. I told the court exactly what I saw happen. I didn't back down on my story then, and I won't back down on it now. Never. On the afternoon Dyanne died, I saw Randy Jackson enter Dyanne's apartment then return to the hallway with her blood all over himself and his clothes. That's what I saw. I lived right down that hall from Dyanne and that's exactly what I saw."

"Maybe you made a mistake," Punt said. "That's possible, you know. Eyes can play tricks. You described the killer as a tall man with a Z-shaped scar on his left cheek."

"Right. That's what I saw."

"Randy's a tall man, that's for sure, but if you'll notice, Randy's scar is on his right cheek, not his left cheek."

Nicole studied Randy as if she'd never seen him before.

Punt continued. "I'm suggesting that you saw that facial scar so often in the courtroom and maybe during the times you double-dated with Dyanne and Randy that its image became embedded in your thinking. I'm also suggesting that because of its familiarity you imagined remembering the scar on the man you saw leaving Dyanne Darby's apartment, the man you believed in your mind to be Randy Jackson."

When Nicole looked at Randy again, her eyes widened as if she were seeing him for the first time.

Punt continued. "Nicole, Randy did not enter Dyanne's apartment that afternoon. He didn't call on her until early evening. They had a dinner date. If you saw someone leave her apartment in the afternoon with blood on his clothes, you probably did see the killer. But it wasn't Randy Jackson."

"Then who was it?"

"If anyone had known that for sure, Randy wouldn't have spent twenty years in prison. Do you have any idea who the killer might have been?"

"No. None. If it wasn't Randy, then why did the jury believe it was Randy?" Nicole asked.

"Nobody knows exactly why any jury reaches the decision it reaches. That holds true of the jury at Randy's trial. Many things play a part in a jury's decision. Randy had no alibi for the time of Dyanne's death. He said he was at home alone. Nobody could prove that he was home alone, and …"

"And nobody believed him?" Nicole asked.

"He had no corroborating witness to the fact that he was alone. His alibi amounted to no alibi at all under those circumstances. Your testimony that you saw him leaving Dyanne's apartment in the afternoon went a long way toward convicting him. He had her blood on him, that's true. He explained he had touched her body, tried to see if he could help her before he realized she was dead and called the police."

"And the jury didn't believe that."

"Right. They didn't. And in addition to that, Randy's court-appointed lawyer did little or nothing to help him win his freedom. At the time of Randy's trial DNA evidence was inadmissible in the courtroom. But things have changed. DNA evidence is permitted and that's what won Randy's exoneration—twenty years too late."

Nicole looked at Randy, then she looked back at Punt, glaring at him for a few moments before she burst into tears, lowered her head to her knees and sobbed. We all squirmed in discomfort at her outburst.

At last she raised her head, still gulping for air, fighting for composure. "What have I done?" she muttered. "What have I done?"

"Perhaps the only thing you've done is make a mistake," Punt said. "Anyone can make a mistake. And what's past is past. We haven't come here to fault you for your mistake. But we have come to ask you to help us find Dyanne's killer. We've no interest in seeing you brought up on a perjury charge for a lie that you could easily admit was an error, a case of mistaken identity. But I'm thinking that if you made one mistake, maybe you made others. Maybe if you think carefully you can recall facts about the killer that might help us identify him today. Are you sure the man you saw leaving Dyanne's apartment was a tall man?"

"Yes. I'm absolutely sure of that."

"What did you compare him to in order to estimate his height?"

Nicole hesitated a long time before she answered. "To myself, I suppose."

"You suppose?" Punt looked Nicole up and down as if measuring her height. "You're about five feet four inches? Is that a close estimate?"

She nodded.

"So if the man you saw was taller than you, that makes him a very tall man?"

Nicole looked as if she might sob again and Punt spoke quickly.

"Nicole, why don't you tell us again what happened the night Dyanne died? Maybe you'll remember some detail that could help us find the real killer. Memories fade with time. We all know that, but we also know that certain special incidents remain lodged in our minds, popping up like lighthouse beacons on a dark shore."

For a long time, Nicole hesitated and I thought she might refuse to say any more to us at all, but after taking a few deep breaths, her story began to pour forth like gall from a ruptured liver.

EIGHTEEN

"ON THE DAY DYANNE died I had worked an eight hour shift at Sloppy's and I had to sub that night for a barmaid who'd gone up north to celebrate Christmas with her family. I envied her for having a family that cared about her. But if it hadn't been for that extra duty, Dyanne and I probably would have double-dated as we sometimes did. Me with Slone. Her with Randy.

"At that time, Dyanne was my closest friend. We had no family that cared a hoot about us. Her stepfather lived somewhere in Michigan near the boundary waters. My alcoholic mother lived somewhere in Alaska—Homer, I think. Dyanne and I were on our own. There's a saying around here: If you're lucky enough to live in the Florida Keys, you're lucky enough. Dyanne's luck ran out. I guess we chose to live in Key West because we couldn't go any farther. A local poet—Shel somebody—wrote that Key West's where the sidewalk ends. It was where life would end for Dyanne."

I'd turned on my mini tape recorder, but I turned off my ears when Nicole repeated highlights of Dyanne Darby's murder that we already knew. When she finished talking, Punt was generous in his thanks.

"You've been kind to admit us to your home and talk to us, Nicole. We appreciate that. We hope you'll keep us and our quest in mind. Think about the day of Dyanne's death—about the minute details. It's hard to remember exact happenings from so long ago, but if any once-forgotten events pop back into your mind, please give me a call at my office. We need to find the person who murdered your friend."

"I'll phone you if I recall anything I think might be of value."

We all thanked Nicole as we left the house. Even Randy

muttered a thank-you. Once back in Maxine's car, nobody spoke until we reached Punt's office and sat again before his desk.

"Guess we wasted our time talking to that bitch," Randy said. "So she made a mistake—one big mistake that cost me twenty years." He rose and stormed toward Punt's desk, shaking his finger in Punt's face. "You let her off far too easy."

"I didn't go there to harass her," Punt said. "If you'll remember, that wasn't the point of our trip. I think we got everything we went for. She promised to help us find Dyanne's killer if there's any way she can do so. I think she'll do that. I think she's feeling guilt-ridden over her mistake. You never know what she may remember that could help us once she starts some in-depth thinking about that murder again."

"Some memory she has!" Randy spit the words.

"I told you that talking to her was a starting place—only a start."

"So now maybe it's time you listened to me—to ex-con Randy Jackson who's been there, done that. I know and we know that DNA evidence from Dyanne's body's on file in police records. That evidence freed me. What we need now is a DNA specimen that matches that filed specimen. And I'm going to find it. When we have that DNA, we'll have the killer."

Randy turned, gave his chair a kick, and started for the door.

"Hold on, Randy," Punt said. "The first thing to do, the smart thing to do, is to convince the police we can offer them the names of viable suspects. We have to convince them to reopen the case. They may balk. But if they agree to reopen, then it's time to ask the police to collect the DNA. They'll do it right and there'll be no mistakes. If we do the DNA collecting, there's a chance we'll make an error that'll cause the police to ignore our samples."

"And forget about reopening the case," I added.

"I'm not going to make a mistake," Randy countered. "Nails, hair, skin, body fluids. I can get that stuff from the guys I suspect and present it to the police on a silver platter. Then they'll have to listen to me."

"Sit down a minute, Randy," Punt said. "Let's go about this investigation with logic and lots of forethought. Of course you can ask any or all of your suspects for a sample of his hair or his saliva. What if he refuses your request?"

"I'll find a way to get what I need."

"Perhaps so," Punt said. "But what will you do with it once you have it?"

"Give it to the authorities," Randy said. "What else?"

"DNA specimens have to be carefully collected and handled. There must be no guesswork as to the identity of the person who has supplied the specimen." When Punt turned his back to open a file drawer, Randy headed for the door again.

"Wait." Punt spoke softly, but there was no mistaking the command. "I want to show you one sure way to collect DNA—a way that conforms to police procedures."

Punt set a paper cup with a paper cover on his desk, a box of Q-tips, some envelopes, some tape. Taking one Q-tip, he stuck it into his mouth, rolling it against his cheek. Then, without touching the cotton portion of the swab, he poked it through the cover on the cup.

"We'll let it dry. That'll take a few minutes."

I thought Randy might bolt for the door, but he sat and remained seated. Reaching into his file drawer again, Punt removed brochures about DNA fingerprinting and gave us each a copy. Maxine and I began reading the information, but Randy sat staring at the cup and the Q-tip.

When Punt felt sure the saliva on the cotton swab had dried, he opened an envelope and without touching the cotton, he dropped the Q-tip inside.

"Please note that I'm not licking the envelope to seal it. If I did that, my own DNA would be on the envelope and two DNA samples in or on the same envelope might cause a problem to analysts later."

Punt sealed the envelope with tape. "If the police were to use this sample, they'd want the donor's name and the date the sample was collected written on the envelope. Randy, after reading the brochure and watching my demonstration, I hope you realize that there are specific procedures that must be followed. If a DNA specimen the police collected and the DNA sample at the crime scene are identical—you have a match. You've found the guilty person."

Without speaking, Randy stood, urged Maxine to her feet, and headed for the door.

"Randy, wait." Maxine held back, but Randy took her wrist and pulled her through the doorway and outside. Then turning, he gave us a scathing glare.

"I'm doing this my way," he shouted. "I'm collecting the DNA first and then telling the police where they'll find the suspects. It'll save everybody a lot of time—time that s.o.b. killer could be spending behind bars instead of walking free."

The door slammed, but in moments, Maxine reappeared in the office, gripping Randy's hand as she pulled him along behind her.

"My Randy, he agree to ask the Reverend Soto's advice before he begins his DNA collecting."

"Good plan, Randy," Punt said. "I remember Soto's name on your suspect list."

"Low on the list," Randy said, much more subdued that he'd been a few minutes ago. "I put him on my list only because he was one of Fisher's divers. Soto helped me out of prison. Ma's right. I need to talk to him before I go on the DNA search alone."

"Good thinking, Randy," I said, doubting my opinion mattered to him.

"I tell my Randy that it's too late tonight to be talking to Soto. We'll wait until morning when we have fresh minds and cooler thinking."

Punt and I nodded, and this time Punt walked with Maxine and Randy to the door and to their car where he opened the door for Maxine and helped her inside.

When he returned to his office, we both heaved sighs of relief.

"We're working with a loose cannon, Keely. We've got to stop him before he does something that'll cause his arrest. We've got to get him away from Key West for a few days. Maybe if we tell Soto all that's transpired, he'll help us."

"Think he could get Randy on another TV show in New York? Or maybe some other distant city?"

"That's a big order. But if Soto can't help, maybe we could

get Shelley Hubble working for Randy again. She's a reputable attorney and the police would listen to her. What's even more important, Randy might listen to her, too. Maybe we, working along with Hubble and Soto could help him find a job. A job would at least slow down his DNA collecting activities—might even stop them long enough for us to get a better plan going for us—and for him."

"You heard what he's said, Punt. I believe him when he says he's tried for a job, tried and failed time after time. And we can't blame employers for not hiring an ex-convict with a hair-trigger temper and no special skills. Would you like to have Randy working for you?"

Punt shook his head. "And Maxine told me he smokes pot. Not a lot, but now and then. Maybe just enough to entice him to wanting something more upscale. I know how that goes, Keely. A guy starts with a little and ends up frantic to have a lot. People never know what a druggie might do. They're unpredictable. A guy needing a fix is one desperate person. I know from experience."

"Maybe we need to talk to the Reverend Soto—tonight, Punt, even if it's late. Tonight, before Randy and Maxine talk to him tomorrow."

"I have another idea. Just thought of it—an idea I'd like to try before we talk to anyone else."

"I'm listening."

Punt tapped his wristwatch. "It's late, Keely, but we have a whole lot of evening ahead of us, and I have a friend living on Big Pine who owes me a favor."

"First you have a useful friend in the police department. Now another good buddy on Big Pine. You going to call in all your markers on Randy's behalf?"

"Not so. Maybe on behalf of Keely Moreno. Maybe on behalf of Maxine. Maybe on behalf of the Fotopolus and Ashford Agency."

"Okay. Okay yet. So who's the guy on Big Pine and what makes you think he'd give Randy a job?"

"His name's Shrimp Snerl and oddly enough, his name fits his occupation. He's captain of a shrimp boat."

"Sounds like a logical nickname for a shrimper."

"There's another logical reason for the nickname. You'll see when you meet him. His boat's the *Midnight Moon* out of Big Pine Key."

"A romantic name for a shrimp boat." I smiled, thinking of the unromantic shrimp boats I'd observed at the Key West docks.

"A few years ago during our beach bum days, Shrimp dreamed of owing a shrimp boat. Not many of the guys hanging out on the beach thought of having a dream, but I remembered some of my own dreams, unfulfilled, of course. Anyway, I persuaded Beau to lend Snerl the money to make a down payment on *Midnight Moon*."

"And it worked out, right?"

"In many ways, yes. It worked out. When Dad lends money, he kisses it goodbye—calls it a gift rather than a loan. Says it keeps him from getting down on people who may stiff him. Anyway Dad lent Shrimp the money to buy the boat and Shrimp cut down on his beach time and readied the craft for action. He had trouble hiring on a crew, so I volunteered to go out on his first run. We had great luck—filled the trawl nets night after night before we docked at Key West to sell the catch."

"I suppose he paid off his debt then and there."

"No. But he made payments on the loan, and today he owns his boat free and clear. Let's drive to Big Pine and talk with him. He usually leaves on a Saturday and stays out five or six days. If he'd give Randy a job, just this once, it'd get Randy out of our hair until we set some plans in place for helping him in a logical way."

"Shouldn't you call Shrimp Snerl first? We might make the drive to Big Pine for nothing if he's already out on a run."

"He told me he usually leaves on a Saturday afternoon. But I suppose shrimping schedules aren't set in stone. I'll give him a call and see what he's doing."

Punt searched in his Rolodex until he found the number he needed, punched it on his phone pad, and waited. After six rings, I'd started to congratulate myself on suggesting the call when a woman answered and Punt activated a conference call.

"Punt Ashford here, Ma'am. May I speak to Shrimp Snerl, please?"

"Shrimp ain't here right now."

"Do you know when he'll be in?"

"Ha! It's Friday night at the Moose Hall. Big cash drawing. If'n Shrimp should happen to win the pot, he could be there all night—or until the cops bring him home."

"Thanks for the information," Punt said. "If he comes in, will you tell him Punt Ashford's on his way to the Moose Hall to talk to him?"

"Will do."

Punt replaced the receiver. "Let's roll, Keely. Need to stop by home first?"

"No, but I'll call Gram. She'll want to know where I am and who I'm with."

Punt pulled me toward him as I keyed in Gram's number, told her of our plans. After I replaced the receiver, Punt gave me a long kiss that might, under different circumstances, have altered our plans for the evening had not our need to find temporary employment for Randy loomed so great in our thinking.

After closing and locking his office, Punt took my hand as we walked the few steps to the Karmann Ghia. I looked forward to this evening off Key West and away from the person who wanted to see me dead. As we drove along, I kept a lookout for any car that might appear to be following us, but I saw none.

"Relax, Keely. I'm watching, too. If anyone's tailing us, I'll demand an explanation." Punt reached for my hand and his fingers squeezed mine.

I love the Karmann Ghia, love the looks of it, the feel of its smooth ride in spite of all the gear shifting. The one thing I dislike about the car is the bucket seats. They allow little opportunity for snuggling, but Punt always assures me that will come later in the evening. And it does.

Right now we were driving along the highway leading to Big Pine Key, and the moon looked like a Halloween pumpkin rising from the horizon. A full moon. I hoped it was a good omen as we lessened the distance between us and Shrimp Snerl. Shrimp Snerl. Certainly an unromantic name. But I looked forward to our meeting.

NINETEEN

PEERING INTO the rearview mirror, I thought I saw a tan Acura tailing us. I nudged Punt, but the Acura zipped around us in a no-passing zone, streaking toward the Boca Chica bridge. After another ten miles of peering over my shoulder, I relaxed. Nobody was following us, and we drove on following the car ahead of us as many wise drivers do when they travel Highway One. We went with the flow.

We'd almost reached Ramrod Key when flares lit the sky and we heard shouting.

"What's going on over there?" I peered to our left, expecting to see a police car.

"This must be a contest night—ride the mechanical bull contest."

"Ever tried it?"

"No." Punt laughed. "I value my back."

Punt slowed down as much as he could without drawing the ire of those behind us. Others must have been gawking, too. Nobody honked at us. We watched a man in a baseball cap and jeans riding on the back of the mechanical bull. Someone manipulating levers in the background controlled the speed of the ride, but we couldn't see that person.

"Guy who sticks on longest wins a prize," Punt said. "Don't know what the prize is, but whatever it is, it's probably mousemilk—not worth the bother if you want to keep your spinal disks intact."

"Maxine said Randy won a hundred dollars one night." I wished Punt hadn't reminded me of the threat note. Mousemilk, indeed! I started watching over my shoulder again.

"Relax, Keely. Nobody's tailing us. I'm watching in the rearview mirror."

"So, if you're watching, you must think there's a possibility we're being followed." Punt didn't reply, but the warmth of his fingers against mine helped me relax.

After we passed the Torch Keys and entered the Niles Channel bridge, Punt slowed to thirty-five miles per hour.

"Do you think such a radical speed limit really saves Key deer lives?"

"Nobody can prove one way or the other. Sometimes I think posting a special speed limit just makes the deer refuge workers feel needed. Sure gripes lots of drivers."

"Wonder where the Moose Hall is?" I peered at every building we passed. Sea Center Marina. Shady Pines Court. Post office. "Punt, why not use your cell phone? We could call the Moose and ask directions."

"We'll find it."

We reached the stop light—the only one between Boca Chica and Marathon—and still no Moose Hall. Punt turned left onto Key Deer Boulevard. Here the traffic moved at thirty miles per hour. I saw no deer.

Methodist church. Road prison. Watson Field. Blue Hole. We drove over eight miles. Didn't know Big Pine covered that much land.

"There it is to our right." Punt slowed down. Wow! What a crowd. We searched for a few moments before we found a parking place some distance away and off in a palm thicket. "You're coming in with me, aren't you?"

"Sure. No way am I sitting here alone. I read about the Brandt case—serial murderer. Lived right here on Big Pine before he killed his wife and his cousin, dismembered their bodies, and then hung himself up north around Orlando."

Punt raised the top and locked the convertible before we approached the doorway of a large building. I didn't need to tell Punt we were at the wrong place. The sign outside read LION'S CLUB. Another sign on the door said BINGO EVERY FRIDAY. We stayed only long enough for Punt to get directions to the Moose Hall.

We'd passed our intended destination on the way to the

Lion's Club without noticing it in spite of the many cars parked nearby. We found a place to leave, as in abandon, the Karmann Ghia and Punt took my hand as we stumbled over rough ground to the door. Of course Punt had no membership card, so he had to ask the doorman to page Shrimp Snerl. A kind official standing behind the doorman invited us inside to wait. The hall smelled like a dirty ashtray and smoke stung my nose and throat and made my eyes water. The high-decibel level of voices made conversation impractical.

Jeans and T-shirts were the costume du jour, and men and women majoring in having a good time shouting at each other sat at tables that ringed a main floor. People without seats huddled on the sidelines like gulls in a storm. Crowds make me nervous. There's always the danger a crowd will turn into a mob.

These people were intent on drinking beer and eating chips and cheese on crackers. No mob activity seemed eminent. I wondered which one of the revelers might be Shrimp Snerl. I perused the crowd, trying to form a mental image of what he'd look like. I expected to see a whale of a man—someone like Gus Helmer. Wrong. The man who finally appeared to greet Punt with a slap on the back had to stand on tippy-toes to reach Punt's shoulder. Shrimp.

Captain Snerl was a toothpick of a man—small boned, thin. Looking into his beady black eyes, I remembered an English teacher who tried to teach us to avoid clichés. Said she could string a necklace with all the beady black eyes she'd blue-lined from student essays. So I tried to think of Shrimp's eyes as black snails, ebony snails dropped in whites so yellow they made me wonder if he had jaundice.

"Glad to meet you, Keely." His handshake belied his fragile appearance and left me wondering how many of my fingers needed splints. And for such a little guy, he had the booming voice of a Bible-belt preacher.

"Need to talk to you, Shrimp," Punt shouted. "Want to ask a favor."

Shrimp eyed the crowd, then eyed Punt again. "Sure thing, man. How about a couple of beers? Soon as this drawing's over, I'll be with you all the way all the day."

"No beer for us, but thanks. Mind if we wait outside? You take your time. We'll stick around."

"Okay, man. Be right with you." Shrimp escorted us to the door and outside and I welcomed the clean air. Would he return for us, I wondered. We sat on the top step and waited. I counted the cars passing on Key Deer Boulevard and after a long time I reached the conclusion that two out of every ten cars are red.

When we heard the crowd inside roar and cheer, we jumped up. And just in time. The door burst open and people poured out like water gushing over a dam.

"Five hundred big ones," one man shouted. "Butch's always a lucky so and so."

"Dang it," another man said. "Been comin' here for years and never won a cent."

"Going to give up on raffles." The first man tossed his ticket stub onto the graveled parking lot.

When Shrimp appeared, he invited us to sit in his pickup while we talked. The truck looked new except for the ominous bullet hole in the driver's-side door. Shrimp saw me staring at it and laughed.

"It's a decal, Keely. Realistic, right? Stuck it there to get a rise out of my wife."

"And did it?" I asked.

"You bet." He opened the passenger door and Punt helped me onto the seat where I sat between them, pressing close to Punt. Or was Punt pressing close to me?

The truck interior smelled of hemp rope and WD40. Clean smells. Smells I seldom associated with shrimp boats or shrimpers.

"Good to see you again, man. We need to get together more often. I miss my old beach pals. We had us some good times, right?"

"Right," Punt said.

"What can I do for you, man?" Shrimp asked.

"Got a friend who's down on his luck. Thought maybe you could use him on your crew for a week or so."

"He got any experience around shrimp boats?"

"No," Punt admitted, "but he's smart. He'll catch on—guarantee you that."

"What's his name? Anyone I know?"

"Name's Randy Jackson. Ever heard of him?"

"Nope. Can't say that I have. What kind of work does he usually do?"

"He's been out of work for a long spell, been out of the Keys for a long spell."

"Doin' what?"

Punt sighed. "Doin' time. Twenty years of it. He's been exonerated by the court, and now he needs work." Punt told Shrimp the whole Randy Jackson story along with the fact that Randy's mother and I had received death threats.

"The guy's a hothead," Punt admitted. "I want him off Key West while I'm trying to investigate that twenty-year-old murder."

"What makes you think I need a hothead on *Midnight Moon?* A shrimper's no place for a prima donna. And I don't want to tangle with an ex-con. Randy Jackson sounds like bad news. Don't think I want to go there."

"Maybe we can make a deal," Punt said. "Instead of you paying Randy, I'll pay you to take him off my hands for a few days."

"You sound downright desperate, man."

"Not quite, but almost. What do you say?"

Shrimp pulled out a cigarette, lit it, and took a few drags before he spoke again. "Tell you what, Punt. I'll give him a bunk for a week. You can pay me five hundred earnest money in case he decides to tear up my boat or start a mutiny. But if he turns out to be a good worker, I'll return your five and pay him the regular shrimper's fee."

"Sounds like a plan to me." The men shook hands and Punt reached for his billfold and peeled off five bills. "When do you go out next?"

"Tomorrow. Two o'clock sharp. Bring him to the Key West shrimp docks a little before two. I'm having some repairs made there and once they're done, we'll be off."

"Where'll you be going?" Punt asked.

"Man, you're asking for my trade secrets. I never talk about my route or my destination. All I do is brag about my catch once I get back."

"Fair enough, Shrimp. I'll have Randy at the docks on time. Don't go without us. I'll remind him to bring along sunscreen, too. He hasn't seen much sunlight lately."

"Good idea at that. But we'll work by night, sleep by day."

"What kind of jobs will he be doing?"

"The usual. Galley duty. Winching in the nets. And sorting out trash."

"Trash that's been dumped into the sea?" I asked. "Cruise ship trash?"

Shrimp laughed. "No. To a shrimper, anything that isn't a shrimp is trash or by-catch. We sometimes pull in a lot of other fish and turtles along with the shrimp. Someone has to sort them out and pitch 'em overboard."

"Oh." Now I remembered reading about environmental laws forcing the shrimpers to replace their old nets with new ones that would release loggerheads and greens before the crew hauled them aboard. Those laws never made the shrimpers happy, so I avoided that subject.

"Tell him to pack light," Shrimp said. "He'll have only a small bunk with a storage space underneath it. I'm not running the *Queen Mary,* you know."

"I'll make that clear to him." Punt opened the truck door, alighted, then helped me to the ground.

"See ya tomorrow, man," Shrimp called after us as we made our way back to the Karmann Ghia.

"Good job, Punt. You talked him into it. Hope Randy comes through for you and you get your five hundred back."

"A risk is a risk and I feel that one's a good one. But there's one thing we've forgotten. We need to give Randy the hard sell on the plan. We need to convince him that taking this job would be in his best interest. And we need to do it tonight. If he refuses to sail on *Midnight Moon,* there's no way we can make him go."

"So let's talk to him. Tonight. He'll need some time to get his things together."

"I'll drive him to the shrimp dock tomorrow if he's willing. So let's go see what he says right now. If he refuses this job, we're back to square one."

TWENTY

WE WERE CROSSING THE Niles Channel bridge when I began worrying about Shrimp Snerl and his offer to allow Randy on his boat.

"Should we call Randy before we get to Stock Island?" I asked. "Maybe we should make sure he's home. Or if he's not home, maybe Maxine can tell us where he is."

"Let's arrive unannounced. Remember that element of surprise. It could work to our advantage—again. Call him, and he has too much time to think over his options."

"Yeah, you're right. If we present our offer face to face, we'll have a better chance of persuading him to our way of thinking. Maybe Maxine will overhear us and help him make the right decision. Shrimping with Shrimp. I like the sound of it."

We drove through the soft night. The mechanical bull on Ramrod sat in silence, but a bit farther on, the sound of the steel drums drifted toward the highway and cars still crowded Mangrove Mama's parking lot.

"Need a drink?" Punt asked.

"Not unless you do. I'd rather get on home and talk to Randy."

"Right." Punt drove faster, but still within the speed limit— not an easy task on a highway where the speed limit changes a dozen times between Big Pine and Key West. A few minutes later, Punt took a left onto Stock Island and when we reached the Jackson trailer, we saw the gray Ford parked nearby. Leaving the Karmann Ghia, we walked to the trailer. I looked overhead, wondering if Lavonna the iguana lay on a branch doing guard duty, but I didn't see her.

"What're you two doing around here this time of night?"

The gruff voice startled me and I grabbed Punt's hand before I realized Randy was lying in his hammock. At the sound of his voice, a light flashed on over the trailer steps and Maxine appeared silhouetted in the doorway.

"Randy, we have some great news." I stepped closer to the hammock.

"I could use some good news for a change," Randy replied without rising.

"Why don't you all come inside?" Maxine called. "Got plenty of space here, and maybe we need to talk in private."

"Good idea," Punt said.

Maxine opened the door wider and stepped back. At first I thought Randy might refuse to join us, but he heaved himself from the hammock and followed us. The trailer smelled slightly of spaghetti sauce and garlic bread, totally pleasant fragrances.

Punt, Randy, and I sat on the couch, trying to ease into positions that would allow us to face each other. Maxine pulled a folding chair from a slot between the closet door and her bed at the back of the trailer and joined us.

"Spit it out." Randy looked at Punt. "What's your great news?"

Maxine busied herself making us iced tea while Punt told Randy about Shrimp Snerl and *Midnight Moon*. Randy's scowl didn't change as he listened. At the end of Punt's spiel, Randy said three words.

"What's the pay?"

The question startled me. I hadn't expected Randy to jump at the chance to work on a shrimp boat, and I thought he'd have questions about accommodations, work requirements, and stuff like that.

"Your pay depends on the catch," Punt said. "Good catch, good pay. Poor catch, poor pay. It's all relative. But it's your chance to prove yourself—at least prove your worth to Captain Snerl."

"It's also my chance to lose a week's time in collecting DNA." Randy's scar began to brighten. "The DNA samples rate tops on my list of important things. I can go shrimping anytime. Anytime at all." Randy stood and began to pace—a difficult feat in a small trailer. Maxine kept dodging, allowing him space between the couch and her bed.

"Yes," Punt said. "Yes, you can go shrimping anytime—anytime someone will take you on, anytime a captain will risk his boat, his crew, and his reputation to give you a job. Not everyone's hiring right now. Shrimp's doing me a favor by taking you on for a trial run. If you do a good job, he might hire you again."

"Randy," Maxine cut in. "Give it some thought—a lot of thought. I know shrimping's some of the hardest work around, but ..." She broke off mid-sentence and curled her tongue over her gold tooth.

"Don't think I'm afraid of the work, Ma. You know better than that." Randy stared at the floor. "But now that Punt Ashford's willing to help us investigate Dyanne's murder, that's top priority with me. A week on *Midnight Moon* would be wasted time as far as our investigation's concerned. A whole week lost."

"Maybe you could think of it as a whole week gained in the employment field," I said. "And while you're at sea, Punt and I'll be working on your DNA idea and on getting the police to consider the suspects you mentioned."

"There's another thing, too," Punt said. "Once you make good with Captain Snerl, the police'll give your requests to review suspects more attention. A man with a job carries more weight with the police than an unemployed drifter."

"They may even want to listen to you and hear your views," I said. "It would certainly be a boon to them and their careers to be able to say they'd solved a cold case others had given up on."

Randy scowled, sighed, stared at the ceiling. His body language told me we'd won our case.

"Okay, people. You win. I'll sign on with Captain Snerl for one run and we'll see how it goes from there."

"Good decision." Punt rose to stand beside Randy and shake his hand. "Keely and I'll pick you up tomorrow afternoon around one o'clock. That'll give us plenty of time to drive to the shrimp docks, meet Captain Snerl, and get you settled on the *Midnight Moon*. You're going to be glad you made this decision, Randy. It could turn your life around and point it in a better direction."

We left the Jackson trailer before Randy could change his mind.

"Well, Punt, we got what we wanted—and needed. We'll have a whole week to work on the investigation without Randy's help."

We drove onto Key West and Randy stopped at my office. "How about spending the night at my place?" he asked. "I feel, well, I feel that every night you spend here alone, you're putting yourself in danger."

"You're sweet to be concerned, Punt, and I appreciate it. But not tonight. I'd have to wake Gram up to tell her or she'd worry when I didn't appear in the morning. We always check on each other, first thing."

"So leave her a note," Punt said. "You've got a key to her place. Leave a note on her coffee grinder. Or anyplace she'd notice quickly."

So that's what I did. It didn't take a lot of talk from Punt to persuade me to see things his way. The memory of the rock through my window, my time at the ER, and bruises that still hurt hastened my decision. I wrote a quick note, left it on Gram's breakfast table, and we drove to Punt's place.

Even with the lights gleaming from the widow's walk, the mansion held an empty and deserted atmosphere without Jass in residence. But I smiled as I remembered she and Beau still had another month to enjoy their trip abroad. Due to my nightmares, I felt in no position to make a full commitment to Punt, but I liked the dream-free nights we spent alone at the mansion.

"How about a swim?" Punt nodded toward the pool where hibiscus bushes surrounding the water gave privacy to anyone caring to swim. "It's a warm night and we've had a long day. A swim will refresh us. How about it?"

"Let's go for it. Is the water heated?"

"Not tonight. Didn't think we'd be using the pool."

"No problem. If it's chilly we can warm up in the shower later."

We climbed the stairs to Punt's apartment and once we stepped inside, I headed for the drawer where I kept a few of my things and reached for my black bikini. Punt took it from my hand and replaced it in the drawer.

"Let's call this skinny-dip night. Been thinking about it all day long."

"It's bright moonlight, Punt. Anyone passing by could see us in spite of the hibiscus bushes."

"Oh come on, Keely. Nobody's going to be looking. It'll be us and the moon and the water."

"Okay, Punt. Your call." I sighed, but I was as eager as he. "There's nothing like the feel of cool water against bare skin."

"I can think of a thing or two, but we'll talk about that later." He handed me a robe and grabbed one for himself. We slipped into them and walked barefoot down the apartment steps and to the pool. Then Punt headed back upstairs.

"Wait a sec, okay? I'm going to snap off the widow's walk lights. This night's going to be between us and the moon."

I waited, and presently the widow's walk became silhouetted in moonlight. Punt returned, and in the shadow of a hibiscus bush he removed his robe and then mine and led me toward the pool. We both made smooth dives into the water, surfacing to blink moisture from our eyes.

"It doesn't get much better than this." Punt pulled me to him and we kissed with the man in the moon watching in envy. "You're concave where I'm convex. Could I talk you into a little sex?"

"You're a poet and don't know it." I slipped from his embrace. "Beat you to the other end." I started with a strong crawl, but Punt overtook me, drawing me to him while we both did a smooth side stroke that pressed our bodies together in a demanding way.

"We should have thought of this a long time ago."

Now we stood in water chin deep for me and he cupped my breasts in his hands then lowered his face into the water and kissed them. When he surfaced, he asked, "Have you ever done it in the water, Keely?"

"No. Have you?"

"Not telling. Want to experiment? We could teach each other as we go along."

Facing me, Punt began walking through the water until I felt the pool wall behind me. I clung to him, my arms around his neck, pulling him close, close until no space separated us. We were involved in a deep kiss when we heard a car pull into the driveway, heard a door slam. Then footsteps sounded on the apartment steps and a voice called.

"Punt? Punt, are you home?"

"It's Consuela," Punt whispered, his lips close to my ear. "Keep quiet and maybe she'll go away."

She didn't go away. "Punt? Punt?" she called again. "Your car's here. I know you're in there. Come to the door. I've got something for you. Something you'll be interested in."

"You and Consuela got something going?" I caressed a part of him that had gone limp, and he put his hand over my mouth before I could say anything else.

"I don't know what she's doing here. But we can wait her out. If she comes near the pool we can submerge until she leaves."

Consuela knocked and called to Punt a few more times then we heard her come back down the stairs. All was quiet and we waited to hear her car start. Surprise. The next thing we knew she was standing in the moonlight at poolside, but she hadn't seen us.

"Grab a breath," Punt whispered.

I had barely inhaled when he pulled me under beside him. We stayed down as long as our breath lasted, but we couldn't help splashing when we surfaced. Consuela stood at poolside like an osprey searching for a fingerling.

"Oh, so you have company tonight, Punt." Consuela laughed in a coy way that would have turned my stomach had we been meeting under different circumstances. "Very, very, very sorry to intrude, but I have something special to show you."

Consuela's green sarong parted thigh high as she stooped to hold an object toward us. In the moonlight, it looked like a plastic baggie.

TWENTY-ONE

"CONSUELA," PUNT SAID. "You're trespassing. You've no business here. Go. You're intruding. Please leave. Now."

"I've brought you and Keely something special. Come and take it, then I'll leave you to whatever it is you're doing." Consuela picked up our robes, her spike heels click-clacking against the poolside brick as she brought the garments to us.

"Leave now or I'll call the police." Punt's voice pulsed with anger.

"Using what for a phone?" Consuela pulled Punt's cell phone from the pocket of his robe and laid it out of reach on a chair beside the baggie she'd been carrying. "Come up here. Look at what I've brought you. I want you to admit I've helped you in your investigation. Out now. Out and up."

She click-clacked closer to the pool edge, thrusting our robes toward us as if we should put them on while still in the water. "Don't be shy. A little skin never embarrasses me."

When she saw we weren't going to take the robes, she turned and dropped them on the chair beside the cell phone, the baggie.

"Come on, you two. I'm not going to hang around forever waiting on you. Out!"

"Follow me, Keely," Punt whispered.

Punt began easing us around the rim of the pool, shielding me from Consuela's gaze as much as he could while he moved toward a ladder near the diving board. With an aggravating grin, Consuela followed us, click-clacking every step of the way and looming above us like a bad omen as she stepped closer to the pool's edge. Punt's next move startled me so that I swallowed a mouthful of water.

Choking and gasping, I saw him thrust himself up, grab Consuela's ankle and yank her into the pool with us.

"The ladder, Keely!" Punt shouted. "Go for it!"

I scrambled up the ladder, skinning my shin on the top rung, but running on toward our robes. What is there about being nude that makes one feel so vulnerable? We both were dressed again before Consuela stopped thrashing in the pool.

"Sorry you forgot to bring a robe." Punt scowled at her while she struggled up the ladder and stood on the bricked patio beside us. Her green sarong clung to her body like Saran wrap, but she took advantage of that, slicking her hair behind her ears, flicking water from her eyes, then rising on tip-toe and turning like a model to give us a good view of her voluptuousness.

"You're mean, Punt Ashford. My favorite sandals are still in your pool."

"If you think I'll dive and get them, think again. I want you out of here."

"Punt," I broke in. "Let's see what she's brought you. Then I'm guessing she'll leave and maybe arrange to pick up her sandals tomorrow."

For a moment Punt's shoulders slumped, then he straightened and spoke.

"All right, Consuela. What have you brought us?"

Consuela padded to the lounge chair and holding the baggie between thumb and forefinger, she thrust it toward Punt.

"What is it?" I craned my neck to peer at it, but I couldn't make out the contents.

"It's DNA," Consuela said. "A DNA specimen from one of Randy's suspects."

"Looks like a condom to me," Punt said.

"Right." Consuela tossed him a coy smile. "A very used condom I managed to swipe from Gus Helmer. Take it to Randy. Let him deliver it to the police. And give me a break. Don't tell Randy where you got it."

Punt dropped the baggie into his pocket. "Leave now, Consuela. Right this minute!"

Consuela turned to leave, taking mincing steps as she padded barefoot across the brick, the grass, the gravel, and then stepped into her car.

"I'll come back for my sandals tomorrow," she called over her shoulder.

"Don't you dare!" Punt said. "Our pool boy will retrieve them and deliver them to your door."

"That will suit me fine—if it's the broad-shouldered blond I've seen working here. And count me as one of your investigators. I have my ways of getting evidence."

Punt didn't bother to answer, and I rolled my eyes and stood there shivering in the moonlight. Consuela had squashed all romance from our late night skinny dip. And she'd done it intentionally. All three of us knew that.

Once upstairs, not even the thought of a warm shower, the soft bed, or the reflections in the ceiling mirror revived our earlier mood. I felt cold and exhausted, and I could tell that Punt's heart still pumped as much anger as blood. We did share a warm shower, massaging each other with jasmine-scented soapsuds, but the machinations merely added to our sleepiness.

There are worse things than falling into bed with the man you love. We pressed close to each other, cuddling and enjoying being together. Punt fell asleep before I did and I lay there counting his even breaths that felt warm and comforting against my neck. I eased closer to him and although I didn't remember dozing, I guessed I'd slept only minutes before I heard a noise at the door. Someone was pounding on the door and shouting. I bolted upright, pulling the sheet to my chin and waiting for Punt to take charge, go to the door. He lay motionless, his breathing slow, steady.

"Punt." I nudged him. "Punt wake up. Someone's pounding on the door. Punt! Punt! Maybe Consuela's returned for her sandals."

Punt didn't move. The pounding continued and a voice shouted words I couldn't understand. Then I could understand them all too clearly.

"Keely! Keely!" Jude Cardell's voice beat on my eardrums. But how impossible! Jude died months ago. Someone had come here impersonating him. Someone had come here trying to frighten me—maybe the person who'd been threatening me.

But no. In the next moment, a man crashed against the door and came barging into the apartment. Jude? He looked like Jude. A Jude look-alike. I couldn't imagine anything worse. Could this man be Jude returned from the grave? He wore jeans and sandals and a sweatshirt. From somewhere a light gleamed onto his bald head. He looked around, dazed at first, then he gave a triumphant smile when he saw Punt and me lying on the bed.

"Punt!" I screamed. "Punt! Help me! It's Jude. He's after me. He'll kill me. Help. Help!" I lay there screaming, yet no sound came from my mouth. It was as if someone had pushed the mute button on a remote control that silenced my voice.

Punt didn't move. But Jude rushed to the bed and jerked me to my feet, twisting one arm behind my back until I felt sure it would break. Jude had always had a knack for knowing just when to stop. Many times he'd left me battered and bruised, but only once had he actually broken bones—my jaws.

I tried to scream again, and again my voice failed me.

"Ki-ki-ki-Keely." Jude used the nickname I remembered with such horror—the name he always used before the bad things began. "Ki-ki-ki-Keely. Come along with me and I'll show you a good time. A time you'll never forget. I've brought my favorite toys and we'll play until dawn, even longer if you beg me."

"Leave me alone!"

"Beg me, Ki-Ki-Ki-Keely. I love to hear you beg."

"Punt will hear you. He'll call the police." Jude's malevolent grin chilled me.

"Punt doesn't care anything about you, Ki-ki-ki-Keely. Not a thing. Why, if he cared for you, he'd be out of bed this minute trying to rescue you. And you can see he hasn't moved an inch. Fat lot he cares about you. You should have seen him in action a few years ago on Smathers. Oh, the dolls he played with! You think he was spending all that beach time building sand castles? You dumb broad!"

Jude pulled a padded club from his waistband and pushed me ahead of him toward the splintered door. I stumbled down the steps, falling face down into the gravel when I missed the last three steps.

"Get up, bitch." He grabbed my hair and I felt a handful of it part from my head before I managed to get to my feet. Now he pulled a fillet knife from his waistband, removed it from its sheath and strode toward the Karmann Ghia. I heard the canvas tear as he slashed the top of the convertible. Would he knife me next?

"Help!" I screamed. No sound. Punt had forgotten to turn the widow's walk lights on after our swim, and now moonlight filtered through clouds that dangled like black webs in front of the moon. Jude and I were alone in the near dark. Only moments passed before I heard the tinkling of broken glass and I knew he was breaking windows in Jass's greenhouse. What if he entered the greenhouse? He could do that easily enough once he'd broken enough of the glass. What if he slashed her prized plants? Jass would never forgive me for not protecting them. But she wouldn't have to forgive me. I'd be dead in a few minutes.

This born-again Jude left the greenhouse and returned to yank me to my feet. Then he brought the padded club down on my shoulder. Next on a breast. Next on a thigh. He knew the places that were the most painful, the places where cuts and bruises wouldn't show later. I continued my soundless screaming until he pushed me into the pool. The water soothed my bruises. For a few moments I felt revived. If I ducked under the surface, maybe he wouldn't be able to see me. If he gave up finding me and left now, I could make it to safety. I could hide, only coming up to breathe. I could hide until he left.

He jumped into the pool with me. I grabbed a deep breath and submerged.

"Ki-ki-ki-Keely! Where are you, shitface? Come to daddy—if you know what's good for you."

Somewhere I found the strength to swim underwater and I swam to the ladder. Surfacing quietly, I looked around until I saw him on the other side of the pool. But he saw me at the same time. My only chance of escape was to climb the ladder and run into the street. Maybe someone would see me there. I had given up all hope of waking Punt.

The ladder rungs cut into my bare feet but I kept climbing. I had just reached the top rung when Jude grabbed my ankle and yanked me back into the water.

"Ki-ki-ki-Keely! You weren't trying to get away from me, were you? We've only started having fun. There's much more to come. Much, much more." He struck me across the mouth and I spit a bloody tooth into the pool. Next he ducked me, each time holding me under until I felt close to drowning. Then he'd let me up, but never long enough for me to grab a full breath.

At last he of tired of that game. "Let's get out of the water, Ki-ki-ki-Keely. Let's play a little game of tag. You go first."

He goosed me as I climbed the ladder, holding me back now and then so he could goose me again. The minute I stepped onto the pool's edge, I began to run. Gravel cut into my feet as I headed for the street. Even though it was late, I hoped someone would see me, rescue me. For a moment I didn't hear anyone behind me, and in an agonizing burst of speed I ran right into Punt's arms.

"Keely!" Punt put one arm around me and held my wrists in a vise-like grip with his other hand. "What are you doing out here?"

I couldn't speak for a few moments, then at last I relaxed against Punt. "Nightmare. Horrible nightmare." I cried until I thought I'd never be able to stop, but all the while Punt was leading me upstairs and to his bed.

When I calmed down, Punt brought me a cup of hot tea and some crackers. "When I felt that empty bed, I thought you had awakened and gone home. You do that now and then and I thought this was one of those times. Then I heard someone splashing in the pool and saw you running toward the street."

I clung to Punt, wanting to tell him about the nightmare. That's what my therapist said I should do. But I'm unable to pull the horror of the dream back into my conscious mind again.

"Punt, I'm so sorry. So very sorry. This's the first nightmare I've had in weeks. I thought perhaps I'd conquered them. But we can both see I haven't. I can never have a normal life as long as Jude returns in my dreams."

"Never say never. You don't hear me complaining about your

nightmare, Keely. I'm sorry you suffer so from them, but I'm more than willing to play rescuer if you'll only give me the chance."

I ate the crackers, drank the tea, and we fell back into bed again.

"Maybe tomorrow, Punt. Maybe I can talk about it—us—tomorrow."

TWENTY-TWO

THE NEXT MORNING, the aroma of coffee and frying bacon drifted to me, but in spite of the enticing smells, I didn't hurry to get up. Punt had shoved aside the wicker screen that usually separated the bedroom and kitchen areas, and I saw him standing near the stove. A white terrycloth towel secured around his waist contrasted with his tanned skin. I wondered if he missed his carefree days of bumming on the beach.

"Rise and shine." He glanced in my direction, grinned, and blew me a kiss.

I sat up, dangling my legs over the edge of the bed, feeling for my slippers, but the "rise and shine" part of his command required more strength than I could muster. Mornings following one of my nightmares left me feeling drained and useless. Punt poured two glasses of mango juice then sat beside me as we enjoyed the treat.

The juice revived me. A few minutes later I felt stronger and I slipped into my robe while we shared scrambled eggs, bacon, and toast at his glass-topped table. In spite of the hearty breakfast, I faced the day slowly. It wasn't until the last toast crumb disappeared that I glanced at my watch.

"Punt! It's almost noon. I had no idea. Why didn't you wake me sooner?"

"Didn't know we had a schedule."

"We have things to do today. There's Randy and the shrimp boat and …"

"You were sleeping so soundly, I didn't have the heart to wake you. You had a hard night."

"We had a hard night—Consuela in person. Jude in phantom. I'd like to forget."

"We need to talk, Keely. When we going to do that?" Punt rose and stood behind my chair, leaning to kiss my forehead. "When?"

"Not today. Please, not today. Give me a little more time. I'm carrying so much baggage it's wearing me out."

"So I'll help you carry it."

"You have a few bags of your own, remember?"

"Maybe we should have a joint session with your shrink. How about it?"

"I'm not sure. I hate the thought of a third person mucking through the private details of our relationship. There are special moments we've shared that I want to keep private, moments I want to enjoy in the secrecy of my heart."

"So what can I say?"

"Nothing more right now. Okay?" I rose, kissed him on the hollow of his throat where his pulse throbbed against my lips. When we stood apart again, I began loading the dishwasher while Punt wiped the table and the stove.

"We'd better hurry to Randy's place. Be sure he's getting ready to leave at one o'clock as promised."

"Right." Punt snapped my rear with a dish towel, then we both scrambled to get dressed for the day—cut-offs, T-shirt, sandals—the local's uniform of the island. Sometimes the tourists catch on to our casual dress code, but seldom. They seem to prefer their up-north slacks and collared shirts or Hawaiian shirts and shorts.

Saturday—a whole weekend off. It felt good to leave my jumpsuit in the closet. I gave Randy a wake-up call to alert him to our imminent arrival.

"Good!" Punt exclaimed. "At least he's up and about."

"You thought he might not be?"

"You never know. A guy like Randy might decide he has other mullet to fry. He wasn't totally sold on taking a week's run on a shrimper. And he knows nothing about Captain Shrimp Snerl. His name alone could be a turnoff. I'm going to call Maxi-Taxi."

"Good thought. I forgot we can't get three in your car. But it's a ways to Stock Island. Why not drive to Randy's place, then call the taxi?"

"And leave the Karmann Ghia unattended on Stock Island all the time we're at the shrimp docks? Thanks a lot, but no thanks. It'll be safer here in my carport."

I didn't argue, and when Maxi-Taxi arrived, we got in and the driver nosed his way through the midday traffic on North Roosevelt. A huge pick-up with Alaska plates cut ahead of us at the left turn signal onto the highway, but our cabbie kept his cool. I grinned. Punt scowled but he didn't offer any backseat advice.

I never tire of gazing at the water from the Boca Chica bridge. A few boats were motoring in from half-day charters. I felt envious. Lots of sun and almost no wind. A travel brochure kind of day in living color. The driver turned at MacDonald Avenue, and when we reached the Jackson trailer, Randy scowled at us from an aluminum chair on the open-air porch. A duffel rested at his feet. Today he wore a No Name Key T-shirt with threadbare jeans and boat shoes. A faded sweatshirt lay across the duffel. Punt and I slid from the taxi. I looked around for some sign of Lavonna, and seeing none, I stepped closer to the trailer.

"Morning, Randy." Punt greeted Randy with a handshake and a scowl. I smiled and nodded.

"Ready to go?" I asked. "Taxi's waiting."

"Ready as I'll ever be, I suppose." Randy kicked at the gravel with the toe of his shoe and lowered his voice. "I appreciate you getting me this gig, man. And I'll do my best to perform whatever duties Captain Snerl has lined up for me. But as soon as we dock, I'm ready to begin rounding up some DNA."

"You know how I feel about that." Punt spoke softly, keeping his back toward the taxi driver. "First show the police a viable suspect, then consider getting the DNA."

"We think differently, don't we?" Randy's gaze never left Punt's face.

"Where's Maxine?" I asked, desperate to change the subject, to avoid a last-minute argument that might nix our plans.

"Working," Randy replied. "Where'd you think?"

"I thought she might want to go with us to see you off."

"This's no pleasure voyage, Ms. Moreno. No ticker tape. No champagne." Randy stood, picked up his duffel, and headed toward the taxi. He sat beside the driver. Punt and I shared the back seat. We said little on the ride to Land's End Village and the shrimp boats.

After Punt paid the driver, we walked along the planked dock. Several rusty-hulled boats trimmed in black bobbed in the water, lashed to dock cleats with lines encrusted with brine. Dark masts and riggings rose silhouetted against the sky like the devil's jack-straws. Overhead, gulls screamed into the tradewind that fanned my cheeks, and closer at hand a pelican showered us with water as it splashed into the bay in pursuit of a pinfish. I tasted brine on my tongue, my lips, and tried to avoid thinking about what else might have been in those drops of water. A dead-fish smell on the dock filled my nose—even the back of my mouth. For a moment I held my breath. Then I exhaled slowly, trying to accustom myself to the odor.

"There it is, Punt." I pointed to a boat where three men were checking lines and nets. *"Midnight Moon."* A glamorous name for such a clunker of a boat. I wondered what Randy might be thinking and if he'd be able to deal with the smells that wafted around us. But I guessed a prison cell didn't smell like rose-scented eau de cologne.

At that moment Captain Snerl saw us, waved, and motioned us aboard. Punt grabbed a dock piling for support then stepped over the gunwale and onto the gray deck. Turning, he offered a hand to me and then to Randy. The crew had raised the boat's iron outriggers until they formed a black V against a blaze of sky.

Punt introduced Randy to Captain Snerl and the two men shook hands.

"Welcome aboard." Snerl's voice boomed into the afternoon. "We'll cast off in a few minutes, but there's plenty of time to introduce you to the boat, show you to your quarters. He led us toward the pilot house, then paused when I reached out to touch what looked like two blobs of rouge-colored fabric attached to the mesh of the trawl nets.

"Those pink things are chaffing gear. They help protect the nets from wear while we drag them along the sea bottom."

"Your radio in good order?" Randy asked.

I guessed the appearance of *Midnight Moon* along with his past experiences with Mel Fisher's dive boats and the sea were making him wary.

At Randy's question, Snerl motioned overhead. "See that tallest mast pointing to the sun? Well, that's the radio antenna. Never have had any problem keeping in contact with shore."

Captain Snerl led us into the pilothouse and lowered a chart rack hooked in place above a bunk bed. Unrolling the chart and securing it into place, he pointed to some numbers penciled in near the Gulf coast.

"Those figures mark my choice of fishing waters for this trip."

When I eased closer for a better look, Snerl released the chart and it made a loud whooshing as it curled into a tube overhead. I jumped in surprise.

"Why don't they fold those things?" I asked, laughing at my own discomfort.

"Maps are folded," Snerl said. "Charts are rolled. Sometimes I need to measure distances on a chart. Folds in the paper could throw off my calculations."

I resolved to ask no more questions that would point up my ignorance of the shrimp boat scene.

"What will my job be?" Randy asked.

"You'll have an assortment of duties." Snerl led us into the galley. I tripped over the coaming, but Punt steadied me. "Randy, you'll set the table for the four of us. You'll bus the table after each meal." He pointed to a pan on the stove. "I've got a pot of chowder simmering for tonight, so the clean up'll be easy."

We stepped back onto deck and Snerl continued. "You'll help man the buoy once we've reached our fishing spot." He pointed to a long chain attached to the bottom of a cane pole that had two battery lights and a white flag wired to its tip. The bottom of the pole passed through the center of three thick squares of Styrofoam. "You'll help lower this equipment into the sea. The chain serves as an anchor, and the pole will float upright on the foam. I'll steer the boat around that light in an ever-widening circle. The pole will be our focal point of reference as to our position—our location in the sea."

I wondered how far away the boat could travel and still allow the crew to see such a small light, but I'd bite my tongue before I'd inquire. I smiled when Punt asked the question for me.

"That small light shows up from a great distance in the dark of night," Snerl said. "So far I've never been lost at sea. We'll have plenty of work for you, Randy. You'll also help us discard the by-catch, help ice down the shrimp in the hold." He looked directly at Randy. "You sure you want to go with us?"

Randy hesitated only a moment before he replied. "I'm sure. I thank you for the opportunity."

Snerl showed Randy to a bunk in the bow, lifted the mattress and opened a storage area underneath. "You can stow your gear in there."

Randy dropped his duffel into the bin and replaced the mattress. Snerl led the way back to dockside. Grabbing a piling, Punt hoisted himself onto the dock and turned to offer me a hand.

"Thanks for the boat tour," Punt said. "I wish you all success on this trip."

"Thanks, Punt. I plan to dock right here on Friday around midday."

"We'll be here to meet Randy."

Randy gave us a wave and walked to the other side of the boat and stood gazing into the distance. We found a splintery bench at dockside and sat to wait until the *Midnight Moon* put out to sea. I didn't think Randy would change his mind and leave the boat, but I wanted to be certain that he'd be off-island for a few days. We watched and waited.

"Punt, it's wonderful of you to give Randy a chance."

"Tell me again how wonderful I am. I like the sound of your voice wrapped around those words. But in all fairness I have to admit that it's Shrimp Snerl who's taking all the chances by hiring Randy on for a few days."

"I think Randy really wants to work, and I hope he can tolerate shrimping. Sounds like heavy duty to me—working at night, sleeping by day. Wonder why those shrimp aren't out and about in the daytime."

"You'll have to ask a shrimp about that. How about some ice cream?"

Punt got no argument from me. We walked to the Half Shell Raw Bar. It wasn't such a scary place in the daytime with all the tourists crowding around. Punt bought two coconut sherbet cones to go and we resumed our vigil at the *Midnight Moon*.

"Punt, I know you think we should present suspect names to the police first to get their attention, but I sort of agree with Randy. I think the police would be more interested in pursuing an investigation if Randy worked through Attorney Hubble and presented DNA samples first and then gave the police names of suspects to be investigated."

"You may be right," Punt said. "Maybe there's no absolutely right or wrong way to approach this investigation. Guess we might be wise to collect what DNA we can before Randy returns and insists on doing it for us—his way. That's the scary part— his doing it for us and maybe getting so rough with someone that he earns himself another term behind bars."

"We have the suspects' names—all divers. Maybe we could ask Attorney Hubble to present those names to the police. That should, at least, get the police thinking about an investigation."

"That's one plan, but in the end we'll need Randy to explain to the police in detail why one of those men had motive or opportunity to murder Dyanne Darby."

"And Punt, should we consider Beau a suspect? Randy wasn't clear on that. Don't know how he felt about your dad."

"It wouldn't be hard to get a sample of DNA from Dad."

"It wouldn't? With him abroad? How can you manage that?"

"I've a key to his house—supposed to check the place every day to be sure no druggies have claimed it for an overnighter. That happens down here. Some unsavory character sees a vacant house and that place becomes fair game for illegal activities."

"So you check his house every day. And…?"

"For instance, there's bound to be a hairbrush lying around— one he left behind. I'll just snatch a few hairs, tuck them into an envelope, and there we'll have a DNA sample. No hairbrush available? I might be able to take the mouthpiece from his scuba gear. The police have ways to get DNA from dried saliva."

"Okay. Sounds workable. Now what about the other four divers?"

"Surely the Reverend Soto will be cooperative once we tell him our plan. I can't believe he has anything to hide."

"I'd be embarrassed to approach him and ask for a DNA sample after all the effort he's put into getting Randy freed. Such a request would be a slap in the face."

"Ask and it shall be given unto you. Seek and ye shall find. Aren't those the reverend's mottoes? Don't think he'd fault you for taking advice from the Good Book."

"Okay, I'll talk to Soto if you'll get the hair sample from Beau's brush. And that's enough plans for starters."

The next time we looked up, we saw the *Midnight Moon* leaving the dock. Randy stood at the gunwale staring in our direction, but he didn't return out waves.

TWENTY-THREE

PUNT CALLED ANOTHER taxi, directing the driver to the Ashford mansion. When we arrived, we climbed the steps to Punt's apartment and then relaxed while we enjoyed a Coke and our reprieve from the day's activities.

"Shall we go out to dinner tonight?" Punt asked. "How about Louie's Back Yard or Rooftop Café?"

"May I take a rain check, please? I'm exhausted and I need to get home and see how Gram's doing. Saturday's always a big day in her shop. Sometimes she overdoes, forgets about her weak heart."

Punt sighed. "Your wish is my command—I suppose. But I'll have to admit that I'm ready for some rest, too. I'll drive you home and maybe we can plan tomorrow's activities on the way."

"Right. We need to get on with this investigation while Randy's away." We both stood and headed downstairs. "Tomorrow's Sunday. Since Reverend Soto's on our list, maybe we should attend his church service and talk to him afterward."

Punt had been walking ahead of me, and now he stopped so abruptly I almost stepped on his heel.

"Keely! Look!"

I looked. Someone had slashed two tires on the convertible and the knife still protruded from the back tire. We ran to the other side of the car. Those tires there were flat, too. One had slipped from the rim and lay in the gravel.

"This's my fault. Someone's after me and making you suffer on my account. Oh, Punt! What'll you do?"

Punt wrapped his arm around my waist and pulled me close, his face deadly pale.

"It's not your fault. Don't think in those terms. You're being paranoid." His voice throbbed with anger, and his next words snagged in his throat. "And what I'll do is call a garage, have the tires repaired or replaced. Then I'll find the s.o.b. that did this. Leaving the knife behind isn't the mark of a genius."

"It's that easy? Replacing the tires, I mean on a car that old?"

"There are ways of getting it done. I may be using a rental for a while. There may be a few of those at the airport, but …"

His voice trailed off as he began circling the car, looking for clues that might indicate the perpetrator of the vandalism. The mansion grounds had never been gated and locked. Years ago, Beau had planted a privacy fence of hibiscus that had kept trespassers at bay—until last night.

"In all the years we've lived here, Dad's never had this kind of trouble before. Maybe we'll have to post a guard."

"When do you suppose it happened? Last night? I didn't hear anybody around, but then, I was busy having a nightmare."

"Suppose Consuela had anything to do with it? She was mad as a bee in a bottle when she left here dripping wet and without her sandals. I probably shouldn't have pulled her into the pool."

"I don't think Consuela's the type to slash tires. She's often an enigma but …"

"Yeah, right. She's a mysterious bombshell. But slashing tires is pretty much a guy thing." Punt gave a bitter laugh. "Ironic that we took a taxi to Stock Island, hoping to keep the car safe."

Once again Punt called Maxi-Taxi and drove me home.

"Where's your bike?"

"Chained to a pole in the alley."

We both ran to look, thinking the bicycle might have been damaged or stolen, but it was where I left it. I held my breath to avoid inhaling the garbage odor that had taken up residence in the alley.

"Let's haul the bike inside, Keely. Then you'll be sure to have it when needed."

We unlocked the bike and wheeled it into my apartment. I thanked Punt, and when he left me, I knew he was already on his cell phone calling Sears' garage, hoping it hadn't closed for the weekend. Gram was heading for my door, and I decided not to tell her about Punt's car. No point in causing her needless worry.

"What happened to Punt's car?" Gram asked almost before we exchanged welcome hugs.

"What makes you think something happened to it?"

"He never arrive in taxi before. Tells me something malo."

So I told her the story, skipping the parts about Consuela in the pool and Jude in my nightmare. Although it was only late afternoon, Gram closed her shop and insisted I share a piccadillo dinner with her. Piccadillo…My favorite Cuban food.

We climbed the narrow stairs to her apartment where I set the small table for two while she warmed the peccadillo, black beans, and yellow rice on the stove. I mixed a fresh onion and tomato salad and slathered garlic butter onto slices of Cuban bread, heating them under the broiler. We needed nothing else. My mouth watered long before I got a taste of the ground beef laced with sliced olives, raisins, and kippers. For years after Mom died, Gram and I shared meals like this one. Cuban soul food. It soothed both our hearts and our stomachs.

Once we finished eating, we talked for a while, then I cleared the table and washed our dishes before I returned to my apartment. Too early to go to bed. Plenty of time to pick up the clutter of clothing that lay here and there if I wanted to do chores. I didn't. Instead, I went to bed, falling asleep almost before my head hit the pillow.

The next morning the telephone awakened me and I reached for it, half asleep, half awake. Punt's voice brought me to attention.

"G'morning, Keely. May I pick you up in a little while and we'll go to church?"

"What about your car?"

"I have a replacement."

"Punt! That's great. I mean …"

"Relax, Keely. You know I wouldn't give up the Karmann Ghia for any new car. You'll see me driving a Conch cruiser. Nobody'll get much pleasure in vandalizing it. Can you be ready in an hour? The Reverend Soto does a ten-thirty service at a community church a few blocks off Flagler."

"I'll be ready."

What to wear! Sometimes I attended a small early-morning

service at St. Paul's, a few blocks from my shop. But I knew the Reverend Soto's church service in a newer part of the island would be more formal. I reached to the back of my closet and pulled out the navy-blue skirt and white blouse. Forget that. It wouldn't do this morning. I remembered ripping the skirt vent. Someday I'd mend it. But not today. Some other day. I hung it back in the closet behind my collection of jumpsuits.

I reached for the green silk that Punt always liked, the one I wore to dinner when we went somewhere special. After laying it on my bed along with my green sandals and multi-colored purse, I paused to gulp some orange juice and eat a slice of toast before I dressed. I wasn't a big breakfast eater, but no sense in getting toast crumbs or juice on my good clothes.

I liked the swish, the smooth feel of the silk as it slithered onto my body. During the night my hair had coiled into ringlets. Tugs with the hairbrush smoothed it into looking as good as it ever looked. Damp tradewinds work havoc on curly hair. But I managed to be ready and waiting when Punt arrived. Brakes squealed as he stopped at the curbing, and when I saw his car and stepped outside, I broke into giggles.

"Where'd you ever find it, Punt? The Reverend Soto's congregation may refuse to admit us if they see this car first." Someone had painted the ancient Chevy an electric blue that almost, but not quite, hid spots where rust had eaten through the chassis. Daisy decals decorated the hood and roof. Someone had painted a huge fish, silver and purple, on the passenger side with the words KEEP WHALING stenciled in red above it.

I walked around the car. The driver's side carried the likeness of a loggerhead and the words THE SHELL GAME. The trunk bore the words CONCH CRUISER.

"Where'd you ever find it?" I shook my head and slid onto the passenger seat when Punt opened the squeaking door for me, taking care that the rough seat didn't snag my dress.

"The guy at Rent-a-Wreck had it in his fleet. Didn't take much talk to persuade him to rent it to me for a few days—or a few weeks, if it takes that long to replace the tires on the convertible."

"Let's hope it takes only a few days. People will think you've lost your mind when they see you driving this."

"Naw. They won't. People have accused me of a lot of things, but never of being a car snob." When Punt closed the driver's door it sounded like the lid falling off a rusty bait bucket. I didn't mention the faint stench of cigarette smoke that clung to the car's interior.

A few tourists had gathered on the sidewalk to stare at the cruiser, and curiosity about the crowd drew Gram outside. I grinned and shook my head. She gave me a shrug and a palms-up gesture then waved us goodbye.

"Punt, we can't park this thing in front of anybody's church. Maybe we can find a spot on a side street and walk a short distance."

Punt chuckled, amused at my embarrassment as much as at his own skewed pleasure in driving the weird car. We drove to Flagler and then on another block or so to the church. Punt humored me and found parking near a schoolhouse in the next block.

"Neat church," I said as we approached the stucco building with a bell tower and a bell that pealed "Amazing Grace" into the warm morning.

Inside the door, an usher gave us bulletins and then led us to one of the few empty pews near the back of the sanctuary. I guessed the church might hold three hundred souls and it was obvious that the faithful arrived early to get a good seat down front. The scent of candle wax hung in the air. Uneasy, I glanced over my shoulder. Surely killers didn't attend church. My nervousness rubbed off on Punt. He glanced back, too.

"Relax," he whispered and took my hand. "This's a safe zone."

Sunlight streamed through the stained-glass windows, and a blue-robed choir sat in a loft behind the minister's pulpit. Announcements. Prayer. Hymn (all six verses). Scripture reading. Choir anthem. Collection plate. And at last the sermon.

The Reverend Soto stood in the pulpit wearing a high-collared white robe that reached almost to his shoe tops. A green stole hung around his neck and a braided green belt cinched the robe at the waist. I'd seen his garb before—the day he emceed the TV show in New York. Today he spoke on the Ten Commandments and I had to elbow-prod Punt to keep him alert. At the end of the service, everyone paraded forward to receive communion, and my watch hands pointed to noon before the service ended. After the benediction, Soto approached and welcomed us, referring to our meeting at Margaux Ashford's funeral. It amazed me that he remembered us. Maybe he'd taken Memory 101 at Seminary.

"Sir," Punt said. "We'd like the pleasure of taking you to lunch. Would your schedule allow that?"

"Nothing I like better than an invitation to lunch, unless it's an invitation to breakfast or dinner."

"Good," I said. "We've enjoyed your service very much."

"Thank you." He looked down at his robe. "Give me a few moments to change, okay?"

"Certainly," Punt said. "We've parked a short distance from the church. I'll go get my car and we'll pick you up at the door."

"Fine," Soto agreed, and my heart sank. What if he refused to get into that car?

But most of the stuff I worry about never happens. When we pulled up at the church, he stood waiting, dressed in chinos and a golf shirt. He looked at the car, smiled, and shook his head.

"I'll be using this for a few days," Punt said, "until some new tires come in for my convertible."

"The Karmann Ghia, if I remember correctly."

"Right." Punt grinned as he pulled onto Flagler, pleased that Soto had remembered his car. "Reverend Soto, would you and Keely like to lunch at Pier House?"

"It's one of my favorite places," Soto said.

I nodded my agreement and Punt drove us to Old Town. The parking attendant at the Pier House gated lot rolled his eyes, but he found us an empty slot. Once Punt had locked the car, he led the way past an aviary of tropical parrots and on past a growth of sea grape, elephant ears, and bird-of-paradise that thrived along the path leading to the restaurant. The fragrance of grilled fish and steaks reminded me of my scant breakfast.

"Shall we dine on the deck?" Punt asked.

We both nodded. The waiters wore shorts and identical hibiscus-flowered shirts that matched the fabric of the umbrellas shading each round table. Our waiter found us a spot near the deck railing where we had an unobstructed view of the beach and the sea. Gulls perched on the railing in defiance of the sign: Please do not feed the birds.

We studied the menu for a few moments before ordering. I chose the seafood salad special, but Punt and Soto chose heartier fare—the surf and turf special that included steak, broiled yellowtail, and red-skinned new potatoes. We were more than halfway through our meal before Punt drove to the point of our meeting.

"We know you're acquainted with Randy Jackson," Punt said. "He's having a hard time finding a job and adjusting to life on the outside. Thinks the only way he'll find work is to prove someone else killed Dyanne Darby. He's come to my detective agency, and at Keely's request, I'm trying to help him."

"And you think I can be of assistance?" Soto asked.

"It's a long shot—a very long shot," Punt said, "but maybe you can. This's a bit touchy—perhaps more than a bit. We're not here to hurt feelings or to point fingers of accusation."

"Punt, get to the point," Soto said. "If I can help you, help Randy, I'm more than willing to try."

Punt leaned close to Soto and spoke softly as he explained Randy's list of murder suspects and his need for DNA samples from them.

"In his mind, Randy believes the guilty person must be one of the *Atocha* divers he worked with at the time of Dyanne's death. Keely and I believe that you should be cut from that list because you did so much to help free him from prison, but in this case we want to humor Randy."

Punt explained about Randy's temper, about our getting him a temporary job off-island while we tried to do some of the DNA collecting.

"So what do you want from me?" Soto asked. "Perhaps something simple like a tuft of hair, a saliva sample?"

"The hair would be good," Punt agreed, then he blushed when he noticed Soto's bald head.

"Oh, I can spare some hair. My head hair tends to grow over

my collar, and don't forget my beard. You bring along scissors? An envelope?"

"I have manicure scissors in my purse," I said while Punt fumbled in his pockets until he produced a small envelope. I hoped Soto didn't notice that the envelope had come from his church, one that Punt had failed to drop into the collection plate.

"Let's finish our meal," Punt said. "Food has high priority over DNA samples today."

So we finished eating and topped the meal with pieces of Key lime pie before we returned to our car. Pausing beside the cruiser, Soto, raised his chin.

"Why not take the sample from the underside of my beard? How big a sample will you need?"

"Just a small snip," Punt said.

Soto leaned against the whale door, raised his chin, and pulled a tuft of hair from the underside of his beard. I found my manicure scissors and snipped. Punt opened the envelope, I dropped the hair inside, and Punt pulled a roll of tape from his pocket and sealed the envelope.

"Thank you very much, sir," Punt said as he wrote Soto's name and the date on the envelope.

Only then I noticed the parking attendant watching us with mirthful curiosity. I raised my eyebrows at him and his rudeness before he rolled his eyes at me in disdain.

We drove Soto back to his parsonage near the church and in a flutter of thank yous for the church service, the lunch, the hair sample, we left him.

TWENTY-FOUR

After seeing the Reverend Soto back to his church and parsonage, Punt drove to the school where we'd parked before the worship service and stopped the car so we could talk in privacy.

"What now?" I asked.

"That's always the question. What now? Getting the tuft of hair from Soto was easy enough. Who shall we approach next? Arnold Soto. Gus Helmer. We've covered two suspects out of five—if you count Beau as a suspect."

"I think we'd better count him. If for no other reason, it'll appease Randy. So we still have to talk to Slone Pierce and Ace Grovello. There are other things I'd rather do on a Sunday afternoon. One of those two may be the person who's after me, Punt—me and Maxine."

"I think you can scratch Dad from the suspect list, but don't write Gus Helmer off. We may have his DNA in a baggie, but what do we really know about him? That he's worked for years as a shrimper. That's he's your foot reflexology client. That he's a married man who cheats on his wife with Consuela."

"You think a guy who'd cheat on his wife might also commit murder?"

"Let's just say Helmer's not a straight-forward guy when it comes to women and it's a woman's murder we're investigating. You can't deny that Helmer's strong enough to slash tires."

"That's for sure."

Punt pounded on the steering wheel. "And I don't think we can dismiss Arnold Soto too quickly either. In his youth he must have been a strong diver to hold a job with Fisher, yet today he seems frail, maybe not muscular enough to slash a tire, but he's smooth—a very smooth operator."

"Right. Most ministers are smooth operators. And yes, I know he worked hard in Randy's behalf—perhaps now he's working just as hard to cover up his own long-ago sin."

"Any minister could easily use his robe, sash, and stole along with his position of trust in his community to cover up a darker reality."

"But I like Arnold Soto," I insisted.

"Yeah. So do I."

"If he were guilty, don't you'd think we'd have a gut feeling, a strong hunch that would warn us? I don't have such feelings about the man."

"Nor do I, Keely. But …"

"Yeah, but. Okay, let's move forward. If we count Beau out for the time being, that leaves Slone Pierce and Ace Grovello. Do you think either of those men will give us a DNA sample?"

"We can ask. If they consider our question an insult and say no, then that's it. If we'd take DNA from an unwilling person, it could cause trouble later."

"I suppose the person could complain to the court."

"Yeah. Might cause a mistrial if the case came to trial. Maybe our DNA request would seem less insulting if we pointed out that a DNA mismatch could put a person in the clear. That's what happened to Randy."

"I think anyone might feel insulted at being considered a murder suspect."

"Okay." I sighed. "So we're going to offend both guys. Which one do you think we should we offend first?"

"We're within a few blocks of Slone Pierce's house. Why not stop and ask if he'll talk to us? We can park around the corner from his place so we won't attract attention from his neighbors and so we won't give him much lead time in coming up with a reason to refuse our request."

"Slone Pierce scares me, Punt. He's not my client, but I see him around town. There's something about his eyes. They're like marbles of black ice that reflect no warmth."

"He'll know we've been here to talk to his wife about her testimony at Randy's trial. No doubt the two of them have discussed that visit."

"Maybe she kept our visit top secret. She impressed me as the type who majored in keeping things to herself, especially things that might upset her husband. I have a hunch the Slone-Nicole marriage wasn't made in heaven."

"Would you rather talk to Ace Grovello first?" Punt looked at his watch. "The afternoon's slipping by. Personally, I'd feel more comfortable talking to Slone Pierce in broad daylight."

I sighed. "Okay. Let's go for it. Let's roll."

Punt turned the Conch cruiser onto Flagler and we drove the few blocks to the Pierce address, parking around the corner. Two guys on skateboards spotted our cruiser and approached us in a whir of wheels. One gave our rear fender a resounding slap that made us both jump in surprise.

"Neat chassis, Mama-o," the first guy called, whacking the fender again with the flat of his hand, winking, and looking at me while blowing kisses into the air.

"Party tonight at Hog's Breath, man," the other guy called to Punt. "Bring the broad along. We'd like to meet her."

Punt bounded from the car, but before he could say or do anything both boys whirred on down the street, hitching up cutoffs that were riding precariously low on their hips. For a moment I smiled at Punt's dark scowl.

When we walked toward the Pierce home, the coral rock fence around the property reminded me of a fortress wall. I took care to keep the gate in my peripheral vision while Punt stepped onto the porch and knocked.

At first nobody answered and Punt rapped again—louder and longer. In a few moments Nicole appeared in the doorway clutching her robe at the waist. I wondered if that was her only at-home garment and I suspected that we had wakened the Pierces from an afternoon nap.

"We meet again." Her lips formed a sullen pout. "How may I help you?"

"We'd like to talk to Slone for a few minutes," Punt said. "Would that be possible?"

"He's not home," Nicole said. "Want to leave a message?"

"No," Punt replied. "Can you tell us when he'll return? We'd like to talk to him today if it's possible. Need to talk to him before he gets involved in the work week."

"He's not home." She clicked the lock on the screen door that separated us as if we might try to barge in. "And I don't know when he'll be back. Probably not anytime this afternoon."

"What the hell's going on out there?" The voice growled from deep inside the house. "Get back in here, Nicole. Now."

Before Nicole could obey or refuse, Slone stepped into the living room doorway and stared at us from a distance. He wore nothing but a towel secured around his waist, and his heavy body reminded me of a sleek seal—oily, damp.

"So it's Punt Ashford—and friend." Slone glared at us, looking me up and down at the same time he hitched his towel tighter. I knew then we might as well leave, that he wasn't going to be helpful in any way, but Punt faced Slone's hostile attitude head-on.

"Slone, we'd like to talk to you on behalf of Randy Jackson. We have …"

"I've read all about Randy Jackson," Slone stepped closer to us. "Know more about him than I want to know."

"Then maybe you already know that he's a free man now, a free man who's trying to find the person who should have been in that prison cell instead of him."

"I'm totally uninterested in Randy Jackson's past life or present goals, and I don't want you or him nosing around my house again while I'm away, bothering my missus. Got that clear?"

"We've come to help you prove you had nothing at all to do with the death of Dyanne Darby. You could easily give us undisputable evidence right this minute that'd prove without a doubt that the police need to search elsewhere for the guilty person."

Slone cocked his head and looked at us through half-closed eyelids. "How you going to do that, gumshoe?"

"All we need's a DNA specimen from you. If your DNA

doesn't match the DNA found at the Darby crime scene, nobody will ask you anything about that murder."

Now that Slone stood more willing to listen, Punt poured out the story concerning Randy's suspicions of the divers.

"You mean you intend to take any DNA sample I might let you have directly to the cops?"

"Yes," Punt said.

"Ha!" Slone said. "Don't try to con me. Don't try to tell me the cops are going to listen to a gumshoe. I don't know what you're up to, but I think you're trying to get me involved in a murder investigation. Well, no way am I going to allow that. Me and Beau are pals, right. But there's no way I'm going to let Beau's no-good son cause me to get the police on my tail."

"But…"

"No buts." Slone clicked the lock on the screen, opened the door, and stepped onto the porch steps. "Get off my property. Now."

I was already off the porch and halfway to the gate when Punt spoke.

"Thank you for your time and trouble, Mr. Pierce. We won't be bothering you again anytime soon."

Punt didn't give Slone the pleasure of seeing him hurry away. We walked at a normal pace back to our car, then we drove toward Punt's office.

"What now?" I asked. "Punt, I don't like Slone Pierce. He might be the one we're after—a murderer."

"That's a possibility. Maybe he's afraid Nicole might remember he's the one."

"She could be blackmailing him with the threat of telling, right?"

"If she remembers, Keely. It's all speculation on our part."

"If he's innocent, why's he carrying such a chip on his shoulder? Why wouldn't he talk to us about a DNA sample? And he's strong enough to slash tires."

"Good questions. Good point. No sure answers." Punt pulled the cruiser into his parking slot and we went inside. His office had a closed smell, but Punt shut the door and didn't open any windows. We both sat in the chairs in front of his desk.

"Punt, I've got an idea."

"So let's hear it. I'm ready for an idea, a good workable idea."

"It's about saliva. You mentioned saliva on a sealed envelope. You were careful to tape closed the envelope containing Arnold Soto's hair. Well, why not trick Slone Pierce into licking an envelope and mailing it to us? Then we'd have his DNA."

"Sounds good so far. How are we going to get him to mail us an envelope?"

"Everyone likes free things. Maybe we can send him an ad—an ad for something he needs and uses. Something expensive that he'd really like to own. Maybe a piece of diving equipment. A dive mask? A scuba tank? Or maybe a free dinner and cocktails for two for anyone who'll sign up for a demonstration of some piece of diving equipment. Sign up, with no obligation to buy. I get lots of those kinds of ads, don't you?"

"Keely, I think you're on to something." Punt turned to his book shelf and pulled down a catalog, began thumbing through the pages. He looked at ads for scuba tanks, snorkels, motors. "Look at this!" He held the catalog toward me and pointed to an ad for a No-Fail Depth Finder. "We could offer dinner for two to anyone stopping by to examine this. An offer like that would attract almost any diver, fisherman, boat captain."

"Hold on a minute. Would the police frown on tricking him into supplying us some DNA?"

Punt thought for a moment. "They might. That DNA might not be admissible in court, but I think the police would be curious enough to check it out. If it was a match, then they'd find a legal way of getting the specimen they needed."

"How we going to make an ad?"

Punt pointed to his computer and printer. "I've been sending out flyers for our PI business and I've learned to create graphics. Let's give it a try. Let's name our make-believe place of business Seaman's Paradise and say it's opening next month at a Key West location soon to be announced. We'll call this offer a Grand Opening Special."

"We can promise more details to those who sign up."

Punt made several tries before he came up with a single-page ad that suited us. "We'll do it in red and black with lots of white space," Punt said. "Read a book on advertising that said red sells and white space sells."

When Punt finished working with color and space details, font size, and script style, he ran off a copy of the ad. After that he created a return envelope. All the recipient had to do to receive a free dinner for two was to check the box marked "I am interested, please send more details," slip the page into the enclosed stamped envelope and drop it in the mail.

"This looks very professional, Punt. You should go into the ad business."

"Not unless the PI business goes belly up."

I read the come-on again. "Free dinner and cocktails for two at Louie's Back Yard, corner of Vernon and Waddell. Ocean view porch dining, indoor dining or deck dining at transom level. Live music on Thursdays. This offer good any time during March." I grinned. "Sounds so good it makes me want to sign up myself."

Punt addressed one envelope to Slone Pierce and the other to No-Fail Depth Finders.

"I'll use my post office box address for the return envelope."

We studied the come-on, reading it several times before inserting it into the envelope, sealing it, stamping it. We drove to the post office on Whitehead and mailed the letter.

"I need to go to Beau's house and check it out," Punt said. "Want to go along?"

"Think I'll beg off if you don't mind. I need to get home. Tomorrow's a work day and I have several appointments. Need to see if I have plenty of supplies and a shelf full of clean towels and slippers. My thoughts have been so fragmented, I'll need time to organize."

"Of course," Punt smiled and drove me home. "I'll call you tomorrow after your last appointment and maybe we can make plans for approaching Ace Grovello. He should be an easy mark compared to Slone Pierce."

"I don't know, Punt. He came in for one appointment, but he didn't return for a second. Maybe I offended him."

"You're not the type to offend people, Keely." Punt pulled me to him for a quick kiss. "Do you have clients all day tomorrow?"

"Just in the morning. An afternoon client called saying she had to cancel, so I told her I'd reschedule her to Monday evening. I don't usually take evening appointments, but I liked the woman. This time I made an exception."

"How about seeing Ace Grovello tomorrow afternoon?"

"A rotten way to spend a Monday afternoon, but we do need to talk with him."

"Right. Why don't I call you in the morning to make sure your afternoon's still open. We can finalize plans then."

"Good idea."

We shared a farewell kiss, and as usual, it left me sorry to see him go and eager to hear his voice again even if it meant a visit to Ace Grovello. That couldn't be any worse than our visit to Slone Pierce. Could it? I tried to bury all thoughts of warning notes, warning phone calls, broken windows.

TWENTY-FIVE

ON MONDAY MORNING, after a weekend of freedom from my office, I welcomed getting back into the routine of meaningful work, peaceful work compared to investigating a murder. I checked my appointment book. No first-timers today. I sighed. That meant I wouldn't have to explain the age-old idea behind foot reflexology. In addition to that, I'd know my clients were returning as satisfied customers.

Since finding the death threat on my door last week, I'd begun opening my office carefully, casually peering in all directions before I walked slowly and calmly to give Gram a good morning kiss. If anyone were nearby lurking or watching, that person would see no sign of fear in my actions or my demeanor. There's a lot to be said for presenting a strong front to the public. It's a bit of positive action that bolsters my confidence.

This morning the fragrance of coffee already scented the air. Gram stood behind the espresso machine making lattes for three customers sitting at her coffee bar. Two more tourists sat beside them perusing a menu, so I blew Gram a kiss from the doorway and returned to my office. After a light breakfast, I straightened my apartment, pulled the privacy screen in place, and opened the drapery across my window to let customers know I was ready for business.

Punt called me moments before I expected my first client.

"Love you, Keely. Never forget that."

"I won't forget. Never. All's okay at your place this morning? No slashed tires?"

"All's well here. You have a good night?"

"Yes. No nightmares. No death threats written or verbal. No rocks crashing through the window."

Punt laughed. "Sounds downright boring. I'm calling to reconfirm our plan to visit Grovello this afternoon. That still fit into your schedule?"

"Yes. I suppose so, but this one really makes me nervous. I keep wondering why he didn't schedule his next appointment. He paid in full for six treatments, but he didn't schedule number two, nor did he demand his money back."

"Don't sweat the small stuff. Consuela will get on his case. She'll be afraid of losing her freebie."

"I promised her the freebie whether or not Ace returned."

"You might mention that you appreciate his business when we pay him our surprise visit this afternoon. We could use it as an opener—a reason for our call."

"I suppose we could, but I refuse to look like I'm begging for his business. I have enough clients without having to give would-be customers the hard sell."

"Right. Maybe you can think of it as a soft sell. I'll pick you up a little after two. That sound okay?"

"Yes. I'll be through working by then. You still driving the cruiser?"

"Sure. We could walk, if the cruiser embarrasses you. His B&B's only a mile or so from your office. But I think it'd be wise to have quick transportation handy."

"You're right. I prefer the cruiser to walking and I'll be ready when you get here."

My day passed as scheduled. Two clients, then lunch. Gram had started closing her shop from eleven until one and placing a SIESTA TIME sign in her window. She said it gave the shop more local color, but that was an excuse. She closed for a couple of hours on doctor's orders. At age seventy-two she needed the rest. She put in a full workday not counting the siesta break. I never mentioned age to her. That was a no-no and I didn't like to go there.

After lunch, my first client arrived late, but it didn't ruin my schedule since I allow an hour between sessions to rest my hands and my psyche. More goes into foot reflexology than a massage. I need to draw on the earth and the air for psychic strength that puts me in touch with elements that I never totally understand. Those elements, in turn, put me in touch with my patient's inner needs. Sometimes I used to go alone to the beach, stand barefoot in the sand, feel the sun's warmth against my skin, and breathe in the scent of the sea. That ritual restored my inner strength. But I hadn't done that lately. Not since the death threats.

The early afternoon passed quickly and I told Gram my plans. I waited in front of my office, ready to slide into the Conch cruiser before Punt had to stop and search for a parking place. He arrived promptly and we were off. The cruiser still reeked of cigarette smoke that I tried to avoid inhaling by taking shallow breaths. Punt drove down Duval before he turned on Whitehead. The distance to Ace's B&B was farther than we'd expected. Glad we hadn't tried to walk.

"There it is." Punt pointed to a gate in a croton hedge. "The Sand Dollar."

He parked a block from the entry and we walked back. The croton hedge surprised me. The multi-hued green, red, and yellow leaves are bright rainbows of color that attract the eye, but the locals know that the leaves can brush permanent stains onto clothing. The stains don't show immediately, but eventually the smudged spots appear and the wearer wonders where they came from.

A brass arch marked the doorway into The Sand Dollar office that consisted of little more than a highly polished teakwood desk, a steel four-drawer file cabinet, and a swivel chair, empty at the moment. A corkboard at the left of the desk announced prices and checkout times. Ace Grovello had a good thing going here. Rates started at $200 per night and checkout time was ten A.M.

"May I help you?"

Punt and I both looked up in surprise as Consuela swept into the office and took a stance behind the receptionist's desk. She reminded me of a cormorant today—jet black hair, long neck, black eyes. She tossed us a supercilious grin.

"What are you doing here, Consuela?" Punt failed to hide his irritation.

"Sometimes when I've been good to Ace, he lets me work here at the desk."

"We'd like to speak to Mr. Grovello," I said before she could go into detail about the why of today's employment.

"He's out at the moment." Consuela lifted an eyebrow. "Do you have an appointment?"

"No." Punt peered around Consuela through an open doorway. "Could we wait for him in the courtyard?"

For a moment Consuela appeared flustered, making fluttery motions with her hands. "Will you tell me the nature of your business, please?"

I spoke before Punt could say anything. "You know Mr. Grovello's a client of mine, and …"

"Oh," she said. "You're here on a business call?" She didn't wait for my reply. "Well, I suppose it'll be all right for you to wait in the garden. Mr. Grovello dislikes hearing it called a courtyard. He should be back in a few minutes—although he never advised me that he expected callers."

Punt eased us toward the patio and we entered a tropical garden, a courtyard surrounded by sleeping units whose doors opened onto this patch of greenery. Consuela led us to lime-green patio chairs pulled near a round umbrella table whose glass top covered an array of sand dollars arranged in cream-colored sand.

"May I bring you some iced tea?" she asked.

"No thank you," Punt said. "We'll be content to wait here until Mr. Grovello arrives."

And wait we did, unable to speak freely for fear of letting Consuela know the nature of our business with her boss—at least her boss for today. An hour passed before we saw Ace Grovello walk through the front gate. He stopped briefly to talk with Consuela at the desk, and then strode toward us, belly leading body—a thing I remembered from our previous meeting. A shaft of sunlight glinted on his doubloon pendant, and again he reminded me of a Mack truck intent on running us down. Punt and I both stood.

"Miss Moreno, I believe?" He reached to shake my hand. "Nice to see you again."

"Thank you, and please call me Keely. I'd like you to meet my friend, Punt Ashford."

Punt and I sat and Ace joined us, relaxing into a chair he pulled into position across from us.

"How may I help you people today?" Ace asked.

I sensed Consuela eavesdropping, but Punt spoke, keeping his voice low. "I'm a private investigator, Mr. Grovello. Keely, along with Maxine and Randy Jackson, has hired me to look into a cold-case murder that took place on Christmas Eve around twenty years ago."

"And your investigation has brought you to my door?" Ace acted neither ill at ease nor angry—merely curious. I saw Consuela in her desk chair, leaning toward us.

"Yes, it's brought us to your door as well as to several other doors. Are you familiar with Randy Jackson's story, his present plight?"

"Randy Jackson." Ace rolled the name around on his tongue as he repeated it slowly and looked into the distance as if trying to recall some memory hiding in the recesses of his mind. "Randy Jackson." After a few moments, he looked directly at Punt. "Isn't he the convict the courts exonerated some months ago? A convicted murderer the court released into society?"

"Yes," Punt replied. "Randy Jackson is that person—that innocent person."

"I suppose he has a burr up his butt after rotting away in a prison cell all those years."

"Mr. Grovello." Punt impaled Ace with his steely gaze. "Randy Jackson has more than, as you so delicately phrase it, a burr up his butt. He has a burning desire to see the person guilty of murdering Dyanne Darby convicted of that crime, a burning desire to see that person imprisoned."

"So why are you here this afternoon? Why are you telling me this Randy Jackson hard-luck story? And Miss Moreno—Keely—how are you involved in this sordid matter?"

"Keely's involved because she's received death threats from some person who doesn't want her to stir up an investigation into this case."

"And why would Keely want to, as you say, stir it up?"

I hate it when people talk about me as if I'm absent, or incapable of speaking on my own behalf.

"I want to bring this case to police attention again because Randy Jackson's mother is my friend and because she and her son need my help—and Punt's help. Also, I abhor the thought of a murderer walking the streets of Key West."

Punt could tell my anger was about to boil over. He rose and stood behind my chair as he drove to the point of our call—Randy's suspicion of the long-ago divers and our need for DNA specimens.

"It would be an easy matter for you to clear yourself of all suspicion by letting us collect some DNA material," Punt said. "Randy says you were one of his diving buddies years ago."

"Hah!" Ace roared and rose, glaring at Punt on a level. "And what do you propose to do with my DNA material should I happen to go along with your scheme and provide it? Answer me. What are your plans? Do you have a license to make such a request of ordinary citizens?"

Punt pulled out his billfold, opened it. "I have a private investigator's license, Mr. Grovello."

Grovello turned away. "Hah! A PI license doesn't impress me. I think you're up to something underhanded. If the police wanted DNA material to be used in Randy Jackson's behalf, I feel sure they'd send an officer—an officer of high rank to request and collect it. I'm having nothing to do with a private investigator."

"As you choose, Mr. Grovello," I said.

"Ace. You may call me Ace. And I do want to book another reflexology appointment with you. Sometime soon. Should have done it while I was in your office, but I had a strict schedule that day."

"You're changing the subject, Mr. Grovello," Punt said. "I'm sure Keely welcomes all clients, and of course, that's her privilege. But as far as cooperating with us on the DNA request, you've made your position clear. Perhaps you're afraid of what your DNA might reveal to the police."

"I'm not afraid of your investigation, Mr. Ashford. Not at all. I consider criminals beneath my consideration. And I consider private detectives only a step or two above them. Now will you please leave my premises before I call authorities and have you evicted?"

I stood, and Punt took my arm and we headed toward Grovello's office. Consuela rolled her eyes and gave us another supercilious glance as we left the building and stepped onto the street. We didn't speak until we reached the cruiser and eased inside it.

"What do you make of Ace Grovello, Punt, and Consuela?"

"I don't know. We made him very angry. He seemed even hotter than Slone Pierce. And I suppose Consuela managed to overhear our request and his response."

"Yet in all his anger, he wanted to set up another reflexology appointment. I don't want to work with him again, but I think I need to. And I will. Maybe I can get information from him that you or the police can't. He's a bragger. I might be able to lead him into revealing information we need."

"Maybe. I don't want you taking needless chances with any of the suspects, especially Slone and Gus. Those guys are rough and tough and ready to protect themselves in any way that's necessary."

"And then there's Consuela. I didn't expect to see her today."

"One never knows exactly what Consuela's up to. Maybe she's merely after a more elegant bed. Grovello's a smoother operator than Slone and Gus. He has to meet the public every day in order to keep his place in the upscale tourist business."

"So let's get out of this neighborhood. If Ace tries to make another appointment with me, I'll welcome him with my ears wide open."

"Good idea, but take care. Let me know when and if he books. I'll be at Celia's having an espresso—available if you need to call me."

"I'd appreciate that."

"So far we're getting nowhere with our DNA collecting. In a few days Randy'll be back. Maybe we've done enough, failed enough to convince him that collecting DNA's a job for the police. But there's one more thing we can do. We can go to Beau's place, pick up his scuba mouthpiece and have it ready for examination."

"And who are we going to get to examine it?"

"I think approaching Shelley Hubble's our best bet. The police and the court authorities know of her previous work for Randy. They'll be more likely to listen to her than anyone else."

"What about Jeff Bremmer—our friend on the police force?"

"Right. What about him! He hasn't reported to us on his research concerning previous burglary charges against the divers. Some buddy! I'm not interested in turning the DNA evidence we have over to him."

"Maybe he couldn't get the info you asked for without arousing suspicion. Cut him some slack. Tomorrow, if we're lucky, we may get a letter from Slone Pierce."

"Maybe. It's a little soon, but maybe. How about some dinner, Keely? I'm starved."

I looked at my watch, surprised to see that darkness had fallen and it was almost seven o'clock. "Can't take time to eat tonight, Punt. Remember? I told you about my client who needs a makeup time. She's scheduled tonight at eight."

"You have to eat. Not good to miss meals."

"I'll make a snack after I'm finished working with her. See you tomorrow afternoon after work. That okay?"

"Guess it'll have to be. I'll call you if we get a letter from Slone. Mail comes around two o'clock."

Punt drove me home, gave me a goodnight kiss at my doorway, and once I was inside, he drove away, leaving me to think about Ace Grovello—and Randy.

TWENTY-SIX

My evening client came and went. By that time Gram had retired for the evening and I had no desire for dinner. I picked up an avocado from my kitchen countertop where I had placed it to ripen a few days ago. It seemed soft to my touch, so I cut it open, removed the huge center seed, and peeled one half of the fruit. Pulling a jar of mayo and an almost-fresh croissant from the refrig, I made a sandwich, added a bit of salt and a squeeze of lime juice. Aah! My almost favorite sandwich. My mouth watered, and the tartness of the lime juice along with the bland taste of the fruit told me I had made the perfect snack for this hour of the night.

Once in bed, I lay awake thinking about Slone Pierce and Ace Grovello, hating it that they had been so uncooperative concerning the DNA testing. How would Randy react to that news when he returned from shrimping? In my mind, both Ace and Slone had clouds of guilt hanging over them. Surely an innocent person would have offered a DNA sample with no reservations. Why hadn't those men done that? Maybe one of them was guilty. Or maybe they both were innocent. I had ambivalent feelings about Soto. Who could guess what his work in Randy's behalf might have been covering up? And Beau? I refused to consider the possibility of his guilt.

Punt called early on Tuesday morning.

"Bad news, Keely. Nikko phoned last night. That Brighton case I mentioned has taken him to Orlando and he needs a detail person in Miami—me."

"When will you be back?"

"Maybe not until Wednesday afternoon. But don't worry.

This'll give us another day to hear from Slone Pierce, and Randy won't return until Friday. We'll still have a couple of days to get the DNA we have retrieved, carefully labeled and ready to submit to Shelley Hubble—if she's willing to help us. How about my picking you up late Wednesday afternoon? We'll get Beau's scuba mouthpiece and have it ready to take to Hubble along with the other specimens. I think the scuba gear will work better than the hairbrush."

"Sounds good to me, Punt. I don't plan to go fishing tomorrow afternoon, so I can be ready whenever you get here."

"Good thinking about the fishing. I hate to see you going on the water alone. Play it safe and stay close to home."

I hate it when Punt tries to tell me what to do. Reminds me too much of my years with Jude Cardell. But it had been my idea to forego fishing, not Punt's.

"I'm not staying home because I'm afraid, Punt. Have you looked at the weather report today? Weatherman's predicting high winds. Twenty and above. Smallcraft warnings are in effect as we speak."

"Sorry you'll miss your afternoon on the water, but there'll be better days—days when we can go together."

"I'll miss you while you're gone. Take care. Are you flying to Miami?"

"No. Driving. It takes longer, but it's less hassle—no airport security delays. No last-minute cancelled flights."

"You're driving the cruiser?"

Punt laughed. "No. I'm renting another car, an unobtrusive car, a car suitable for a private investigator."

After Punt broke the phone connection some of the sunshine disappeared from my day. I ate breakfast at Gram's coffee bar. She snorts and fumes when I try to call a French vanilla cappuccino my breakfast, but that's all I felt like eating. For lunch I appeased her by bringing us take-out salads from Fausto's—lots of green leafy stuff that promises good health.

Tuesday passed slowly as did Wednesday until the moment Punt returned late in the afternoon from Miami. He reported that all was well concerning the case he and Nikko were investigating up north.

"Any mail from Slone Pierce?" I asked the moment Punt finished telling me about his trip and his business in Miami.

"Haven't been to the post office yet. Why don't we go there now and see what's in the Fotopolus-Ashford box before we drive to Dad's house and pick up his scuba mouthpiece?"

"It's a plan." I locked my office door, stopped for a moment at Gram's shop to tell her our decisions. When Punt arrived—in the Conch cruiser—we left Duval in a cloud of exhaust fumes.

Luck smiled on us and we found a fifteen-minute parking place in front of the post office. We eased our way through a throng of business people eager to push the day's outgoing letters through the mail slot, and the keys on Punt's key ring jingled as he sorted through them to find the one to his private box. I peered over his shoulder when the brass door opened easily, revealing an assortment of letters and ads.

"Here it is, Keely!" Punt flashed a familiar envelope at me for a few seconds before he slipped it into his briefcase.

"What luck!" My nape prickled with excitement. "He fell for it! That gives us one more bit of DNA for the police."

"Right!"

Then a worrisome thought hit me. "Punt, will the authorities toss out a sample that the donor was unaware of providing?"

"I'm not sure. Guess we'll have to learn about that later. Maybe Randy won't think to ask that question."

"Slone Pierce could say that someone else licked the flap and mailed the envelope for him. His secretary or …"

Punt laughed. "I don't think salvage boat owners can afford secretaries. According to Dad, Slone's business is strictly a one-man operation and Slone's the man for all seas and seasons."

"He could have asked his wife to sign up for the freebie and mail the coupon. What if he did that?"

"Keely, let's not make problems where there may be none. Let's mark this sample from Slone, give it to Attorney Hubble if she agrees to help us, and let her deal with any complexities. In the meantime, how about taking a quick drive to Dad's house? I missed checking on it yesterday, so we'll take care of that detail first and then find his scuba gear."

"Okay." I was following Punt to the cruiser when a new idea popped into my mind.

"Punt, when people take reflexology treatments, they touch things. Things like sign-in sheets. The portable foot bath. The treatment chair. There'd be several opportunities for a client to leave fingerprints. Right?"

"I suppose so. But there would be a mingling of many prints even if Maxine didn't rub them away when she cleans."

"Would there be enough DNA in a fingerprint to make it of use?"

"As I understand it, there could be. When was the last time Maxine cleaned your place?"

"I can't remember, but I can look it up on my appointment calendar."

"When Ace came in, did he pay cash or by check or credit card?"

"He paid cash—lots of cash. He paid in full for my special offer of six treatments. But I've already deposited the bills. I never leave cash around the office."

"If Ace calls for an appointment, schedule it, okay?"

I hesitated only a moment. I felt torn. I dreaded facing Ace again, but I wanted a chance to get his fingerprints. "Yes. Yes. If Ace he calls for an appointment, I'll schedule it. After our chat in his courtyard I may never hear from him again."

Punt sighed. "Covertly picking up Ace's fingerprints is probably an idea that won't work at all. He's no dummy. He knows that if he's in your office there's a strong chance he'll be leaving evidence, DNA fingerprints or perhaps something else, that we could use. And he knows you're no dummy either. He knows you might be waiting for the chance to trap him."

"So what do you suggest?"

"Let's forget about Ace right now. Let's go to Dad's house and see if we can find a scuba mouthpiece."

We drove down Simonton Street, turning left on Truman Avenue until we reached Grinnell and then headed on toward the ocean. On this crowded island, building contractors have no way to go but up. Beau and his second wife disliked the high-rise condos near the airport as well as those on the other side of the island with a gulfside view. They chose to buy a picturesque home a century old and decorated a century ago with gingerbread trim hand-carved by Conch sailors whiling away spare hours during long voyages.

When we stopped in front of the Ashford home, night-blooming jasmine already scented the air. All along the street, bougainvillea vines climbed the palm trees to the balconies of the old Conch houses where they spilled over, dropping pink, purple, and scarlet petals like a rainbow of confetti onto the sidewalk below.

Punt parked in front of the house and I could sense neighbors peeking from behind their curtains, eyeing the cruiser and no doubt wondering what sort of people were approaching the Ashford home. Punt turned and waved, giving a playful grin to whoever might be watching.

"I feel the eyes on us, too, Keely. They don't recognize the cruiser, but I hope they'll recognize me and go on about their business."

Punt led the way through the gate in the picket fence and we walked up a sidewalk lined with pots of lavender hibiscus, an eye-catching advertisement for Jass's tropical plants. At the top of the veranda steps, he paused to insert his key into the brass lock and open the door so we could step inside and look around. The house smelled of a dampness that threatened to turn into mildew, and Punt snapped on the air conditioner, setting it on low.

"I always check the outside doors first for any sign of forced entry," Punt said. "Then I take a quick scan of the ground-floor windows. That's where vagrants might break in."

I shuddered. "That's creepy. Don't the police patrol empty homes on the lookout for any unusual activity?"

"Sure they do, but they can't keep a round-the-clock vigil. During one vacation, Dad paid a full-time guard to sit in the driveway. That was the time someone broke into the back porch and removed any small object good for resale. Druggies take what's easy and handy—what'll sell for enough to get them a fix for the night."

When Punt found nothing out of place, he snapped off the lights but left the air conditioner on. We headed for the carport.

"Dad's scuba gear's out here in one of these locked cupboards." Punt fingered the keys until he found one that fit the largest cupboard. The door creaked open, and I backed off as spiders scuttled to hide behind an assortment of scuba tanks, hoses, snorkels, swim fins, dive masks.

"He could start his own dive shop," I said.

Punt picked up two mouthpieces and a snorkel tube. "These should hold enough DNA to be useful."

I held the equipment while Punt relocked the cupboard. We left the house and drove to Punt's office.

"Now we've gotta label all this stuff, right?" I asked.

"Right. We'll label and number each object we've collected and place everything in a box for safekeeping."

I found a pen and paper. "I'll make a numbered list that corresponds with the objects. We should print out four copies. One for your safe. One for my office. One for Randy and Maxine. And one for Shelley Hubble or Jeff Bremmer—if either of them agrees to help us."

We made short work of the task and Punt set the box in his office safe and twirled the knob.

"Punt, if anyone really wanted something inside that safe …"

"Don't worry about that. Only Nikko and I know the combination and it's complicated."

"I'm sure you're right about that. But if stealing something from that safe was a life or death matter, the thief could take the whole safe, load it onto a truck and drive away."

"Do you know how much that safe weighs?" Punt asked.

"No idea."

"Well it's too heavy for anyone to lift, probably too heavy for two people to lift even if they majored in weight training. I've got the exact weight around here someplace, but I'm not worried about the safe being stolen. Besides the deterrents of weight and a heavy duty lock, it's bolted to the floor."

I sighed. When Punt doesn't worry about a thing, he thinks nobody should worry about it. No point in arguing with him about the safe.

"Who shall we call to help us?" I asked. "Jeff Bremmer at the police department or Shelley Hubble, the attorney?"

"Since Jeff hasn't exactly been a ball of fire when it comes to getting the divers' rap sheets checked for burglary, maybe we should try Hubble first."

Punt had his hand on the telephone directory, ready to look up her number when the phone rang. We both jerked back in surprise, then laughed at our nervousness.

TWENTY-SEVEN

"Ashford and Fotopolus," Punt said.

"Thought it was Fotopolus and Ashford," I hissed, grinning and poking him.

He put his hand over the phone and winked. "Only when Nikko's in town."

"Jeff here, Punt. Sorry it's taken me so long to get that info you wanted."

"Thanks for the effort, Jeff. I know dealing with the department can be time consuming."

"According to their rap sheets, only one of the five divers you mentioned had a past burglary conviction."

"Gonna tell me which one, or do I have to guess?" Punt pushed a button, setting the phone for conference call. "Keely Moreno's here listening in."

"Fine with me," Jeff said. "A jury found Slone Pierce guilty of burglary in December of 1979. He broke into the Boog Powell Marina, made off with lots of cash and diving gear that the police later found hidden at his home. He did some jail time, served a large part of his sentence as an orderly, and then, due to his continued good behavior both as a prisoner and an orderly, the court released him on parole. He's had no more run-ins with the law since that time."

"Good work, Jeff," Punt said. "This information may be a lot of help to us. A big thanks to you."

"Glad to be of use, pal, and sorry it took me so long to get back to you. If there's anything else I can do, give me a call and I'll give it my best shot."

Punt broke the phone connection and started making notes on a yellow pad. "So, I'll cancel all my negative thoughts about Jeff and his getting back to me. For a while I thought he wasn't going to make it."

"So Slone Pierce may be the guy who threatened me and Maxine." The back of my neck tightened as I remembered his smoldering eyes, his sleek heavy body. "He may be the guy who murdered Dyanne Darby."

"He may be. May is the important word here. The information I read said that a significant percentage of people convicted for murder also had a past conviction for burglary. Slone Pierce's burglary conviction in no way tells us for sure that he's the one who murdered the Darby woman."

"Maybe not, but in my mind it raises him to the top of our suspect list. A few days ago I read about a study that showed that four people out of every hundred are sociopaths—people born without a conscience, people who can murder with no guilty feelings. Slone Pierce could be one of those. There's something about that cold look in his eyes that chills me. If he were innocent, why wouldn't he give us a DNA specimen? Why did he make us go to the trouble of tricking him into leaving his saliva on the flap of an envelope?"

"I'm asking myself those questions, too, but at the same time I'm reminding myself that Ace Grovello has a cold look about him, too. Ace also refused to let us have any DNA. Just because Ace has no burglary conviction on his rap sheet doesn't remove him from suspicion. And Gus Helmer used to turn you off, too, until you began working with him as a client."

"Okay. I won't say a negative word about any of Randy's suspects again. So what do we do now?"

"Let's call Hubble. We can offer her the DNA we've collected even though we have none from Ace Grovello. We can let her check on Slone's past burglary conviction—can't let her know Jeff dug up that info for us. But if Jeff found it, Shelley can find it in the same way."

"All right," I agreed. "Maybe she'll agree to talk to us about this case, about the possibility of helping Randy again."

"Maybe she'd even be willing to talk to us tonight. It's still early."

Punt keyed in Shelley's number, leaving the phone on conference call. The phone rang five times before a man's voice spoke.

"Attorney Hubble is unable to take your call at this time. Please leave a message, your name, and your phone number at the sound of the beep, and Ms. Hubble will get back to you as soon as possible."

Punt replaced the receiver before the beep sounded.

"Damn! I wish we could have talked to her right now."

"Maybe we should have left a message. She might be listening and breaking in to talk to the callers whom she finds of special interest. Sometimes I do that."

"Or if she looks at her caller ID, she may recognize my name and return my call. Let's wait around a bit."

Punt brought us small bottles of sparkling lemonade from Nikko's refrigerator and found a bag of chips in his bottom desk drawer. For a few minutes we munched and sipped without talking, but the phone remained silent. If Attorney Hubble knew Punt had telephoned, she obviously thought returning his call could wait until tomorrow.

"Maybe in the morning," Punt said, sighing.

I was staring at my drink when a follow-up idea struck me. Why hadn't I thought of it sooner? I leaned forward, tapping the bottle with my fingernail and organizing my thoughts.

"What's wrong, Keely? Need another soda?"

"I just remembered something. Our talk about Ace leaving fingerprints in my office and about my booking another appointment for him brought it to mind. Maybe it's something important. Or maybe not." I jumped up and started toward the door. "But when I finished Ace's treatment last week, I offered him a glass of lemonade. Not a bottled drink, but homemade juice from fresh fruit. I do that for all my clients. It was nothing special I did just for Ace."

"And he drank it?"

"Yes. He drank it and set the glass on the bookcase near my desk while he reached for his billfold to pay me. My phone rang, distracting me. That's when Ace paid and left my office without rebooking. Punt! That empty lemonade glass may be on the bookcase where he set it. It may have his fingerprints on it."

"What day was that?"

"Last Thursday morning."

Punt reached for his desk calendar and began checking dates. "Almost a week ago. This is Wednesday. Last Thursday would be a week ago tomorrow. You say Maxine cleans for you. When does she do that? What day of the week? And how thorough is she?"

"She cleans on Saturdays. Saturday afternoon, and usually she's very thorough. But I've asked her to skip cleaning my office. She only does my living quarters."

"So the glass may still be where Ace left it."

"It may be. I'm too busy to keep count of every glass in my place of business or in my apartment either, for that matter. But if the glass's still there and if what you say about DNA is true, then that glass may have Ace's DNA on it—either fingerprints or dried saliva around the rim. Maybe both."

"Let's go take a look."

As we left Punt's office, he turned out the light, closed the door and locked it. Then he reopened it, snapped a light back on, and relocked.

"Your worries are beginning to rub off on me, Keely. It's early evening, but a light left on could be a deterrent to an intruder later."

Dusk darkened the street outside Punt's office, and an on-shore breeze reminded us that the sea surrounded our island. We drove through bumper-to-bumper traffic toward Duval Street. If New York is the city that never sleeps, then Duval must be the street that never sleeps. Teenage boys scooped the loop in conch cruisers that looked even gaudier than ours. Three tourists on mopeds rode adjacent to each other, fanning across two lanes of pavement and slowing traffic to a crawl. To Punt's credit, he didn't honk at them. Maybe he refrained because so many other horns blared and a police siren wailed from a distance.

"Tonight's cops are too busy with the mopeders to notice this car." Punt parked in the tow-away zone in front of Gram's shop and we hurried into my office, snapping on lights as we went.

"There it is!" I almost tripped over a chair in my hurry to reach the bookcase. Punt grabbed my hand in the split second before I would have grabbed the glass.

"Wait! Don't touch! Where can I find tongs, a plastic bag— a big one?"

"Some detective I'd make! I might have smudged my prints over any prints Ace left last week."

Although my hands shook, I found a pair of tongs and a Ziploc bag. While I held the Ziploc open, Punt dropped the glass inside.

"So now we may have DNA from all five of Randy's suspects," I said. "Surely Shelley Hubble will listen once she hears our story and relates it to Randy's plight."

We were about to return to the cruiser when Gram rapped on my door then stepped inside.

"Gram!" I hurried toward her. "Are you all right? Can we help you?"

"I be fine. But hear news on radio few minutes ago—news you may need."

"What news? Give."

"Radio man say Nicole Pierce recants, that be the word he used, recants her words before judge, before jury people, words about Randy Jackson."

"What else, Gram?" Punt and I both stepped closer to her. "What else?"

"That's all I hear. Police sirens too loud. You want to know about this, yes?"

"Yes, Gram. Thanks for stopping by to tell us. We'll learn more about it tomorrow. Or maybe on the late TV news."

I saw Gram to her apartment, told her good night, and when I returned, Punt stood talking on the phone to someone at the radio station—and scowling.

"Guy hung up on me. Says to read about the recant in the *Citizen* tomorrow."

"This could be a break for Randy!" I hurried with Punt back to the cruiser which hadn't been towed away at the owner's expense. We drove to his office, speculating about the news break Gram had heard. It could mean a lot of things. Maybe Nicole had remembered who she saw leaving Dyanne's apartment on that long-ago night. Maybe this. Maybe that.

The inside light still gleamed, and when we entered Punt's

office, everything stood as we'd left it. Punt opened the safe, added the latest DNA fingerprint to our collection, and relocked the safe.

We were about to begin congratulating ourselves on our success due to my sketchy housekeeping when we noticed the red light blinking on the telephone.

"How did we overlook that?" Punt asked, reaching for the phone.

"Maybe Shelley Hubble decided we're worth her attention after all." We both sighed when Nikko's voice flowed from Punt's answer box.

"Nikko here, Punt. Calling from Orlando. I know you've barely had time to get home from Miami, but I need your help again. This time in Fort Lauderdale. Come as soon as you can and then phone Pete Branson. He'll be expecting your call and he'll put you up for a day or so at his condo. Try to get here before eleven if you can."

Nikko gave his phone number along with Pete Branson's and that was that. It was a three-hour drive to Miami and maybe another hour on to Lauderdale. Punt could never make it before eleven.

"Wish I'd been here to talk to him," Punt said.

I wished that too, but I didn't say so. I hated the idea of Punt being off island again so soon. I wondered how long he'd be away. Nikko's "a day or so" sounded vague. Maybe ominous. I straightened up both physically and mentally, vowing never to allow myself to fall into the habit of being dependent on a man for my sense of personal worth and well-being.

"Drat!" Punt pounded on his desk. "As the junior partner, I've no choice but to go."

"Anything I can do while you're away? I mean I don't want to approach Shelley Hubble alone. That's a job for both of us. But is there anything else I could do? Pick up mail or something?"

"I'm not expecting anything important in the mail, and I'll be in easy touch with Nikko. If Ace should call for a reflexology treatment while I'm away, you might want to put him off until I return."

"No way." I sounded braver than I felt. "Ace might have been the killer Nicole saw leaving the Darby apartment. I can take care of myself. Gram will play watchdog. Consuela's the one who bothers me. What if she comes around insisting on helping us?

She may ask about her contribution to the DNA box. She may even come up with another contribution—from Ace."

"Just tell her we don't need her help." Punt grabbed my hand. "Keely, before I leave for Lauderdale, I want to drive to Nicole Pierce's place—talk to her. Maybe ask her if she recanted because she's remembered something important."

TWENTY-EIGHT

I SHUDDERED AND HOPED Punt hadn't noticed. "Couldn't that wait until you get back from Lauderdale? It's late to be calling on anyone now. I doubt the Pierces would welcome you with open arms."

"I'll take my chances. I need to hear Nicole's thoughts on the recant—and anything else she might have remembered. My body may be in Ft. Lauderdale tomorrow, but part of my thoughts will be here, working on the Darby murder. I need to have all facts available."

"You need to get on the road. I know you're a careful driver, but I hate the idea of you starting this late and then crowding the speed limit to make up for time lost talking to Nicole Pierce—or Slone."

"I'll be brief. If you don't want to come with me, I'll drive you home."

"Some choice. Okay, let's head for Flagler. Guess I'm betting that nobody there will give us the time of day and you'll be on your way north almost immediately."

"We'll see. I promise you the stop'll only take a few minutes. When we get there, you can wait in the car if you're reluctant to face the Pierces."

"No way. I'm not afraid. Well, only a little bit. They both make me nervous."

Flagler's a wide street, and it seemed busier than usual tonight. A few blocks from the Pierce home we saw blue-and-red flashing lights. Punt reached for my hand. When we drew closer we saw police cars, fire truck, ambulance—all with headlights on. A traffic cop had parked his car across both lanes of the street, diverting traffic.

"Detour, please. Detour. Congested area."

"What's going on?" Punt asked.

"An emergency. Detour. Please keep moving."

People in the cars behind us began honking horns, and Punt followed the cop's orders. We were turning down the side street detour when we saw the yellow-and-black crime scene tape that cordoned off the Pierce residence.

Punt squeezed my hand as he drove slowly and at last found a parking place on this narrow side street. "That tape spells bad news, Keely. Let's be inconspicuous, but let's walk back and see if we can find out what's happened."

"Someone's dead. You know that's what's happened. A murder or an unexplained death." My teeth began to chatter and I felt my hand grow cold even in the warmth of Punt's fingers. "Nicole? Slone? Which one lies dead? Maybe she killed him in self-defense. Maybe after all these years she realized he murdered Dyanne Darby. Maybe she accused him and he came after her. Or maybe after she recanted, Slone killed her before she could tell police he was the murderer."

"Easy, Keely. Easy. We've both got to keep open minds. Let's melt into the crowd of gawkers and walk toward the front of the Pierce house. Maybe we can talk to a cop. Ask a few questions."

"Police will be tight-lipped. You know that. They'll order us to move on."

"I'll take that chance. I'd like to hear what the onlookers are whispering, too. Sometimes curious neighbors pick up info the police never intended to leak."

So we kept to the shadows, trying to attract no attention, stopping when we reached the coral rock fence around the Pierce property. I clutched Punt's arm.

"Punt! They're removing a body." We watched as four uniformed cops carried a stretcher bearing a blanket-shrouded form off the Pierce porch, down a few steps, and then slid it through the open doors of an ambulance. In moments the vehicle drove away. No sirens. No flashing lights.

"Maybe the person's still alive," I said with little conviction, knowing if that were true, sirens would be wailing. "Maybe they're taking someone to the hospital."

"Dream on, Keely. Dream on. But one of those cops in the yard's Jeff Bremmer." Punt stepped closer to the fence. "What's going on, Jeff? Got any details?"

Jeff turned long enough to recognize Punt, step closer and whisper. "ME hints suicide. Chief has an APB out for Slone." Jeff hurried into the house and a man standing next to Punt beside the fence shook his head and whispered.

"So Nicole's dead. Slone's missing. Go figure."

All around us people spoke sotto voce. We hung around in the strained silence a few minutes longer, but when nobody had anything else to say or whisper, Punt headed toward the car and I gave a relieved sigh, more than ready to go with him.

"The spouse is always a suspect, Keely."

"Sure," I agreed. "Wonder why Slone has disappeared."

"Jeff said the medical examiner hinted at suicide. Maybe she left a note. Maybe she felt so guilty about causing Randy to sit in jail for twenty years, that she took her own life in remorse. Wish I didn't have to go to Lauderdale tonight. But I guess we'll hear more about all this on TV later this evening. The media will be full of it tomorrow."

"And maybe it wasn't suicide, Punt. And maybe Slone isn't the guilty one. Maybe Dyanne Darby's killer heard about Nicole's recant on the radio like Gram did, and killed her before she could say anything more—anything that might incriminate him. The killer could be anyone."

"No use speculating. By the time I return from Lauderdale we'll know a lot more about the case. In the meantime, you take care. Keep a low profile and don't do any nosey poking."

I tried not to resent Punt's orders, but I made no promises, and I didn't intend to nosey-poke. Every day I pick up newspapers and read about some stranger's murder, but when such a death happens to someone I know, it's like I've personally been caught in a rifleman's crosshair. Life's fragile. The world's a dangerous place. I never related well to Nicole Pierce, but there for the grace of God…Grim thoughts filled my mind and I wondered if they were filling Punt's mind, too.

We rode in silence for many minutes before Punt spoke.

"Keely, there's one thing you could do for me—and for Dad. It's the house."

"Check on it for you?"

"Right. I promised Dad I'd take a look-see every day and it's no problem as long as I'm on the island. Nikko didn't indicate how long he'd need me up north, but it sounded as if it might be for more than a day. He's eager to drop this case into the 'done' file and get home. Would you mind checking Dad's place for me? You got the time?"

"Be glad to do it. But if you don't mind, I'll do my checking in the mornings. I'd feel safer that way. I know we looked the place over earlier today, but an early-morning look-see will tell if there might have been a problem during the night. Right?" What if Slone Pierce had decided to hide out in Beau's empty house? Lots of the locals knew Beau and Jass were on an extended trip abroad. They knew Beau and Slone were friends. Cut the crazy thinking, I told myself, trying to block the thoughts from my mind as Punt spoke.

"Right. An early morning check would be a good deal, Keely. I'd appreciate it." When we reached my place, Punt pushed two keys from his key ring, pulled a spare ring from his pocket, and eased Beau's keys onto it. "Silver one's to the front door. Brass one fits the storage cupboards in the carport."

I pocketed the keys, and Punt walked me to my door. "I'll stop by the airport, and pick up a different rental car, and leave immediately. Still have my bag packed. No problem there."

We said a lingering good night, then I watched until Punt disappeared, driving into the clamor of Duval Street.

I tossed and squirmed all night, trying to find a comfortable position, all the while suspecting that my discomfort lay in my mind and my negative thoughts rather than in my body. The next morning Gram telephoned me, wakened me just as I'd dropped into a deep sleep. I had to force cobwebs from my mind before I could respond.

"What's up, Gram?"

"Hear TV news. The Nicole woman dead. Police find husband. You know these people, you and Punt?"

"Yes. In a business way we know them. It's a sad situation." I snapped on my TV, eager to hear more details of yesterday's tragedy.

Gram gave a harrumph, making it clear she wanted no part in the Pierce problems.

"Special coffee beans due to arrive from Hawaii. Kona. Would you come over? Help me deal with heavy bag and with Jose? He be the delivery man today. Take day off from Strunks."

"Can't he lift the bag for you?"

"Jose be with a bad back today. No like to ask him to lift. We can do it together."

"Okay, Gram. I'll be over soon as I've had a bite of breakfast."

So we lift the bag of beans to spare Jose's back, then we have bad backs. I thought Jose should seek a less demanding job, but I corked that idea. I knew Gram'd have her wheeled cart ready. We'd use it, and nobody would have to lift the beans far. Maybe I'd have some free minutes to check on Beau's house before my first client arrived.

I ate breakfast, straightened my apartment and my office, listened to the TV news. Nicole had died from a gunshot to the head. Slone was in police custody being questioned. I felt more at ease, knowing Slone Pierce's whereabouts. But how long would they hold him? The rest of the announcer's chatter gave me no new information. Now we'd never know if Nicole had recalled the identity of Darby's killer. A single bullet had silenced her. I switched the TV off.

No Jose. My first appointment arrived, but still no delivery truck. Midway through that appointment, Jose stopped his truck out front and honked. I excused myself, met Gram at her doorway and wheeled the cart to the truck. Jose managed to lower the beans onto the cart and get Gram's signature on a receipt before he and his truck traveled on down Duval.

My day got off to a bad start and it didn't improve as the hours passed. I hoped Punt would call me from Fort Lauderdale. He didn't. My second appointment turned out to be a no-show—an hour wasted. Had I known, I could have used her time to take a look-see at Beau's house. My third appointment arrived late, expecting me to give her a full hour's treatment. And I did. That left me almost no break before my next client. By four o'clock I felt exhausted. And I hadn't kept my promise to check on Beau's house.

"Where you go now, Keely?" Gram called when she saw me unlocking my bike.

"To Beau's place. Be back in a few minutes." I explained my mission. "How about having a late supper together? I'll stop at Fausto's and bring us something warm and Cuban."

"Not good idea for tonight." Gram's earrings bobbed as she shook her head. "Muy tired. No hungry. Long day. I close shop at five and retire."

"Another time, then." I blew her a kiss and started to pedal down Duval. The day was still warm and sunny, but the wind had increased and I returned to my apartment for a sweater. I paused to make sure I had my cell phone in my pocket and the keys to Beau's house. I'd call Gram when I got back to be sure she was okay. I didn't like her to skip supper any more than she liked me to skip breakfast.

I had to fight the wind, pump hard, launch all my weight onto the pedals. Styrofoam cartons and cups scudded down the street along with an aluminum can and a paper bag from Fast Buck Freddie's. Trash never sleeps. I smelled rain in the air and felt goosebumps rising on my arms, but only a few sprinkles dampened my sweater before I reached the Ashford house. After chaining my bike to a palm inside the picket fence, I paused to look around. Lights were blinking on in the neighborhood, and clouds cast deep shadows onto the porch although it was not yet five o'clock.

Pulling the house key from my pocket, I climbed the steps to the porch and paused again. Why had I told Punt I'd check on the house? I regretted having been unable to do it this morning as I'd planned. I hated to admit the house frightened me and that the possibility of Slone Pierce's presence scared me even more. I poked the key into the lock, determined to put my fear behind me.

TWENTY-NINE

AFTER INSERTING THE KEY in the lock, I'd opened the door when someone called to me.

"Miss? Miss? There's nobody at home there. May I help you?"

I turned to face a puff-ball of a woman, short and fat and wearing a caftan that flowed around her ankles. Her headband echoed the turtle pattern in the caftan.

"I'm Keely Moreno." In the mist of rain and the rising wind, I left the porch and crossed the yard to extend my hand toward the woman. "I'm a friend of the Ashfords and I've come to give the house a quick check while Mr. Ashford's away."

"I'm Daisy French from next door," Puffball said. "We neighbors keep an eye on Beau's house, too. But we never have problems around here. Glad to meet you, Keely. Give me a call if you need any help. I'll be right inside."

I thanked the woman then I climbed the porch steps again and unlocked the house. I was sorry I'd entertained the thought that Slone Pierce might come here to hide out from the police. I tried to calm my fears by remembering that he was in police custody. Once inside, I checked the three doors that opened to the outside before I examined each window. No smashed glass. All locks in place. I breathed easier.

I considered placing some markers here and there throughout the downstairs, a thread on a certain spot on the carpet, or an envelope between two couch cushions. Then on another visit, if any of the markers had been moved, I'd know an intruder had been here.

You've been reading too many detective novels, Keely. Finish looking around and go on home.

I left the house and locked the door, turning to wave toward

Daisy French's house in case she might be watching. In fact, I hoped she was watching. In spite of knowing Slone Pierce's whereabouts, I still felt uneasy as the early dusk and threatening clouds predicted an early evening. Why not skip the carport check? The thought tempted me, but I discarded it and walked around the side of the house. No point in opening the cupboards. They were still locked. Nobody had been here since last night when Punt and I picked up Beau's scuba mouthpiece. I started to leave and return to my bicycle when I heard a tell-tale crunch. Whirling around, I saw a man half hidden by a palm tree.

At first I thought another neighbor had come to check on Beau's property, but chills playing along my arms and across my nape warned me of danger. I grabbed a deep breath, planning to call to Daisy French.

"Don't scream. Keep quiet."

I didn't recognize the guttural voice, and when the person stepped into full view, I understood why. A person wearing a hooded raincoat that blended with the cloudy day began approaching me. A nylon stocking covered his face and head. But nothing covered the pistol in his hand. His? His? It could be a woman. The androgynous outfit made it hard to tell.

"W-who, who are you?" I stuttered and my voice shook, revealing my fear. "What are you doing skulking around this house? You're trespassing on private property, and…"

"Shut up, woman," the voice ordered. "We're leaving this property right now. Together."

"The neighbors are watching. You won't get by with this— with whatever you're planning. Someone will see you and call the police."

My captor chuckled. "No. That won't happen. It's early and most of the neighbors are still at work." He held up a cell phone. "I called the French home the minute I recognized you. Told them their daughter had been injured. They're probably already on their way to the hospital. Come with me now and you won't get hurt. At least you won't get hurt right here."

A gun barrel prodding my ribs prompted my obedience. It surprised me that I managed to keep talking.

"I rode my bicycle here. In the morning, Mrs. French will think it strange to find it still padlocked to the palm. She'll connect the bike to the phony call about her daughter."

"We're taking the bike with us. Where's your key?" He held out a hand. "Give me the key."

I hesitated.

"Give me the key. Now." The gun prodded—harder this time—and the person pressed his body closer to mine and linked his left arm through my right arm. "See, we're old friends walking down the street on a dismal evening. Some people consider walking in the rain romantic. However, I'm not one of them. Hand over the bicycle key."

Now he was clutching my arm and twisting it behind my back. It had to be a man, didn't it? Even through my pain I realized a woman wouldn't have strength for both holding a gun and twisting an arm.

I wear my bicycle key on a lanyard around my neck. With my free hand I jerked it off and handed it to him.

"That's more like it, Keely. I thought I might be able to make you see things my way. Now come with me and we'll collect your bike."

"Someone will see us. I'll shout for help."

He nudged me with the gun again. "You think I won't shoot?"

"That's right. I think you won't. You wouldn't dare. You wouldn't dare risk revealing yourself. The sound of a gunshot would bring neighbors on a run." My words sounded phony even to my own ears and I knew he didn't believe me.

Walking side by side, we entered the front yard and headed toward my bicycle. I wondered how he'd manage to unlock it with a gun in his hand. I needn't have wondered.

"Unlock it," he ordered. "Right now." He chuckled. "You didn't think I'd risk doing it, did you? Unlock the bicycle."

I moved as slowly as I dared, dropping the key as if by accident, but I retrieved it, followed his orders, and unlocked the bike.

"Pull it into riding position," he said. "My car's parked around the corner. Place both hands on the handlebars and wheel it straight ahead and then around the first corner to your left. Forget about escaping. I'll have my gun trained on you every second. You try to ride away, and you're a dead woman."

Could this man be Slone Pierce? Had the TV announcer said Slone was under arrest? Or maybe he'd said the police were holding him for questioning. I wished I'd listened more carefully. Fear-driven thoughts raced through my mind. Why would Slone Pierce come after me? Maybe because Punt and Randy were off island and I was available? How I wished Punt and I had never gone to his house to talk to Nicole!

Again, I forced myself to recall safety rules from the past. Don't let him get you in a car even if he has a gun. Huh! I wondered how often that lecturer had run while someone held a gun to his ribs. Of course, if I tried to escape on my bike, I'd be a moving target and moving targets are hard to hit. I wondered if this man had practice in shooting at moving targets. And I wondered why all these crazy thoughts were rushing through the turmoil of my mind. I was about to be kidnapped, and who knew what else my captor had in mind—yet all I could think of were safety rules that wouldn't do me any good.

Talk, I told myself. Show some spunk. You talk to clients all day, so talk, now when your life depends on it.

"Why are you doing this?" I asked. "If you want something from the Ashford house, go back and take it. But let me go."

"I warned you not to nose into the Randy Jackson case. But you're a dumb broad. You didn't pay attention. Now you've caused me trouble."

"I really can't cause you any harm. I'm no detective. I'm no PI. If anyone gives you trouble it won't be me. It'll be the police who'll soon have information that'll bring the Randy Jackson case back into their thinking."

"You're wrong. You might say you're dead wrong. When the police find your body, they'll face a hot case that'll make them forget about a decades-old cold case."

"Cops may slide unsolved murders to a back burner, but they don't forget them. And in this case, they'll have Randy Jackson and his mother to remind them of Dyanne Darby."

"Hah! The news media will be screaming about the murder

of Keely Moreno. Or maybe I can think of some way to pull this off and make your death look like an accident—or a suicide."

"You're not that smart."

"I'm smart enough to want to get the police involved in a new homicide. I found a patsy to take my place in prison for twenty years, didn't I? I call that plenty smart."

"You won't get by with such a thing again."

"Of course I will. There are people on this island who think you should be doing a little jail time yourself."

"Nobody ever charged me with a crime." My whole body grew hot and I guessed how Randy must have felt when he heard himself accused of a murder he didn't commit.

"You may never have been charged with homicide. But that doesn't make people believe you're innocent. Many folks still wonder what Margaux Ashford might say if she could speak from the grave. And others wonder what Jude Cardell might have said if he'd had a chance to confront the police. Keely Moreno, if you should happen to die—accidentally—some folks would say, serves the broad right."

THIRTY

WHEN WE REACHED THE car, I thought it was the one that had hit me the night I'd been trying to find Gram's heart medicine, but I couldn't be certain. On a rainy day, gray cars tend to look alike. My captor kept his gun trained on me, and held a handlebar on my bike.

"Open the trunk," he ordered. He placed the key in my hand. "Open it. No funny stuff."

I opened the trunk, letting the key hang in the lock as the lid inched up.

"Now lift the bike inside the trunk."

"I can't. It's too heavy."

"Can't be much heavier than a bag of coffee beans now can it? Lift it front wheel first into the trunk."

So this guy knew I'd helped Gram lift bags of coffee beans. Where had he been hiding while he watched? And what other of my activities had he found interesting enough to monitor?"

"Do it now. Move."

The bicycle felt awkward—more awkward than heavy. I managed to get the front wheel onto the rim of the trunk, twist the handlebars and shove the front half into the storage space. After that, the seat and the rear tire slid in with only some hard shoving. I didn't know if I was gasping for breath from exertion or from fear. Maybe both.

"Now crawl in there with it." He grabbed my arm, forcing me closer to the trunk.

"There's not enough room. There's barely room to close the lid on the bicycle."

"These old Lincolns are known for their roomy trunks. Now

get in beside the bicycle and shut up." He goosed me with the gun barrel.

It took me a few moments to get into the trunk. A pedal bit into my shin, and I hit my head on the trunk lid hard enough to bring tears. But that was nothing compared to the head blow when he closed the trunk lid. I lay entwined with the bicycle, feeling blood running down my shin, feeling numb and nauseous from the blow to my head, wondering if the blow had broken my neck. But no. I could still move fingers and toes.

In moments the car started and we eased along the street. My stomach churned from the smell of gasoline and motor exhaust, but I managed to free one arm from its cramped position and grope for a trunk release lever. No luck. These old trunks had no safety devices.

I tried to keep track of our route, and from the traffic sounds around us, I knew when we reached the highway and turned toward Miami. We had gone only a short distance when the car made a sharp turn that butted my stomach against a bike pedal. I thought I might vomit, but I clamped my teeth against the rising gorge. Shortly after the turn, the car stopped, the driver's door slammed, the trunk popped open.

Is this where he planned to kill me? A storm howled around us and darkness blacked out the surroundings, leaving me with no idea of our location. Rain poured into the trunk. I closed my eyes and lowered my head. Would he shoot me in the trunk? No. Wouldn't want my blood on his car. The bike pedal scraped my shin again, but I lay beyond caring.

"Help me, you dumb butt. Push on that bike. Push and lift. We're dumping it. Nobody'll come nosing around this scrap heap anytime in the next few days—or weeks."

I heard a scraping as he jerked my ID tag from the bike.

"Even if anyone finds it, they won't be able to identify it. It won't take long for rain and salt air to turn it into a rust heap. Wish I could leave you right here beside it, Keely Moreno. That'd make my job easier. But finding your body would give the police too many clues. I'm taking you where nobody's likely to find you or your remains."

I wondered where that place might be, but I wasn't about to ask. A lot of crime takes place in the Keys. According to Punt, much of it's never reported. And the local police get so many missing-person reports they don't consider all of them emergencies. Kids run away from parents. Husbands run away from wives. Wives run away from husbands. But if I went missing, I knew there'd be a fuss. Gram. Punt. Consuela. My clients. There'd be a police search for me—or my body.

My captor managed to lift the bike from the trunk without my help. It clattered as if it hit concrete when he threw it down. Then turning quickly, he yanked me from the trunk. My legs were so cramped I could hardly stand, but he didn't expect or want me to stand. Pulling a bandana from his back pocket he folded it into a blindfold and tied it around my eyes. Then I heard tape peeling from a roll and he grabbed my wrists and taped them together. Once he finished that job and taped my ankles together, he lifted me and threw me back into the trunk.

He hadn't gagged me, but I lay in shock, unable to muster the energy to scream for help. He slammed the trunk lid shut and drove off, turning onto the highway and easing into traffic. How could I bear this! I couldn't see. I couldn't move my arms or legs. If I screamed nobody'd hear me.

Gram and I seldom leave Key West. Like many of the locals, we're content to stay where we're planted. But now I remembered my trip with Punt to Big Pine Key. I began to recall a ride to Marathon and Key Colony Beach last year, but so what? What good would remembering do? I couldn't recall more place names except Key Largo and then Homestead which really isn't a Key.

I wished I hadn't tried so hard to remember because now Punt's words replayed through my mind—words about a place were the deer refuge workers buried the deer that died or that had been killed in traffic. He said one time the police had found human bones mixed with the deer carcasses—bones that nobody ever claimed or identified. Was that where I was headed right now—the deer boneyard?

My head ached and I curled myself into a fetal position. All I wanted to do was to close my eyes and sleep. But no. I might be able to do something to save myself from this guy if I stayed awake—if I stayed alert. After a few minutes rain stopped pelting on the trunk lid. I could hear water hitting the underside of the car as we splashed through puddles, but the rain had stopped.

In a few seconds I heard that fact announced from a microphone. "Okay, folks. The rain's over and the night's young. Who's going to be the first one on the bull? Don't be shy. Step right up."

The voice faded into the distance, but I knew where we were. Ramrod Key. The Boondocks. Punt and I passed here on the way to talk to Shrimp Snerl. But where to now? When I felt our speed slow and remain slow, I remembered the night-time speed limit on Big Pine Key. So we were on the Key Deer Refuge. A national refuge. An area where cops strictly enforced the speed limits. I guessed we were traveling a bit below the thirty-five mph limit. My captor would take no chances of being pulled over for a traffic violation.

When the car stopped, I knew we'd reached the one traffic light between Big Pine Key and Marathon. Moving forward again, we took a left turn. Were we heading toward the road prison? The Blue Hole? Was there a place nearby where this guy might dump my body? I remembered the vast expanses of scrub palm and mangroves between the stop light and the Lion's Club. I also remembered desolate country with paths and trails going off the main road, trails that led into nothingness.

We drove on and on and on. I knew Big Pine Key was the largest of the keys in land mass, but surely it couldn't cover as many miles as we had traveled! For a while the road felt smooth, then suddenly we turned sharply to the right. We jounced and bumped over ground rough enough to blow out tires. Maybe this guy was blazing his own trail through the scrub brush. I braced myself against the top of the trunk with my bound hands and against one side of it with my feet.

At last the car stopped. I waited. Nothing happened. Maybe he planned to desert his car along with me? How long would it take someone to find a car with a body in the trunk? What if I screamed? Would there be anyone around to hear? Maybe I could work my hands loose, find a car tool, and beat on the inside of the trunk. Again, I wondered who would hear me.

At last the trunk lid popped and I felt a rush of cooler air. Taking his time, my captor unbound my ankles, but he left the tape on my hands and the blindfold in place.

"Get out."

I can't, I wanted to scream, but I didn't dare. If I couldn't get out of the trunk under my own steam, he might leave me there— forever. I flexed my fingers and my toes. I took some deep breaths.

"Get out. Now!"

From somewhere I found the strength to push myself across the bottom of the trunk, to reach for the side of the opening even with my hands still bound, and to pull myself to a sitting position. Then he grabbed my arm and hoisted me from the trunk to the ground. I sank to my knees with cramps in both legs, but he jerked me upright, not noticing that my blindfold had slipped askew.

I glimpsed a ray of moonlight playing across the rooftop of a small house in front of the car, then a cloud covered the moon, blacking out the area. He pushed me ahead of him to the house, unlocked the door, flung it open. Pulling a flashlight from his pocket, he shone it around the room, and then pushed me toward a bed and flung me down on it while he taped my ankles together again. I dreaded what might be coming next. How could I fight him off with my hands bound? His next words surprised me.

"You can call this your home away from home, Keely Moreno. The house has been vacated. The owners won't be returning this season. I'm leaving you for a while. But never fear. I'll be back."

"Where are you going?"

A slap in the face was my answer. My cheek smarted, but at least I lay on the bed and he couldn't knock me down.

"Don't try to escape. If you should be so unlucky as to get outside, you'll face wildlife. Raccoons, hungry raccoons. Deer. Snakes. Iguanas, wild and determined. Those big lizards can be treacherous. And alligators. There are lots of fresh-water holes in the thicket. A couple of 'gators live in each hole. And in addition to the animals, you could wander into poisonwood and manchineel trees. Natives used to tie a victim under a manchineel and let the sap drip on him. Ate flesh to the bare bone."

At last he left me alone, bound, partially blindfolded, and in the dark. Once he was gone, I knew that all the wildlife wasn't outside the house. Tiny footsteps scurried across the bare floor. Scurry. Scurry. No. I was not alone.

THIRTY-ONE

I BEGAN TRYING TO FREE myself from the tape that almost blocked the circulation to my fingers. I tried to pull my wrists apart with no success. My skin felt so tender I wondered if my wrists were bleeding. With great effort I raised my body to a sitting position. Once upright, I fumbled at my blindfold, and although I managed to jerk it from my eyes, the house was inky black. I could see nothing.

I tried to ignore the nauseating odor of duct tape while I dug my teeth into an edge of it that bound my wrists. After several minutes I felt it loosening and I spit gritty fragments from my tongue. After more struggling, I heard the tape rip apart. My fingers tingled as blood rushed to them. When I finished easing the tape from my wrists, I touched my skin. I felt no blood so I guessed I wasn't bleeding. I flexed my fingers until I could bend them easily before I ripped the tape from my ankles.

Sitting on the edge of the bed, I rubbed my wrists and then my ankles while I tried to work out a plan for coping with my predicament. When I stamped my feet to help restore circulation, the mice sounds ceased. Rat sounds? I tried to believe the creatures I'd heard scampering about were more frightened of me than I of them. I also tried to figure out what sort of house imprisoned me. Could this be someone's abandoned vacation home? If so, why had they abandoned it?

I managed to stand and pull the cell phone from my pocket. What good would it do to call 911 if I couldn't tell the dispatcher my location? Somewhere near Big Pine Key was too vague an answer to be helpful. No use to call Gram. She couldn't hear a hurricane once she dropped to sleep with her earplugs in place. Punt. I could call him and at least tell him I was safe for the moment.

I keyed in his number. Nobody answered. No voice asked me to leave a message. Maybe he didn't have his phone turned on. Maybe this. Maybe that. Lots of maybes, but I knew nobody would rescue me from this forsaken spot anytime soon. Maybe not anytime in my lifetime.

Forget that idea, Keely. Think positive. This's no time for negative thoughts.

Standing up, I took a few tentative steps. Since I'd been flung onto a bed, I tried to visualize a bedroom. I groped my way with hands outstretched until my fingertips touched a wall, then I followed the wall, walking around a dresser, a chest, a chair until I reached a doorway. I entered another room, and after more groping and feeling, I touched a table. Running my hands across its dusty top, I brushed into a candle—and near it a box of kitchen matches.

My fingers shook as I struck a match on the side of the box and blinked at the sudden flame. Never had sulphur smelled so good! I lit the candle, noting its stubbiness, knowing the flame would be short-lived. Holding the candle high, I studied my surroundings. Kitchen. Well, a kitchen of sorts. A wood-burning stove dominated one wall and an ice-box type refrigerator another... Wood stove? Ice box? Primitive! No wonder the owners bailed out. Maybe it had been some druggie's hideout rather than a visitor's vacation home.

I examined the walls and didn't see what I knew I wouldn't see— light switches. Electrical outlets. This house had no electricity.

"Who'd live in such a place?" I began talking to myself. Somewhere I'd read that only crazy people talked to themselves, but Gram sometimes talked to herself and she wasn't crazy. Right now my Keely-to-Keely conversation made me feel less abandoned and alone.

"Who would live in such a house as this?" That question kept replaying through my mind. "Was this was someone's fishing shack? Where would such a shack be located? Was there water close by?"

I asked, but nobody answered.

I remembered reading feature articles about No Name Key— human-interest articles, Punt called them. I racked my brain and details from some of the articles came to mind. A bridge separated No Name Key from Big Pine Key. No Name Key used to be a ferry stop for travelers in Marathon on their way to Key West. But that was long ago. The ferry had been obsolete for years. Today most people avoided No Name Key—unless they lived there, or unless they were tourists determined to catch a glimpse of a Key deer or enjoy a beer at No Name Pub before they trekked north.

Several of the articles had mentioned that many people who lived on No Name were reclusive types wanting little more than privacy. Every now and then the *Citizen* carried headlines about No Name residents taking a vote on whether to bring electricity, water, or telephone lines to their island. Some home owners would have welcomed modern conveniences, but the vote always came out negative and the residents continued to use electricity from their own generators and solar panels and water from their wells and cisterns.

Punt said he knew a couple of artists, brilliant creative types, who lived on No Name on a houseboat, home-schooled two kids and sent them off to college where they both earned graduate degrees. Did those kids ever return at holiday time to visit good old Mom and Dad? I tried to forget other tales—stories of people who'd disappeared and who'd last been seen on No Name. I also recalled newscasts about bodies found here and never claimed by next-of-kin. I didn't want my name on either of those lists.

I began searching for more candles, finding none. My stomach knotted when I realized I held the last bit of light I might see until morning. I used what remained of the lighted stub to explore.

The house consisted of three rooms—two bedrooms and this combination kitchen and dining room. No bathroom. What did I expect? Gold fixtures and a flush toilet? I guessed there must be a necessary house out back, but I didn't need it yet. Thank goodness. I tried both the outside doors. Locked. I found only five windows locked and shrouded with heavy cotton. I hesitated before pulling a drapery aside. What if someone saw the flicker from my candle and came to investigate? A person who enjoyed living in the seclusion of No Name Key might be more dangerous than the kidnapper who dumped me here.

No point in opening the draperies now. My watch hands pointed to midnight. I tried calling Punt again. Still no answer. I thought again about calling 911, but if I told the dispatcher I thought I might be on No Name Key, would she listen to me? Or would she think it a crank call keyed in by some jokester? But I'd feel super stupid if my captor returned and I hadn't tried to call for help.

I punched 911 on the keypad and I had to clear my throat twice before I could respond to the calm voice on the line.

"Where are you, miss?"

"I'm not sure. I may be somewhere on No Name Key. A man kidnapped me in Key West and drove me to this isolated place. I'm in a house—a shack. No electricity. No water. I'm calling you by candlelight and the stub's about to splutter out."

"Are you injured?"

"No. I was bound with duct tape, but I've worked myself free."

"What do you see around you outside?"

"I can't get outside. The doors and windows are locked. I peeked from behind a drapery into total darkness. No moon. No stars. Dark. I suppose I could break a window and escape, but then what? I don't know where I'd..." I gulped before I could continue. "...find any help." I didn't tell the woman I'd be scared to death to be outside with night creatures and trees that could drip poison.

"Stay where you are for the time being, Miss. We'll do what we can to find you using the information you've been able to provide. Give us your cell phone number please."

I gave her my number and she hung up. Stay where you are. The words echoed in my mind. As if I had a lot of choices. I walked to the ice box. No food. That didn't surprise me. People closing a house in the Keys seldom leave food. Too many cockroaches and rodents. Gram says that when humans abandon a house, even temporarily, wood rats living in nearby palms move in the next day. I searched the cupboard for food and had better luck there—a tin of crackers, a can of beans, a can of Coke.

Forget the beans. I couldn't find a can opener and I didn't want to waste candlelight by looking for one. I feasted on saltines, washing them down with Coke that must have lost its fizz sometime during the Ice Age. Food had never tasted so good. When exhaustion overtook me, I stretched out on the bed. After the candle wick hissed and died in a pool of melted paraffin, a waxy odor hung in the air. I didn't realize how much comfort that candle had offered until dark pressed in on me again. What if the kidnapper returned yet tonight? If he had murdered Dyanne Darby, a second murder might offer little challenge to his conscience.

Now with the candle out, I found my way to a window and opened the drapery. I saw nothing but blackness on the other side of the glass. I lay down on the bed again and tried to come up with some plan that might save me. I wondered what it would be like to live without fear, to feel sure that my life was going to count for something to someone.

If I died in this filthy place, Gram would be devastated. She might wonder if her genes held a contamination that caused her next of kin to be murdered. And the Ashfords—not just Punt, but the whole family that had helped me survive Jude Cardell. I couldn't let their faith in me die on No Name Key. I'd prided myself on being a survivor. I'd hang on—someway.

I tried to keep awake and on guard, to prod my brain into creating some life-saving idea, but I kept dozing and I slept fitfully until dawn began to turn the blackness into gray. My whole body ached from yesterday's sojourn in the car trunk as well as from hours on this hard bed.

I tried calling Punt again and my whole being went on red-alert when he answered. My need to talk to him tangled my thought and my words until I paused to sort them out.

"Where are you, Keely? What's the problem?"

This time I forced myself to talk slowly when I repeated the happenings in my life from yesterday afternoon until this morning. How, I wondered, could so much have taken place in so short a time?

"You've no idea who the guy is or where he went?"

"No idea at all. I've looked through the window and I don't see any sign of human habitation anywhere near. I only see scrub thicket. I think I may be on No Name Key."

"That's probably a good guess. I don't know of any other place that has areas as isolated as this one you describe. Here's what I want you to do. Call 911 again and repeat your story. I'll also call 911 and confirm your story so they'll get on the ball with their search. I'm coming to find you, but you're going to have to be outside where I can see you. And carry a pillow case or a towel with you so you'll have something to wave overhead to attract attention."

"I'm locked in."

"Be real, Keely. Heads up! Break a window. And be quick about it. It's time for a serious reality check. That guy could return any time. Take a chair, smash the window pane, and crawl through the opening. Now that it's daylight, get as far from the house as you can. Look for a clearing, stand in it. If you see the kidnapper returning, duck into the thicket. I'm going to rent a helicopter and come looking for you."

"A helicopter? Do you know how to fly…"

"I'll rent a pilot along with the chopper. No point in driving. You'll be easier to spot from the air. I'll be there as soon as I can. Now get out of that house and hide—in plain sight, of course. Don't be afraid—well be afraid if you can't help it, but don't panic. That's the important thing. Don't let fear throw you into a panic."

"I'm not afraid," I lied. "And I won't panic. You be careful, Punt. Remember, this guy has a gun."

"I'll keep that in mind. I love you, Keely. Don't forget that."

Punt broke our connection before I could tell him I loved him, too. I'd make that up to him later. Right now I had to forget about wild animals and manchineel trees and get out of this house. I saw no pillowcase. My head had been on a dirty pillow ticking. Yuck! Now was no time to be worrying about hygiene. I was alive, wasn't I? For right now, that was enough and I wanted the condition to last a long time.

In the kitchen I found a tattered towel before I rushed to the window and peered outside. What did manchineel trees look like? Did they have thorns? Three-leaf clusters? Smooth bark? Shaggy bark? I decided to avoid touching any kind of tree I didn't recognize. That meant none except palms, sea grape, and mangrove. My experience with trees is limited.

I picked up a straight-backed kitchen chair then set it down again while I stuffed some crackers into my pockets, taking care not to smash my phone or miniature tape recorder. Again I picked up the chair and approached a window, closing the drapery across it so glass shards wouldn't fly everywhere when I smashed the pane. After grabbing a deep breath, I gave the window a whack with a chair leg.

The glass remained intact. Maybe I wouldn't be able to use the drapery for padding. I whacked again, this time at the bare pane, and I jumped back when I heard the glass break. Some of it fell outside the window and some inside, and slivers of it still hung in the window frame. Removing a shoe, I knocked the slivers from the frame and put my shoe back on.

I'd started to lift one foot through the opening when I saw the iguana and froze in place. This creature looked nothing like Maxine's pet. It looked as if it might be the granddaddy of all iguanas. It had the dragon-like head, but its body was mostly a gray-brown shade instead of green, and dark gray bands ringed its super-long tail. An orange-colored pouch on its throat throbbed. In. Out. In. Out. I shuddered. The biggest difference between this creature and Lavonna lay in its size. It was super huge and it didn't look as if might go away anytime soon. In fact, it seemed very curious about me as it inched toward the broken window, lifting its head and snorting through its nose.

THIRTY-TWO

BEFORE I HAD TIME TO retreat from the window and search for some sort of a weapon to discourage the iguana, my phone rang. The creature rose and placed its forepaws on the windowsill as if it might try to climb inside the house.

"Keely," Punt said. "I thought of another thing that might help me find you. You might…" His voice faded away as my phone battery died. Frantically, I tried to call him back. No luck. Now I felt totally alone and abandoned and threatened by the iguana. And I needed the outhouse.

I looked again at the window and I thought for a moment the iguana had gone away. But no. When I peered outside I saw it sitting in a patch of weak sunshine right beneath the window.

"Scat! Shoo!" I yelled at the creature and leaned out the window to snap the towel at it.

No response.

"Hello, buddy." I tried softening my voice and smiling at him, but he didn't smile back, nor did he make any sound at all. But that was better than the snorting I'd heard earlier.

Do iguanas bite? When I'd asked Maxine, she'd said they bite veggies and she'd given Lavonna lettuce. I hoped biting humans wasn't one of their favorite pastimes. I knew they could climb. What if this one looked inside again then decided to climb through the window? He might be searching for food and view me as his next snack. Or maybe he was merely surprised to see me and curious about my appearance.

Finding a pan and a spoon, I returned to the window and played that pan like a bass drum. The sudden noise breaking the morning silence shocked me as well as the iguana and it took off, heading for the thatch palms at the side of the house. Once I felt sure the creature wouldn't return, at least for the moment, I crawled through the window and stood on the porch, pan and spoon at the ready, assessing my situation. Not good. I wondered how long this thicket had been encroaching on the house. But at least the rain had stopped and the sun was shining. I'd almost forgotten yesterday's downpour.

The outhouse! Where was it? I stepped from the porch and staying close to the house, I walked toward the back door, watching for the iguana with each step. A short distance behind the house I saw a small shed, complete with a half moon opening carved in the door that hung open on rusty hinges to reveal—a two-holer. Tentatively, I poked my head inside the shed then backed off, brushing at a web that clung like sticky threads to my face and neck. In the next instant, a brown spider scurried across the splintered bench to a hiding place inside one of the holes. I gave up all thought of using the two-holer and relieved myself behind the shed, one ear alert for sounds of the iguana and the other ear alert for any sound of my captor returning. What if he came back for me? What did he want? What would he do?

After returning to the front of the house, I stooped to examine the tire tracks in the mud near the front door. Had I been a true detective I'd have taken a picture of those tracks or perhaps preserved them in a plaster cast. Too bad I'd forgotten to bring a camera or plaster-of-Paris with me. A hiding place. That's the thing I needed most now. If I stayed right here, my kidnapper might return at any moment to do whatever he planned to do. If I disappeared into the thicket I might have to face the iguana, or perhaps some of its near relatives. I hated all my options. Had it been a multiple choice test, I'd have checked "none of the above." But at least the iguana toted no gun.

I stepped into the thicket at the front of the house, walking in the muddy tire tracks, and planning to follow them to the larger road we'd traveled last night. But how dumb! If the guy returned, that's the route he'd probably use. And he might see me before I could take cover. I stepped into a growth of scrub pines at the side of the tire tracks to rethink my escape, and I froze in place when I heard something near me. Branches broke and dried sawgrass taller than my shoulder swayed against a backdrop of sky. Iguana? Alligator?

I held my breath, every muscle tense, until I saw the intruder. A Key deer had stepped into the underbrush, turned, and now stood looking at me with Bambi eyes. I relaxed, glad to see a deer instead of an iguana.

"Hello there, Bambi." I approached the deer, no taller than a Great Dane or a Boxer, and it didn't run. Maybe it wasn't as frightened as I'd first thought. Pulling a cracker from my pocketed cache, I held it toward the deer's nose.

"Bambi want a cracker?" The creature sniffed the cracker, then showed total lack of interest.

The deer's protective coloring made it hard to see against the growth surrounding it. Did deer attack intruders? This one seemed docile. It had no antlers, so an attack seemed unlikely. A doe. It acted unafraid and that told me it might be trying to hold my attention so I wouldn't notice its fawn hiding nearby. I peered around, seeing no fawn.

I walked closer to the doe, but it didn't run until I reached to touch it, and I never did see a fawn anywhere. But in the next moment I discovered a raccoon, in fact I saw three raccoons—a mother and two babies. They sat a few feet to one side of me staring with eyes like polished chips of black coral. I hoped they were ready to retreat instead of attack. All three looked scrawny and their coats were scraggly as this thicket they called home. No wonder. What could they find to eat in such brushy country?

Again, pulling a cracker from my pocket, I tossed it toward them and the mother pounced upon it. Then I tossed two more crackers, hoping each of her offspring would take one and go its way, leaving me to go mine, even though I had no idea of where my way might lead me. Raccoons always washed their food before eating, didn't they? I'd read that somewhere. Ahh! A plan.

"Let's go, gang. Let's wash those crackers." I called to them and stamped my foot, hoping they'd take off toward water. There had to be fresh water around here somewhere. Punt said fresh water enticed the deer and alligators that hung out on Big Pine. There were sink holes that held rain water, and abandoned construction sites sometimes had gravel pits that filled with fresh water. Where there was water, there might also be boats and people. These raccoons could lead me to safety and maybe freedom.

Then I rethought that plan. The raccoons might lead me to water, but any people who lived near that water might not be eager to meet an intruder with a wild tale like mine.

Knowing it was too soon to expect Punt to be flying overhead looking for me, I took consolation in the hope that the Monroe County police might have begun a search. My best plan might be to follow Punt's suggestion, to start looking for a small clearing where he or anyone else flying over could see me. So that's what I did, stopping every few feet and looking behind me to make sure no iguanas or alligators were following.

I walked a long distance, beating my way through the under-brush, before I found a clearing of any kind. I could only hope that none of the trees I'd brushed against were manchineel. So far my skin neither itched or burned. Instead of being on a knoll, the clearing lay in a slight hollow where I'd be hard to see. So far I hadn't noticed anyone out looking.

Fear, worry, and no sleep had left me exhausted and I sat on the ground to rest, planning to stand up and wave the towel the minute I heard a plane or helicopter overhead. I rested my head on my knees, forgetting about any bugs, rodents, or animals that might be near.

"Mustn't doze. Mustn't doze." I repeated the words like a mantra under my breath. I needed to sleep, yet I knew I had to keep alert if I expected to live, to be rescued.

"Don't doze. Keep alert." I changed the mantra and tried to keep track of how many times I'd repeated it. I'd counted more or less to five hundred when I heard a car approaching. I stopped talking as if someone might hear me above the crunching of tires against the ground cover.

I eased farther from the sound of the car, taking care not to send the brush around me swaying overhead and thus alert the driver to my location. Stopping, I peered between palm fronds as an ancient Lincoln passed only a few feet from my hiding place. In that moment I realized that humans could be the most dangerous animals of all.

Ace Grovello! Not Slone. Not Gus. Ace Grovello sat behind the wheel of that Lincoln. There was no doubt in my mind that he'd come back to kill me and bury my body where it might never be discovered. How I wished someone would fly over right now and see him, capture him, hold him for questioning. Questioning for what? Trespassing? Officials probably had never enacted laws against driving off the beaten path on No Name Key. In fact, I wasn't even sure I stood on No Name. Police might be searching on No Name while I stood hiding out in some dangerous spot I'd never heard of.

Ace Grovello. My mouth and throat grew so dry I could hardly swallow. And to think that a few days ago I had massaged the toes of this man who was trying to kill me! To think that Punt and I had sat in his tropical courtyard and talked to him as if he were a rational human being! I wondered what Consuela would think if she knew what I had discovered about Ace. Surely he was the man who had murdered Dyanne Darby. Had he also shot Nicole Pierce? My mind balked at the thought of being near a sociopath who could murder and then hide his deed while another took the rap. How could he have let Randy rot in jail for over twenty years while he owned and managed a successful business, associated with friends, slept with the likes of Consuela?

I sat down, determined that Ace Grovello would never find me in this thicket. He'd look in the house, maybe even in the outhouse, but all he would see would be the broken window. The iguana wouldn't talk, nor the deer, nor the raccoons. I heard the car stop, the door slam. Then nothing. I willed steel into my spine. I'd let the wild creatures scare me and now Ace Grovello frightened me, too. Fear was an upfront choice, but I mustered courage and refused to panic.

A silence fell around me like no silence I'd ever experienced. Where had Ace gone? After a while I stood, knowing I needed to be quiet yet be on my feet, alert and ready to run, if necessary. Ace outweighed me by many pounds, but I remembered his flabby belly and thought I might be able to outrun him if I had to. Maybe I could even follow the trail of flattened thicket that the car had knocked down. That was a plan. Maybe I should have mentioned that to Punt, but surely he'd think of it. And so would the police. But they'd also know that such a plan would make it easier for Ace to find me and perhaps find me before they did. If I followed the trail Ace's car had made, it might lead back to a main road of some sort. But what then? No point in trying to plan too far ahead. I'd have outsmarted myself if I ended up on a road where Ace could pick me up again. Don't panic. Don't panic. I repeated this new mantra and it helped clear my mind.

I began planning how to move more deeply into the thicket and away from Ace and the house. That's when I heard a great thrashing through the thicket and Ace called my name.

"Give up, Keely. Give up or I'll shoot."

I ran and two shots rang out. One zinged past my head and I heard another shot hit a tree. My heart pounded and my chest felt as if it had been freeze-wrapped in hot iron. I kept running. I'd rather die from a bullet than from whatever else Ace might plan for me. Two more shots rang out. I kept running.

THIRTY-THREE

THE SHOOTING STOPPED. Had he run out of bullets? Or did he think someone else might come to investigate the sound of the shots? I stopped running, knowing any noise I made would clue him to my whereabouts. But any sound he made would clue me to his location, so I guess that made us even on the sound-and-clue scale if not on the gun-and-bullet scale. I wondered if he could hear my gasping breaths knot in my throat.

Ace's next crashing through the thicket again took me by surprise. He came at me from the left rather than from behind where I'd been expecting to see him. When I tried to run again, I caught my foot in a root and fell. Terror squelched my breathing, and panic spread like a boiling liquid coating my stomach. I didn't try to get up. But I didn't need to. In the next second, Ace jerked me to my feet. I almost fell against him, I felt so panicked and helpless, but I jerked as far from him as I could when I felt his gun barrel prodding my ribs.

"So you managed to escape from the house, you bitch. I should have used more tape."

He twisted my arm until I sank to my knees in pain. Again, he jerked me to my feet. I felt like a doomed puppet on a short string—Ace Grovello's string. What if he broke my arm?

"I should have offed you last night, given you no chance to get away."

"So why didn't you?" I spoke through lips I could barely move as I sensed a need to keep him talking, although I couldn't imagine what good talking would do other than to delay my demise. I gritted my teeth to keep from screaming in pain when he tightened his grip on my arm.

"I'm a first class thinker—an ace-in-the-hole planner," Ace said. "That's how I earned my nickname. Last night I didn't have my long-range plans firmly in mind."

"You seem to have them well enough in mind today."

"Or course. You can depend on that. But last night you surprised me. I hadn't expected to see you sneaking around Beau's house. I'd gone there looking for Punt."

"I wasn't sneaking. I'd gone there by request."

"Sneaking? By request? What does it matter? I'd known I needed to get you out of my life ever since I learned you and Maxine were talking about the Darby murder. Then when you and Punt came to my place asking for a DNA specimen, I knew I had to act quickly, to stop your prying before it went any farther. I had to make long-range plans, and I couldn't afford to leave any clues."

"Clues that might link you to a second or third murder—or maybe to multiple murders?" I thought of Punt and Maxine and Randy. Would Ace risk more murders? An inner voice told me this man lacked a conscience and would risk anything to save his own skin.

Ace released my arm then grabbed my hand and bent my thumb back until I whimpered in pain.

"I needed time to make careful plans. Sometimes I think better with a few beers under my belt, so I stopped at No Name Pub. Always a mob scene there at night. Nobody'd notice seeing me, except the bartender. Nobody else'd recognize me or remember me."

I jerked my hand free, and although he grabbed my arm, he didn't twist it. "So you planned my murder over a few beers."

"Too many beers. Too many chasers." Ace winced and for the first time I realized he had a hangover. Maybe I could figure out a way to use his muddled head to my advantage.

"A big guy like you let a few beers change your plans?" I massaged my thumb although I hated to let him know he'd hurt me.

"I pulled off the road into a thicket and slept in the car until morning. But now I've thought this thing through. I know exactly what I've got to do. I'll take care of you first and the others later. Like I said, I should have done you last night."

I didn't ask what he planned. I knew. I didn't have to find ways to keep him talking. He spoke sotto voce and in a monotone as if he were alone and speaking to himself. He pulled me along beside him as we tramped through the scrub.

"Nobody's likely to find your body any time soon. Or to connect me with your death. Even if anyone should find you, your body will be in such bad shape that no medical examiner will be able to determine the time of death."

Time of death. Time of death. The words screamed through my mind, drowning out the background sound of our crunching through the thicket. Only when his monotone stopped did I force myself to speak again.

"Why did you kill Dyanne Darby? Why?"

Ace looked at me and shook his head. "The dumb broad laughed at me. Laughed at me! Said she was going out with Randy Jackson. I asked why she'd want to date such a nobody when she could go out with me. She said they'd made the date weeks ago. Said I was a fool for thinking I could walk in at the last minute and find her waiting. I promised her dinner at the Rooftop Café and dancing afterward. She laughed again and that's when I decided to teach her that broads don't laugh at Ace Grovello. She'd laughed her last laugh. I felt justified. What kind of a man would let a broad talk to him like that! I was justified."

I could hardly believe it. This man had killed a woman for wounding his ego. "And Nicole Pierce? Did she laugh at you, too?"

"She was threatening to recant her testimony about seeing Jackson leave Dyanne's apartment. She was a loose cannon. I wasn't about to let the police start looking for some other killer. I had to get rid of her. And now you make number three. Nobody's going to come here looking for you."

"You can't be sure of that," I said. "You're just guessing. Important people in Key West know that Punt Ashford and I've been trying to find Dyanne Darby's killer."

"So what. Trying and succeeding are two different things entirely."

"We've given colleagues our list of suspects and you're high on that list. If I disappear, Punt Ashford will see that all the old-time *Atocha* divers rate the full attention of the police."

"I'm telling you that your body won't be found for months." Ace snorted. "Try to get that through your thick head. Your body may never be found where I plan to hide it. True, you may be listed as a missing person, but it's hard for the courts to build a murder case when they have no dead body and no murder weapon."

Now we'd reached Ace's car and the house where I'd spent the night. I didn't want to ask, but I couldn't hold back the question. "And where is this special hiding place?"

Ace had loosened his grip on my arm and for a moment I thought I might be able to jerk free and run. But run to where? He still had his gun. Could I wrest it free from his grip, demand the car keys, and drive myself away from here? For a few seconds my dream of escape blocked out the sound of his voice, but when he nudged me with the gun barrel, I heard his words clearly.

"I'm going to drop you into the old well behind the house— an abandoned well. Folks around here have no organized-by-the-county water system. Oh, water's piped down from Miami, but it goes to well-organized communities along Highway One— Largo, Marathon, Key West. Water's never been piped to No Name Key. Families here depend on wells or cisterns."

"But that's going to change. Monroe County owners of old wells, cisterns, and septic tanks will soon be ordered to fill them in, to make way for a new water and sewer system. A body in a well will be discovered."

"Dream on! The new septic system plan's mousemilk— smoke and mirror politics. Oh, I suppose it might happen sometime in the next half century. Officials blew lots of hot air about ousting the live-aboards on houseboat row in Key West like they'd have them gone the next day." Ace chuckled. "Took 'em over thirty years to legally force them to rent slips at Garrison Bight. And now they're starting on the live-aboards around Boot Key Harbor. It'll be years before No Name gets a sewer system."

I knew Ace was right. Even now there are a couple of house-boats still lashed to Key West's city bulkhead. Changes never take place quickly in the Keys. Nothing happens fast. That's the way people want it. That's why they choose to live here. And that's what Ace was depending on—that due to political delays, nobody would ever find my body.

I watched a vulture drift on an updraft. "Punt Ashford will have the police on your trail very quickly if I turn up missing. You might even have to beg for police protection if Randy Jackson gets involved in searching for me. Randy's an angry man—and you know why."

"Even if your body's found and identified, and the time of death established, the bartender at No Name Pub will give me an alibi. The other barflies may not remember me, but the bartender will. He'll remember me as the Big Tipper from Big Pine Key. That's where I told him I lived. The No Name Pub's gonna be one of my favorite places for the next few months. Now come with me."

Another nudge with the gun barrel assured Ace of my obedience. He shoved me along as he started around the side of the house. I wondered if iguanas frightened him. Maybe if that big iguana appeared suddenly…or maybe a deer would jump into our path. Maybe a surprise would confuse him. But no iguana appeared. No raccoon family either. And no deer or alligator. I swallowed those faint hopes of delay. What chance would critters have against his gun!

Before we reached the outhouse, Ace stopped and studied the ground as if memorizing it for future reference. Then he nudged me with his gun, pushed me forward.

"There it is. The underbrush has grown up around the concrete square that marks the well opening. But it's there as I remembered it."

In my mind, I had pictured a well as an upright structure of coral rock or brick with a roof protecting its opening from the elements. Where was the pump, or if no pump, where was the windlass and a bucket that could be winched to and from the water?

Ace forced me closer to the concrete square. "There it is under that rotting wood." He pointed at the well with his gun barrel.

I gasped. Not only did I see the low-lying slab of concrete that marked the well, but I also saw the snake coiled on the well cover. Ace tossed a stick at the snake, but instead of uncoiling and easing away on snake business, the creature raised its head, and in undulating S shapes, it slithered toward us, rattlers rattling.

"A timber rattler." Ace backed off as he stated the obvious. "Poisonous as they come. Okay, Keely. Get a stick and prod our uninvited visitor aside. Once you've done that, we'll open the well and see if it still holds water."

I hesitated, wondering if I could find a stick long enough to reach the snake without allowing it to reach me with its fangs. Did snakes jump? Or did they just scare a person to death by slithering?

"Get a stick. Now. Or maybe I should push you closer to the rattler and let nature take its course. If you die from rattler venom, nobody can claim you were murdered."

I forced myself to keep talking. "People finding my body here might wonder why I came to No Name Key to play with snakes."

"Find a stick. Get a strong one."

Most of the thatch palm branches were too tough for me to break off, but I found a dead limb that had fallen from an Australian pine. I picked it up, but by the time I turned around, the snake had departed. Some of my panic left me although I don't know why. Would I rather die from a snake bite or from drowning? Some choices!

"You lucked out that time," Ace gave an evil chuckle. "But once I open the well hatch, you're a goner."

He shoved me ahead of him until we stepped onto the concrete slab. "Don't think for a second that I'm going to make myself vulnerable by stooping to lift that cover. That's your job, Ms. Moreno. Do it. Now. I want to see into that water and I know you do too. Could be anything down there. Water bugs. Recluse spiders. Even water snakes. Open it."

I still had the stick in my hand, so I used it to shove the rotting cover aside.

For a few moments we both stood peering into the black water. Bricks lined the inside of the well and the water surface lay at least ten feet below us. Water bugs and spiders skittered about.

I could almost feel Ace's hands on my back pushing me toward my death.

THIRTY-FOUR

I HAD ONLY ONE SHOT at this ploy—and a renewed determination to live. In spite of my inner journey, my effort to forgive Jude, I'd almost let his aura force me again into the role of victim. No way. I corked thoughts of failure and zoomed into a win-win mode. Turning to face Ace, I looked up at him and held his gaze while I lifted my right foot and then slammed it against his instep. He yelped, jerked his injured foot up, and teetered off balance just long enough for me to shove him through the well opening.

Kerplunk! He hit the water and surfaced bellowing and splashing.

Stepping back from the well rim, a wave of relief flooded through me and I grabbed a deep breath. I heard nothing except his shouts, his spluttering that echoed against brick and rose from a safe distance.

"Bitch!" he screamed. "Bitch! You'll pay for this. You'll …"

Did he still have his gun? Do guns work if they're wet? I peered cautiously into the well, my whole body shaking from excitement and fear. No gun. I did a double take when I saw him standing—with no gun. The water measured neck deep, and he stood wiping moisture from his face and eyes. A spider clung to his left ear lobe, but he didn't seem to notice—yet.

I had expected to see him dog paddling to keep his head above the surface. In a way it relieved me to see him standing. I'd hate to be responsible for killing someone, drowning another person, even in self-defense. Once I reached help, I'd tell the police where to find Ace and let him try to talk himself out of a kidnapping charge along with two murder charges.

My hands stopped shaking, but my heart still pounded. It

took me a few more moments to realize that I had Ace Grovello where I wanted him—at my mercy. I pulled my mini–tape recorder from my pocket and turned it on. Maybe I could top off this triumph by getting a taped confession for the police.

"Ace, what did you hope to gain by killing me? Didn't you realize the authorities would find you out sooner or later?"

No response.

"Ace, how about telling me exactly what happened between you and Dyanne Darby."

"You dumb bitch!" Ace spluttered and slapped at the spider that had begun crawling into his ear canal. "You think I don't know you want to record a confession. Well, that'll never happen. Not here. Not today. Never. Save your little tape machine for your patients' complaints."

"The law might go easier on you if you confessed to the Darby murder, if you confessed to threatening me and Maxine Jackson to keep us from investigating, if you confessed to kidnapping me from Beau Ashford's yard. And what about Nicole Pierce? I'm betting you shot her." I enjoyed taunting him. "They say confession's good for the soul, Ace. How about it?"

I gasped when Ace disappeared. Maybe he'd suffered a seizure. Heart attack. Stroke. Maybe I had killed a man after all. But no. In the next instant his head broke the surface and he brandished the gun in his right hand. I backed off. Do guns work after they've been submerged? I backed off even farther.

"I'm leaving now, Ace. I'm heading for help—Punt, the police, anyone. Want a last chance to confess?"

"You bitch."

"I sympathize with your poverty of vocabulary, Ace."

"Bitch!"

"After I'm rescued I'm coming back here with the police. Don't disappoint me. Don't go away. You wouldn't do that, would you?"

I left the well site and the house with Ace still shouting about a female canine, and I followed our footsteps back to his car. I looked to each side, ready to run in case an iguana or a raccoon might be lurking nearby. Hey! The car! Maybe I could drive away from this horrid place.

I yanked the car door open and slid under the steering wheel. Wishful thinking. No key hung in the ignition. Key West living has taught us locals never to leave car keys lying around—especially never in an ignition. So much for my escape-by-car idea.

I left the Lincoln. Stepping behind it, I began following the trail it had made through the thicket. Ace's two arrivals and one departure had left flattened scrub brush. Walking over the trail required less energy than making a fresh path, and surely Ace's route would lead to a road. All the time I walked, I kept looking for a clearing where I might stand and be seen by searchers flying overhead. But I saw none.

A lumpy black snake slithered across my path. I looked carefully at its tail. No rattlers. Maybe its inner lumps marked breakfast rats. I didn't panic. Maybe I was beyond panic. I wondered what lay beyond panic. Craziness? I hoped I wasn't cracking up. When someone found me, I wanted to be able to tell them a straight story about what had happened to me. I didn't want to jabber like an idiot. I wanted to be able to lead the police to that well and to Ace.

I counted to a hundred to make sure I could make my mind obey. Then I said the alphabet forward and backward. Backward alphabets are hard to say, but I think I got it right. Those exercises kept me from thinking about Ace. But only for a while. Once I thought about him again, my mind whirled. There was a possibility he could escape from the well. Maybe he could find toe holds, hand holds, in the crevices between the bricks and climb out. Or maybe he could press his back against the wall, stretch his feet forward far enough to brace himself against the opposite wall and wiggle his body up, over, and out. I realized I should have pulled the well cover back into place and weighted it down with something—a rock, something from the house, anything heavy. Too late for that now.

The hum of a motor overhead shook me from my morbid thoughts about Ace and the possibility of his escape. I scanned the sky until I saw the helicopter.

"Here! Here!" I shouted, knowing the pilot couldn't hear me

above the noise of his motor. But shouting, the sound of my voice, offered release. "Here! Here!" I'd lost the towel I'd taken from the house when Ace appeared.

I jumped up and down and waved my arms, but the pilot didn't see me. The helicopter flew on past. Was that pilot blind? Couldn't he see the smashed-down trail the car had left? I stood still, hoping to hear the motor again, hoping to see the pilot return. No. That didn't happen. Not then. But after a few more moments, I heard the motor again. This time I hoisted a fallen palm frond and waved it above my head until I thought my arms might break from its weight.

I dropped the branch when I saw the helicopter turn and begin flying low over the area. Again, I jumped and waved, and this time I could see Punt's face at a window. He waved back, but the copter turned away again. No safe place to land, I guessed. Too many trees. Too much scrub brush. I dropped down, deflated, defeated.

Then the copter turned again and flew in lower. I saw something falling from it. A long rope. A harness. Punt and the pilot planned to haul me up.

I couldn't cope.

I didn't have the strength to hang on to a rope or slip into a harness.

I'd fall.

But in spite of my negative thoughts, I jumped up and leaped to grab the rope when the copter flew low. I couldn't work my body into the harness, but I managed to hold on to the rope.

I thought of the vendors at Smathers who sold parasailing rides to tourists. I remembered pictures of marines parachuting into Iraq. I had no parachute. I hung dangling from the end of a rope that I might lose my grip on at any moment. But I managed to cling to it until I felt Punt and a helper tugging me up, up, up.

At last Punt, lying flat and leaning over the edge of the copter doorway, managed to get his hands under my arms and tug me to safety.

"Are you okay?" Punt shouted into my ear as I lay there on my stomach panting and speechless.

I could only nod. It took lots of inner fortitude to hold back tears of panic and exhaustion mixed with relief and joy and to give a weak smile of thanks to the copter pilot and Punt's helper. Motor noise made talking impossible, so we didn't try for conversation until we touched down near a kayak and boat rental business at the fishing camp between No Name and Big Pine.

After thanking the copter pilot and helper, Punt and I waved them goodbye and watched them lift off and head toward Miami.

"Oh, Punt! You've saved my life!" I didn't ask him how I could thank him. "There's an abandoned house hidden in the thicket on No Name. And Ace's trapped there in a well behind the house."

"Drowned?"

"No. Wet and very much alive and angry. And he has a gun—a loaded gun. He had it in his hand when he hit the water. Then he dropped it, but he ducked under the surface and came back up with it. Will a wet gun work?"

"That depends."

The arrival of a police car interrupted Punt's explanation of what the workings of a wet gun might depend upon.

"How'd they get here so fast?"

"I called them from Miami and then called them again from the copter when we spotted you. Also called your gram to tell her you're alive. I knew she'd be frantic when she found you missing last night. Also asked her to call Maxine."

Two officers stepped from the police car—Jeff and Hillie. Jeff's face had flushed to match his red hair. He reminded me of a coiled spring straining for release. Hillie ran his hand over his balding head, looking as laid back as Sunday morning. I wondered how those two managed to work together without driving each other crazy.

Jeff invited us into their car where we sat for a few minutes while I gave a synopsis of my kidnapping and lockdown in the abandoned house. I had barely finished my story when a gray Ford approached and parked alongside us. Again wearing his Hog's Breath Saloon T-shirt, Randy sat hunched behind the wheel with Maxine in the passenger seat and Gram seated behind them. I gasped and reached for Punt's hand.

"How'd Randy know where to find us? The shrimping job didn't work out?" I whispered the questions as if to verbalize them might be a bad omen. Randy slipped a plug of Skoal into his mouth and as he began chewing, the scar on his cheek blazed red.

THIRTY-FIVE

WHEN I STARTED TO LEAVE the police car and rush to Gram, Hillie shook his head.

"Stay where you are."

Punt put his arm around my shoulders, gently restraining me. I settled for smiling at Gram and blowing her a kiss.

"What's Randy doing here?" I perched on the edge of the seat. "How did he find us so quickly?" The officers were busy talking and arguing with Randy, giving Punt and me a chance to exchange a few more words.

"Your grandmother reported your disappearance to the police late yesterday afternoon, and this morning Maxine caught the missing-person news on her police scanner. She drove by for Celia and then she picked Randy up at the shrimp docks because he called to tell her the *Midnight Moon* was docking early. They had a full load, and Shrimp Snerl hired Randy for another run. More information from Maxine's scanner led the three of them here."

"I want to follow you to that well!" Randy shouted to Jeff. "I want to eyeball Ace Grovello. Eyeball to eyeball! I want to hear what he has to say for himself."

"We want no trouble out there," Jeff said. "None. Miss Moreno's been through a harrowing experience. We want to assure her safety—and the safety of all of us."

Randy chewed his tobacco for only a moment before he continued his argument. "I rotted in prison for Dyanne Darby's murder for years while Ace Grovello lived high, building an I'm-On-Easy-Street business and a Mr. Nice Guy reputation. I've got a citizen's right to see that scumbucket now. Right now."

"Mr. Jackson," Jeff said, "as of this moment, Ace Grovello has been neither charged nor convicted of a crime. In the eyes of the law he's innocent until proven guilty. As policemen we are responsible for his safety—and for yours."

Randy pounded the steering wheel with the heel of his hand. "So what're you going to do to him right now? What're you going to say to him? You gonna lift him gently from the well and suggest that he have a nice day? Too bad he didn't drown and save the taxpayers a bundle of trouble and money. Tell me what you're going to do when you reach that well."

"Calm down, Mr. Jackson. We'll arrest Grovello, cuff him, read him his rights. We don't need your help at this time. Maybe later if …"

"Please, officer," Maxine broke into the conversation by opening the car door. She stepped from the Ford, revealing her tank top and blue and white polka dot bloomers, her red-and-white-striped stockings. "I'll guarantee my Randy's good behavior. Please let us go along with you. We'll cause no problem. We're friends of Keely Moreno. We want to see Ace Grovello in handcuffs. It'd purely set our corks a-bobbin'."

Both officers smiled at Maxine's earnest expression, her homespun language and appearance. "Mrs. Jackson," Jeff said, "I guess seeing this guy cuffed and in custody might set our corks a-bobbin', too. He's certainly put Miss Moreno through a bad time. Follow us. But when we arrive at the abandoned house and well, you are to remain in your car. Is that clear?"

"Crystal clear, sir." Maxine slid back inside the car beside Randy and Gram reached to pat her on the shoulder.

We entered the bridge to No Name Key where fishermen flung lines into the waves while pelicans perched on the bridge railing, watching and waiting for a tidbit. Once off the bridge, we followed the concrete road a short distance then turned onto a lane that led into the thicket and then disappeared into the growth of mangrove and thatch palm and weeds. Although by this time tire tracks leading to the old house were fairly easy to follow, stubble still thunked against the bottom of the police car. Jeff braked suddenly as a doe and two fawns ran in front of us. When we reached the house, the iguana eyed us from the front porch. The raccoon family had been peering into the well, but all three of them ran when we drew near.

Jeff stopped the car and he and Hillie got out and approached the well.

"Police!" Hillie shouted. "Grovello, are you able to respond?"

No response. Maybe he was dead. I wondered what Hillie had anticipated. Had the officers hoped to see Ace splash from his watery prison and walk toward them with his hands raised?

"Ace, we've come to take you to Key West." While Jeff talked, Hillie eased to the well and peered over the rim. Then he backed off and shouted.

"Toss the gun to us, Grovello. Give us the gun and we'll pull you from the well."

"I surrender."

Ace's voice sounded hollow and hoarse, and I gasped when his gun appeared spinning in the air above the well. But instead of landing on the concrete slab, the gun dropped straight down and splashed into the water.

"Hold your hands above your head," Hillie shouted. "Tread water. Keep your hands up."

Hillie started easing away from the well opening, when suddenly Randy sprang from his car and dashed to the well. Before anyone could stop him, he leaned over the opening and shot a brown stream of tobacco juice straight down.

"Son of a bitch! Son of a bitch!" Ace enlarged his vocabulary by three words.

I smiled. I knew from the continued stream of profanity that Randy's aim had hit target. Randy tossed an insolent look at Hillie and Jeff, and then strolled toward Punt and me, smiling for the first time since I'd met him. He reached to shake Punt's hand and then he turned to me.

"Thank you, Ms. Moreno."

"You're welcome, Mr. Jackson." I returned his smile. If Punt was surprised, he hid the fact well.

Randy then walked to his car, slid inside with Maxine and Gram and drove away. The officers made no effort to stop them.

By that time backup cops had arrived to offer assistance and one of them drove Punt and me back to Punt's apartment, thanked us for leading them to Ace, and requested that we not leave town.

Punt and I clung to each other for a long time, and I was still shaking as we relived my narrow escape. A long time passed before we could talk slowly and coherently. After we calmed down, Punt helped me take a much-needed shower then we talked some more. We assured ourselves that the law would deal with Ace, who had confessed to the murders of Dyanne Darby and Nicole Pierce, that Shrimp Snerl would hire Randy for more shrimp runs, and that the Fotopolus and Ashford Agency could go on to other business.

"Punt, I've something to tell you. I've thought about your request that I forgive Jude." I paused, and when Punt said nothing, I continued. "I've forgiven him. It was the hardest thing I ever did. I put a positive spin on all his negatives. Jude gave me an appreciation of freedom. His abuse enabled me to call on and find strength I didn't know I possessed. He supplied me with goals to work toward. I'm still relieved that he's dead, but he gave me much to be thankful for. He forced me into a new and better life."

"Thank you for that. I know it was hard for you." Punt and I kissed more deeply than ever before.

"I have something to ask you," Punt whispered in my ear once we relaxed on his couch.

My heart sank. It was true, I had forgiven Jude, but I hadn't forgotten. Until I could wipe old memories from my heart, I still shadow-boxed with the past. I braced my self to hear another marriage proposal, a proposal I wasn't ready for, one I didn't yet feel I could honor.

"Keely, we both need some time to get used to your forgiving Jude, but even so, I'm asking you to be my partner."

"But…"

He touched my lips with his forefinger. "I'm asking you to be my detective partner. Don't tell me you're no detective. You have two solved cases to your credit."

Relief soon replaced my surprise. "I don't want to be a detective, Punt. I've worked hard to establish my foot reflexology business. I like it. I'd hate to give it up. And what about Nikko? What makes you think he wants me as a partner?"

"We've talked it over, Keely. Nikko's going to open a branch office in Miami. We'd like you as our silent, undercover partner here on Key West. Your reflexology business offers a perfect cover-up for your sleuthing activities. What do you say? Will you think it over?"

"Yes, I will." A quick answer gave me time to think. Would Punt be moving to Miami? I didn't ask. "I'd enjoy helping you and Nikko get criminals off the streets. Ace Grovello could have killed me. Nobody would have found my body. This is a special day, Punt."

"Every day's a special day when we're both alive—and together."

I agreed and I showed my agreement in a very special way.